A WALK ON THE WILD SIDE

A WALK ON THE WILD SIDE

M C DUTTON

Matador
Unit E2 Airfield Business Park,
Harrison Road, Market Harborough,
Leicestershire. LE16 7UL
Tel: 0116 279 2299
Email: books@troubador.co.uk
Web: www.troubador.co.uk/matador
Twitter: @matadorbooks

ISBN 978 1 80313 298 3

British Library Cataloguing in Publication Data.
A catalogue record for this book is available from the British Library.

Printed and bound in the UK by TJ Books, Padstow, Cornwall
Typeset in 11pt Minion Pro by Troubador Publishing Ltd, Leicester, UK

Matador is an imprint of Troubador Publishing Ltd

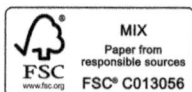

It's all about love of family.

To my wonderful children Helen, Richard and Amanda and Andrew and Nansal

and my darling grandchildren Isabella, Kiera, Rebecca, Josh, Thomas, Bradley, Max, Edie-Rose and

great-grandchildren Thea and Jude.

Nessa you know who you are – Mrs M

"I wouldn't call him a slave. I don't whip him when he does something wrong. Just when he does something good."

Shannon Elizabeth

The ignorant person is totally blind he does not appreciate the value of the jewel.

Guru Gobind Singh

PREFACE

Detective Sergeant Jaswinder Singh, officer serving Ilford, Barking and Dagenham District, please note you have done an upstanding job in capturing one of the largest and most high-powered paedophile ring that England has ever seen. Against all the odds of government services trying to bring you down and your own Metropolitan Police colluding with them too, you still managed to capture and ensure a trial for what turned out to be at least twenty influential paedophiles who worked in government offices, army and various high-powered institutions and one of them was too close for comfort to our Queen and her family. So, in honour of what you have done we, the government and the Metropolitan Police, would like to thank you.

Now that ain't gonna happen. You fucking ungrateful pisspots of humanity. Angry now just thinking about it, Jazz as he was known to his friends and enemies, had hit a point of depression that nearly took him over the edge. He had been on so-called recovery/garden leave for the last three months and he had nothing to do but think, stew and rant. His only friends, he thought, were the vodka bottles he kept in the fridge and the fags that made him cough as he choked on the words in the letter he received from bloody DCI Radley, his boss. The letter inferred he was physically and mentally exhausted and it was suggested he get suitable help during the three months' leave that had been granted.

DCI Radley, with his snotnose university degree without any experience of police work and just-about-shaving boss, was not happy with him.

DCI Radley had left university and entered the fast-track level of the Metropolitan police to advance to senior ranks. He had served his time at Ilford and Barking police station and he now had his eye on a promotion at Scotland Yard as commander. This would have been a huge feather in his cap. He had worked hard to get to know those who made such appointments. The whisper had been that he was shortlisted and he was fairly confident he would pass the interview. Then Singh got involved in tracking and apprehending those involved in a paedophile ring. The Met had worked closely with government departments to get this paedophile ring off the radar. He presumed, for political reasons, it tried to keep those involved in the paedophile ring out of the public eye and out of the courts. To be honest, he couldn't deny he saw who these vile people were and he had backed Singh in bringing them to trial. The ring was dangerous and treacherous. He knew justice was due to the victims but it caused him to lose his grip on his promotion. He recently received a letter from the Metropolitan Committee regarding the promotion interview stating that at the moment he would not be considered. He knew exactly what that meant. He was being punished for not controlling Singh and ensuring that the high-ranking members of the ring were allowed to escape. He hated Singh for putting him in this position and losing the opportunity to rise to a prestigious rank that would have made his family and himself proud. Of course, this would not affect how he ran his station or how he treated DS Singh; well, that's what he told himself. Hatred and despair come in different forms.

Back home in his rented room with Mrs Chodda, Jazz, although reasonably settled and happy living in Mrs Chodda's house, had found Mrs Chodda's matchmaking attempts tiresome. Mrs Chodda seemed to be related to half the country's eligible-for-marriage Sikh women. Coming home after a hard day in the office (Ilford and Barking police station) he would be confronted by Mrs Chodda inviting him into her huge kitchen. This was usually a treat to enjoy her home-made pakoras which he loved but often to be introduced to a young, shy or giggly girl, far too young for him. He was in his forties, for fuck's sake, he told himself. His good manners as a Sikh man, something his work colleagues had never experienced, allowed for the introduction and polite conversation. The mother, aunts, grandmothers would sit in stony silence watching.

This had gone on for a few years with no marriage in sight, much to Mrs Chodda's dismay. She had told everyone how important he was, and would whisper how he was high up in the police force and what a good catch he would make. Mrs Chodda was about to give up when the unexpected happened. Her brother's wife's sister's daughter, Amrit, seemed to catch Jazz's eye. Mrs Chodda was a good woman who attended the Gurdwara regularly and performed *Sewa* (selfless act to help others) by cooking in the Gurdwara for all attendees, but to encourage a meeting between Jazz and Amrit was difficult to condone. Amrit had divorced her husband – something no good Sikh woman would do, and taken her son and lived alone. Well, she was shunned by most of the family for doing such a disrespectful thing but Mrs Chodda couldn't bring herself to shun her and she was invited regularly to her home and kitchen.

After the lack of interest in the all the young, virgin Sikh girls that Jazz had been introduced to, he had, for goodness' sake, showed an interest in Amrit. With a sigh and a resolution that meant if all else failed she would get him married to someone in her extended family if it was the last thing she ever did, meant Jazz was in for a lot of trouble.

The three-month so-called recovery/garden leave finished and Jazz could return to work. He knew the Met would have preferred him to resign but he wasn't going to do that. He was thankful to get out of Mrs Chodda's hair and the uncomfortable invitations to sit with Amrit who appeared more frequently in Mrs Chodda's kitchen than anyone else. He was ready for work and ready to show everyone that he was a fucking hero and not someone to be pushed into a corner. He had no idea what he was getting himself into.

CHAPTER ONE

NOT AGAIN

Back at work and trying to keep out of DCI Radley's way was not easy. Usually upbeat and stupidly optimistic, Jazz got through his days pretty successfully. At the moment he was feeling fed up and depressed. Everyone in the station had noted the annoying strutting peacock of a man who had an answer for everything and took the mickey out of anyone and was seen to fly by the seat of his pants on everything, was not himself. He had become introspective and quiet. No one wanted to admit that they missed the banter and the cheek of the man but the station was a duller place.

Jazz was determined to do anything other than become a lollipop man as DCI Radley was determined to make him. It was sickening because he was a detective sergeant in the Metropolitan police force, not a retired numpty who stood in the rain so the school kids could take the mickey out of him. It wasn't his fault Radley didn't get his promotion. Well, he thought, perhaps it was his fault. Perhaps if he hadn't caught a high-level paedophile ring and ensured the press knew about it and scuppered the idea that MI5 could let the scumbags go might not have helped DCI Radley. But he regretted nothing. Radley was going to make him pay for it, that was a certainty.

Thank God for friends in high places. DI Tom Black, his only friend actually, got him into the Sat Pal case. Just back off garden leave and Radley was busy making arrangements for Jazz to go and do some school crossings at a local school, something Radley said would do Jazz good, to observe the other side of life in Barking. Jazz was about to argue that point when DI Black (Boomer to everyone) entered the room and politely and quietly asked to speak to DCI Radley about something rather urgent. Knowing Boomer, Jazz was very interested in what was going to be said because Boomer was never polite, and never quiet. You don't get the nickname Boomer for being quiet. He was a loud bastard most of the time.

Apparently, Boomer and his team were working on a case involving a Sikh gang leader and Boomer was rather concerned about the racial aspect of following and arresting a Sikh who was well known in his area. He suggested to the press-hungry DCI Radley that there would be repercussions over his arrest that might not be seen as favourable to the police. Some might say, he ventured, that the police were racist and picking on him. DCI Radley looked quite concerned at this and hoped Boomer would have an answer. "Well, sir," continued a far too polite Boomer, "I would suggest that we have a Sikh detective in our midst who would be seen to be running the case and it would take a very stupid person to mention racism if the person arresting a Sikh is a Sikh too. I thought you should have these facts before I move further with this case," said a very thoughtful Boomer.

Not a total idiot, DCI Radley looked from Boomer to Jazz. He knew what was going on and he was being set up. But he conceded it was a sensible plan and he couldn't afford to get on the wrong side of the press or the higher-ups in the Met. He was trying to keep a low profile for a while before thinking about trying for promotion again. A hue and cry of racism at Barking Police Station would just make matters worse.

That was the way Jazz got to work with Boomer on the Sat Pal case. It was a case that would take months to work through and Jazz was eternally grateful for the chance to work with Boomer and away from DCI Radley. His life was looking good again. Of course, that wasn't going to last.

Some might say it was lucky that the case against Sat Pal, a Sikh gang leader, ended with his death in a car accident. It was a case that Jazz and Boomer had been working on for many months. They suspected Sat Pal was organising some sort of takeover by eliminating the Sikh boss who ran a cash-and-carry business in his town. Sat Pal obviously had big plans but what they were exactly died with him. Barking had become a mini multicultural manor for mayhem. Jazz laughed at the thought and reckoned he was a poet but didn't know it!

The case had been wrapped up because Sat Pal was dead and there was nothing to suggest the car accident was anything other than stupidity by Sat Pal's driver who skidded on a curve and stopped the speeding car by hitting a solid six-foot wall killing Sat Pal, his driver and one of his goons. Sat Pal was the power in his gang and it was reckoned they would disband now he was dead.

DS Jaswinder Singh was not happy. He wanted to finish the case. He wanted to bang Sat Pal to rights. The man had caused Jazz months of investigations and to arrest him and his gang of thugs would have been a feather in his cap. He also didn't want to be on DCI Radley's radar, who would be thinking about making him a fucking lollipop man again. Frustrated, fed up and flaming mad, Jazz was in no mood to be sociable.

Not everyone was upset Jazz's case had gone up in flames. Sarah, a civilian manager in the administration offices of Fresh Wharf, thought it was fantastic that Sat Pal was dead and the case was closed. Sarah was a sassy, intelligent forty-year-old and she always got Jazz's attention when she needed it. Being a good-looking blonde helped but they had a cheeky banter and she was known for not taking rubbish from anyone. She knew Jazz would be at a loose end now. It was well known in the station that Jazz hated it when there was nothing to grab his attention. He needed a case to work on, something unusual, something big and certainly something to keep his mind occupied. Sarah desperately needed his confidential help and she knew he would be interested in something no one else would touch with a barge pole. Even she had no idea that what she hoped would be relatively quick and simple would end up complicated, dangerous and deadly.

DCI Radley had made it known to Jazz that when his Sat Pal case finished, he wanted him to work in the schools as a police officer or as a lollipop man. He had thought this might be good experience for Jazz. He also said he was on the rota for school crossings when a lollipop lady or lollipop man was off sick, etc. Jazz was beyond anger. He was seriously affronted by the lack of gratitude by his bosses. He knew exactly what Radley was doing. He was going to make sure Jazz never again took any job that might be interesting, and certainly not dangerous to Radley's promotion. It would kill Jazz to work in these areas and he knew he was being punished for daring to arrest the biggest paedophile ring the country had ever seen against the wishes of the government departments. Next, he thought, they would want him to watch the fluffy bunny brigade at the local sodding zoo! Anger couldn't clear the depressed feelings.

DS Jaswinder Singh was pissed off. He made his way to Boomer's office. DI Tom Black was his title but someone who could shout louder and more often than a fog horn in deep fog deserved the title. Jazz wanted a chat, a look at what was happening in his town and as he was at a loose end, he was hoping for something interesting to work on so Radley didn't put him onto the piddling jobs. That idea was thrown out as he climbed the stairs to the first floor of Fresh Wharf in Barking when he heard coming through the walls of Boomer's office a heated argument between Boomer and his detectives. Boomer was shouting over the top of them something obscene and totally non-politically correct. Jazz was pissed off; he really didn't need any aggravation this morning. Instead of walking towards Boomer's office he turned sharp left into the relatively soothing calm area of the canteen.

A ninety-nine breakfast (two eggs, sausages, bacon, black pudding, fried bread, mushrooms, tomatoes, baked beans and of course two slices of buttered bread and a mug of tea), cooked by the wonderful Milly, was just what he needed. At over seventy years old, Milly still had a glint in her eye and she adored Jazz. He never waited for his breakfast to be cooked or for a mug of tea to be put in front of him with two sugars and stirred to his satisfaction. She always ensured he was comfortable with a gentle question of "Alright, dear?". She reassured him. "Your breakfast won't be long," as she shuffled to the canteen counter to tell off, in her twenty-fags-a-day-for-fifty-years voice, anyone grumbling that Jazz had jumped the queue and they had been waiting for ages for their breakfast. Her cough, deep and painful, filled the air, turning many off the idea of a full cooked breakfast. No one could figure out that in this health-conscious age she had been allowed to continue working well into her seventy years with her obvious health issues. Milly, oblivious to concerns, ran her canteen in the way she wanted to and would take 'no lip from any young whippersnapper trying to come it with her' as she would put it. Some didn't understand what she was saying but most were plain wary of this little East London woman who ruled their break times.

Jazz liked being spoilt. He still had problems with fucking DCI 'Jumped-up' Radley who didn't appreciate his way of working. Most of CID and the beat coppers still treated him with a wariness that bordered on downright rudeness. He was a DS, after all, not some first year, just-out-of-training newbie.

Now he was in big trouble with DCI Radley. They had caught the high-ranking paedophiles and closed the biggest paedophile ring to date. Jazz knew DCI Radley backed him in this. Jazz had to fight MI5 who worked hard to keep the paedos out of the press and out of being charged. Even the bigwigs at the Met, Scotland Yard were after him. It had been a terrifying time but, in the end, and Jazz had to smirk at the thought, he got the newspapers taking it over and all the paedos were going to trial.

So, thought Jazz, you would expect to be praised, given a fucking medal, or at least told well done, but no. He was penalised and told he was working on smaller cases now as if he was a newbie. DCI Radley, whose whole career was based on rising to the dizzy heights of commissioner of police, had been told that his latest application for superintendent at Scotland Yard had unfortunately been turned down. Jazz knew, DCI Radley knew and anyone who was anyone knew it was because of Jazz and his taking the paedophile ring case to the newspapers. The bigwigs walked carefully around Jazz, not wishing to be called racist by newspapers but they would make Jazz pay for his disobedience. He was considered a thorn in their side. The fact he was a successful detective and his arrest rates were higher than most didn't help. They could ensure Jazz never rose in rank and they certainly fell on DCI Radley's application for commander and in polite and politically-correct terms made him aware that he was going nowhere while Jazz caused so much trouble.

Jazz felt sorry for DCI Radley; he had done his best to support Jazz in arresting the paedos. At the end of the day they were doing their job and they did it bloody well. But the atmosphere was toxic and Jazz tried to keep out of DCI Radley's line of fire.

He sat back and took a deep breath. He took a sip of the hot, sweet tea and noted Milly had put at least three if not four sugars in it. He loved Milly, she was such a wonderful woman. This was the most relaxed he had felt for some time. Milly was working her charm and Jazz was almost purring. Going home at the moment was difficult. Mrs Chodda, his landlady, was still on a mission to find a wife for him. She was under the wrong impression that DS Jaswinder Singh ran the Metropolitan police force. It was never anything he had said. He never talked about his work. Mrs Chodda was a good Sikh woman and she didn't need to know what a shitty place Ilford, Barking and Dagenham was with all the crimes he dealt with.

Mrs Chodda, it seemed, had half of all Sikh marriageable women in her family and was bent on fixing up one of them with Jazz who was, in her eyes, the head of the Metropolitan police force and he would make a wonderful and important husband for one of her family. She knew he liked his drink but she also knew that no man was perfect and a good woman would sort him out.

For many, many months every time Jazz went home to settle down with a takeaway and a drink after a long day, Mrs Chodda would entice him into her kitchen with the promise of a plate of pakora specially baked for him, only to find some young girl together with her mother, aunt and anyone else who was interested, sitting there staring at him.

He had manners, although no one in the police station had seen them. But as a Sikh man he knew how to conduct himself in the company of Sikh women and the older generation expected to be treated with due deference and a form of politeness he had nearly forgotten. It was always torture. He had no intention of getting married to anyone. He liked his life. A girlfriend, maybe, but never again would he go through the formality of an arranged marriage. He had tried that and it ended in disaster. Mrs

Chodda was on a mission and Amrit had returned from India.

Amrit was a thirty-year-old female relative who had had the nerve to divorce her husband and take her five-year-old son. Amrit was considered 'used goods' and the mutterings in older company about what she had done was noted and considered above treachery and many in the family disowned her. Mrs Chodda was a kind soul. She didn't agree with what Amrit did but she wouldn't turn her away. No one would want Amrit as a wife. Mrs Chodda was frustrated that all the beautiful, virginal girls Jazz had been introduced to had been turned away, albeit in a charming way, but that he showed interest in Amrit, a used and unmarriable woman for a good Sikh man. Mrs Chodda would never understand what made Jazz tick but if it was Amrit, then she would do her best to push them together. She was now on a mission.

Jazz liked Amrit very much; a feisty woman who had shown her soft side in helping Mrs Chodda and looking after her son. He had liked her motherly ways but at the same time she could put any man in his place if he got out of line. He smiled at the thought. Yes, he enjoyed the flirting and her standoff ways but he knew she was interested. Now she was back and Mrs Chodda was working so hard to get them together with her 'Amrit, go and ask Jazz if he would like anything from my kitchen/ does he need his bed sheets changed/does he need anything, etc'. Mrs Chodda had never done that before.

He really didn't like being pushed into anything and the lure of Amrit was dying fast. He just wanted to be left alone to make his own decisions. Mrs Chodda was turning into a DCI Radley by telling him what to do and pressurising him into doing what she wanted and the thought depressed the hell out of him. He sighed and wondered what was wrong with him. He was never satisfied.

Jazz wanted to stay out of the way for a while. DCI Radley had it in for him, work was quiet and home was tricky. The canteen was a safe haven. Milly brought his breakfast and with a flourish of the hand laid it in front of him and after ensuring he had tomato sauce and salt and pepper, she smiled and left him to enjoy the feast. Every time, a ninety-nine breakfast and the lovely Milly spoiling him always made him feel good. After mopping up the last of the beans on a piece of bread, bloated, full and feeling fantastic, Jazz sat back in his chair happy with the world.

This was just about when Sarah appeared in his sight line. She was making a beeline towards him looking nervous, embarrassed and almost coy. This was not the Sarah he knew from the admin office. A manager of twenty people and an arbitrator between the police, the CPS and the court, she had her hands full. Sarah Philips was a forty-year-old mouthy, intelligent, ballsy girl who had a quick turn in humour and managed to get on with everyone. Being a real looker with a model figure helped as well, he noted. She asked Jazz almost coyly if she could have a few moments of his time. Intrigued, he offered a chair. She sat down, looked around to ensure they were alone and so it began.

Her life would never be quite the same and Jazz, yet again, was walking fearlessly, or as some would say, stupidly and ignorantly, into a festering sewer seen only by those in the darker, murkier corners of life.

CHAPTER TWO

THE BEGINNING

Sarah and Jazz were to meet in the Cranbrook pub that evening. Jazz liked it there and he felt comfortable. It was his local and the barman, Pat, knew how he wanted his drink poured. A quadruple vodka and a small bottle of tonic on the side. Well, as Jazz said often to Pat, "You are piss poor with your measures here. A quadruple vodka is only the same as what you would pour at home." Pat would always nod silently and take the money. Jazz was going to make the one drink last before Sarah arrived. He reckoned he would need a clear head. Sarah wasn't one to mess around with other men or with what she wanted to say so her asking to meet him in private was unusual to say the least. The pub was never that full. It was a bit out of the way for commuters and if you lived close by, there were better pubs to go to. So apart from it being his local, it was pretty discreet for a private conversation.

The Cranbrook pub was past its sell-by date with a tired, almost sixties-style interior. Smoking was banned by law but the walls and ceilings had a long history of smoking causing deep nicotine stains. Jazz had smoked the odd crafty fag there when it was closing time. He told the barman that his odd fag wouldn't do any more damage, and in fact he reckoned it was only the nicotine stains that had kept the wallpaper stuck to the walls. They had both laughed at that worn-out joke.

His tongue was itching for another drink. Sarah was bloody late! He chose to forget the bit about only one drink to keep his head clear. He ordered another quadruple vodka; he had some tonic left in the small bottle. Jazz made sure he sipped it slowly. He was trying to be sensible but it was, after all, his fucking time off. As he was busy justifying another drink to himself Sarah walked in. From the look on her face, she was none too pleased to be there.

"This place is a fucking tip," she said in a disgusted whisper.

She didn't want to upset the barman; he might spit in her drink if offended by her comment.

Relaxed and airily Jazz said, "My darling Sarah, you wanted privacy. Hardly anyone would come here except me – it's my local."

She looked him up and down and thought *my darling Sarah!! Cheeky git!!* Known for her retorts she was ready for a suitable mouthy answer to that but bit her tongue. She knew it was the drink talking. She needed his help and his goodwill. There was no one else she could trust at this stage. So, Sarah smiled, ordered a spritzer from the barman who was quite interested to see an attractive woman coming here to see Jazz. Seeing his interest, Sarah picked up her bag from the bar, slid off the bar stool and suggested Jazz and she move to a table in the corner.

It seemed to take a long time to get started. Jazz used the time to watch Sarah through the haze of the glass that seemed permanently attached to his mouth. He was sipping slowly by his standards and enjoying her uncomfortable fidgeting. She was a good-looking girl; blonde, slim and petite – a perfect combination in his eyes. He was mesmerised by her hair tumbling onto her shoulders in loose and careless sweeping curls. With every flick of her head her hair seemed to caress her face and tumble softly onto her shoulders. He knew the drink was getting to him. She caught his admiring glances and wanting to stop him staring at her in such a way, she cleared her throat to start.

"So," she said, and waited a second. He looked on, mouth open in anticipation. "My husband, Derek…" she ventured hesitantly.

He wondered why it was taking so long. He could see her hands were shaking a little and how annoyed she was with herself. Sarah was always in control of every situation.

"My husband, Derek, you know him, don't you?" she asked.

Jazz nodded. He had only met him a couple of times over the years but he remembered him well. He was sickeningly gorgeous in an understated way. Tall, about six-foot four and slim with black hair and blue eyes that the girls went mad over. Yes, he remembered him well from the office party he came to. He was rumoured to be in the protection command which was within the specialist ops directorate of the Met. The girls at the office party couldn't stop looking and giggling about him and they were fucking police officers, Jazz thought. He didn't like him much. Just because he got to use a Glock 17 handgun and a Heckler and Koch MP5 semi-automatic didn't make him a hero he thought.

"Well," she continued, "something isn't right with him. Actually," and she blushed ferociously at this, "I thought he was having an affair."

Bugger! went through Jazz's head. He just didn't want to get involved in any marital affairs. There were enough officers who strayed and it was best to steer clear of anything to do with it. It usually ended up with a wife making a nuisance of herself at the police station or, if it was an officer sleeping with their married boss, then there was a hell of a fall-out when it ended. *Nah,* he thought, *I ain't getting into anything like this.*

She could see he was not going to get involved and quickly and urgently she added, "But I know he isn't having an affair. It's something else and something a bit sordid and dangerous."

That did it! She could see she had Jazz's full attention now. "Go on," he ventured nodding his head. *Now it sounds a little bit more interesting and Mr Fabulous might not be so wonderful after all* he thought. Sarah was now firmly in it and had to lay out all the details she had before Jazz. She needed his help and she had nowhere else to turn.

She licked her lips, took a deep breath and started. To say this all out loud seemed dirty and wrong and scary.

"He has been distracted lately. We…" and here she hesitated, embarrassed and emotional. She controlled the quivering lower lip and continued.

"We haven't been, you know, close for quite a while. He has his locked room he keeps his work in. It's our loft.

14

We had it converted into a room with skylights with a permanent staircase to the loft."

She looked up at Jazz to ensure he was listening and she could see she had his full attention. She grimaced and added, "I always thought the loft room was going to be for the family we hoped to start but that never happened."

She tried to hide the tears by looking down again. With a deep, regretful breath, she continued again.

"He always keeps the loft room locked. Well, his work is confidential and I think he keeps weapons up there too. I was never allowed up there but I understood how important his work was. He protects some very important people."

She knew she had to tell Jazz but it was difficult. He sensed she was having difficulty and it was all about the loft room. He asked if she had a key to the loft and if she had been up there.

"Nope, I don't have a key but I have been up there. He is away for a week on something important, I never know what or where." She looked at Jazz and smiled. "I picked the lock. You can't work in a police station without knowing how to pick locks."

He laughed. It was very true. With so many criminals going through the station for years, most officers had picked up little titbits of information on entry to various places. Now pushing it on, as she seemed reluctant to do so, Jazz asked what she had found up there. There was a silence for what seemed ages. Jazz finished his vodka and said he would get them both another drink while she thought about it. Sarah nodded in agreement and Jazz ordered another quadruple vodka and a bottle of tonic. Sarah was still on a spritzer. He watched her from the bar under hooded eyes. The brash stance, the ballsy woman he knew had disappeared. She looked defenceless and scared, not the person he knew from work, and he felt sorry for her. He needed to get tough to make her get on with telling him what the hell was going on. Surely it couldn't be that bad, he said to himself. He lit an illicit cigarette. The barman didn't object and he went back to the table, cigarette held between his lips and a drink in each hand. Sarah was grateful for the break. Now for the nitty-gritty of the story.

Up in the loft was Derek's computer, his gun cabinet, locked of course, and a wardrobe. She told Jazz she looked in the wardrobe first and she was shocked at what she found there. After much cajoling from Jazz, she confessed she found a gimlet, a whip, and various leather costumes. This caused Sarah to down half a spritzer in one gulp. "He's a fucking S&M freak," was all she could say. This made Jazz choke on his vodka. *Bloody hell, Mr Wonderful dresses up*. He didn't laugh; he saw Sarah's face. "But that's not all, Jazz, there is so much more," she babbled.

Sarah, who was not into S&M (sadomasochism), took another gulp of her Spritzer and continued. She had gone to his computer next. She said she knew his password. He always used the same one and had done so for years. For someone working in such a highly prestigious and secretive job this sounded stupid to Jazz. She said she found many messages between a woman called Scarlett and Derek. They were, as she put it, 'highly sexual, erotic and fucking dirty'. But she went on, now like a speeding train unable to stop. The messages became almost sinister and threatening and she didn't know what to make of them. She had Jazz's full attention now and he was hanging on her every word.

The latest messages Sarah went on to talk about were the threatening ones. With a quiver in her voice and an uncertainty that she was sane and not totally paranoid, she looked at the table and said, "The latest message hinted of trouble in his family if he didn't do what was asked of him." She looked up at Jazz and said, "I know people into S&M might talk in this way, I am not stupid, but she mentioned my name, for God's sake! She said *Sarah should be careful when she is out. Car accidents happen all the time.*"

Sarah started to cry and rummaged in her bag for a used tissue. She blew her nose and mopped up the tears on her cheeks. "So, Jazz, I don't know what to do. I hate him for cheating on me with this Scarlett and it's unforgiveable what he has been doing but as much as I want to hurt the bastard, I don't want to get him in trouble with his job if it's all just messing around stuff but I am a bit scared and I hoped you would help."

Jazz did wonder if it was all just play-acting in an S&M game. He knew very little about it but presumed it was about control and punishment. Sarah could have just taken a small comment and built it into a humongous conspiracy. It sounded interesting though and to be honest, he didn't like Derek at all. He would take a bit of pleasure in taking him down if he had been messing around with another woman and had dressed up for S&M. He stopped himself smiling at the thought of him in a collar and chain in a leather suit. *What a dickhead!* he thought. Now came the questions.

He asked Sarah why now and she replied because she had had enough of the distance between them and the fact he was never at home these days and when he was he spent hours in the loft room. He was away for ten days working and he went yesterday so she went straight to the loft room to have a look. He would be back in eight days so she wanted Jazz's help to decide what to do and if she should report him or if she was just being paranoid. Jazz had nothing much on at the moment. This was a good opportunity to work away from the station to stop DCI fucking Radley from turning him into a lollipop man and Mrs Chodda at home trying to marry him off to Amrit.

Jazz sat up straight, took a deep breath and told Sarah that tomorrow he would come to her home if that was alright and look in the loft room himself and decide what to do from there. So, taking a business-like attitude he wrote in his diary Sarah's address and they agreed a time. It felt like they should shake hands and leave but Sarah, now very emotional, instinctively hugged Jazz and thanked him. He liked that. When she left, Jazz ordered another quadruple vodka and thought about going home. He reckoned he would leave it until about 10 p.m. and he should be safe to get into his room without Mrs Chodda encouraging him to sit in her kitchen with Amrit. *Bugger that,* Jazz thought glumly. Enjoying his vodka, he wondered what he would find in Sarah's locked attic room.

CHAPTER THREE

THINGS TO DO

The next morning Jazz left the house. He could hear the clatter of Mrs Chodda busy moving saucepans and suchlike in the kitchen. He moved quickly to the door and seemed to escape without that sweet-toned call of 'Good morning, Jazz, have you got a moment?' which he always found so hard to say no to. He loved Mrs Chodda. She was like a mother to him. His mother had died a few years ago and he missed her. Okay, he told himself, perhaps he hadn't seen his mother as often as he perhaps should have, work and all that; but she knew he loved her and he knew she always loved him. He wondered where that sentimentality had come from. It had no place in his life at the moment so he brushed it away and concentrated on how the fuck he was going to avoid DCI Radley today and get out to Sarah's house in bloody Chelmsford. *Who lives that far away from work? It's miles away from the East End,* he told himself.

The walk to the police station in Ilford was uneventful except for a few toerags he knew who nodded as he passed them. They were professional prolific shoplifters and as he had arrested them on many occasions, he reckoned they considered themselves acquaintances of his and always said a friendly hello. Life was weird when it seemed that most people who knew him were criminals. So, shoplifting was going to be the highlight of the charging centre today, he thought. He would inform the office he had seen them. The walk to the station was never a chore, it was a good opportunity to breathe fresh air and smoke a fag or two before starting work. It also gave him the chance to think strategies. He was a coiled spring ready for anything when he got to the station. The trouble was he was coiled for action but nothing came his way. The charging desk had been advised to never call him. DCI Radley had nailed him down to be a fucking lollipop man! All that pent-up energy ready for action turned to resentment and thick, dark anger. As he arrived at the police station an officer shouted good morning as he passed by and Jazz replied with feeling. "Fuck off." Not his best diplomatic response but he was pissed off already and it was only 9 a.m.

He rushed up the stairs agilely taking two steps at a time avoiding the crowd that seemed to be coming down the stairs. He was a good-looking bloke and his suit hung nicely on his slim frame. Women looked at him as he passed them and in a brief moment they noted his Mediterranean look of dark hair and olive skin and the dark shadows around his eyes that made him look interesting. The dark shadows were getting deeper due, some thought, from the drink but at the moment they just made him look alluring. He noted the looks but was anxious to get into Boomer's office before anyone of importance spotted him, especially DCI Radley. He had a plan and the thought of getting one over on DCI fucking Radley gave him a spring in his step.

Boomer was at his desk, growling. Apparently, his boredom threshold was very low and nothing much was happening. He told Jazz that most of the meaty cases in the East End were being looked at by the terrorist squad and a few odd murders were thrown his way every now and then. He knew Jazz couldn't touch anything interesting so him coming into his office didn't light his fire, or words to that effect. Jazz rubbed his hands in anguish. He needed a favour from Boomer and he could tell he wasn't in a good mood. He needed to pitch it carefully to Boomer and make it sound more interesting than it was.

"So, I need your help," was the implored start to the conversation. Jazz looked as pathetic as he could. "I am looking at something I can't talk about even with you, Tom, but, and it's a big but, if it proves interesting, I will be straight back here and giving it to you."

He could see a minute straightening of Boomer's back and he continued, "So, can you please cover me for the rest of the day. I need to leave here to investigate and fucking Radley wants to put me on lollipop duty and that ain't gonna happen."

At this Boomer growled and it turned into a deep noise that began in his stomach and rose to his throat. Jazz wasn't sure but thought it was Boomer laughing.

"Fucking lollipop man with the white coat and big stick. If you do that, I am gonna have pictures taken to blackmail you with." The laughter continued.

"So, what do you want?" was the civil question once Boomer stopped laughing.

Jazz had thought this through. "If Radley or one of his henchmen asks, could you say I was taking old lady statements for something or other because your men were too busy doing real crime work to do it."

Again, that disturbing noise started in Boomer's stomach and just rose to his throat. When he calmed down, he said, "Well, my men haven't got much on at the moment but we did have a stabbing in Green Lane and there were a lot of witnesses so you could be taking their statements. A fucking boring low-life job but suitable for you, I expect, in Radley's eyes."

Jazz raised his eyebrows knowing that was what he was asking for but 'fucking boring low-life job which was suitable for him' sort of dented his ego for a moment. Boomer noted his displeasure and that disturbing noise started again making Boomer cough.

With a heartfelt thank you, Jazz left, wanting to get out of the building before he was seen. Once outside he phoned Sarah who had arranged to have half a day off. She got in at 7 a.m. to do what she needed to do in the admin office and now was ready to meet Jazz in the car park. She had a nice little Suzuki Swift which suited her needs. Jazz was surprised; he thought Sarah with her looks and flair and attitude would have had a sports car. Sarah saw the look and said her other car was in the cleaners so this one would have to do. They laughed at such a stupid comment. Jazz was surprised how quickly they got to Sarah's house. He thought it would take hours but Chelmsford wasn't that far away after all. She lived in a strange place where every road was named after something from a Dickens' novel. She lived in Bob Cratchit Avenue, *a fucking stupid name,* he thought. The house was rather nice though. It all looked very light, clean and pristine around her area. It made him realise how dirty Ilford and Barking had got. Her house was on a corner and had a big green bush thing all around it so you could hardly see the house. They parked in the front garden and made their way to the front door. It was very impressive with a hall, two reception rooms and a big kitchen and utility room. *Her husband must be on a shitload of money to afford this* he thought. *Sarah's wages wouldn't afford this place.*

They went up the stairs and she showed him up the second set of stairs they had installed that led to the attic room. Jazz watched as Sarah opened the door. She again told Jazz she had picked the lock and she ruefully smiled at the thought that her husband would be amazed she could do such a thing. He walked into the loft room and was surprised how much light the windows in the roof gave to the room. It was a *man cave par excellence* Jazz thought. He would love a room like this. There was a wardrobe on one wall, a single bed in a corner and a computer and printer on a large teak desk with drawers full of pens, paper and bits and pieces for writing. The fitted carpet was a neutral light grey and it all looked very masculine. A small table near the door held a kettle and what looked like jars that held coffee and tea and possibly biscuits. *Okay,* he thought, *I've got my own room but Mrs Chodda comes in every now and then to tidy the mess but this room is locked and totally his.* Jazz was very jealous of this lucky fucking Adonis. He hoped he could find something interesting that would destroy such an image. He noted he was getting spiteful in his old age and this made him smile.

Sarah was anxious to show him everything but first he wanted to see the cabinet on the wall. Sarah opened this for him and it contained a variety of firearms. Jazz was fascinated by the armoury he had here. He wondered why he had other firearms in his cupboard. It was half full of what he thought were all the weapons a protection officer would carry. Did he have double of everything, he asked himself, and was it legal? It was definitely getting his juices going. This didn't seem right. He had a Glock 17, a fabulous weapon. Solid black and comfortable to hold. It was easy to reload with a responsive trigger. It was only eight inches long but could fire seventeen rounds. The crème de la crème of handguns.

Then there was the Heckler & Koch MP5 sub-machine gun. He touched it lovingly. This wonderful sub-machine gun was the best known one in the world. It was beautiful. It could fire single shots or it could be turned into a machine gun. God! It had a silencer too. What a fabulously dangerous piece of equipment.

It was like looking at a treasure trove. He loved the weapons and spent more time than he should looking at and feeling them. If Sarah hadn't been there, he would have picked them up and just felt the use of them but she would think he was not taking this seriously. He knew about weapons used, he had studied them, thirsted to have them and had been told by his superiors he couldn't be trained on them. In the past he had been tested psychologically for firearms training and for some reason or other he failed it. It pissed him off but deep down he knew why. His little bit of non-conformity to rules might have something to do with it. *Fuck 'em.* He smiled at that thought. There was a bulletproof vest and the non-lethal Taser X26. Like every other British police officer, he had an ASP Telescopic Baton and rubbish handcuffs. Mr Adonis had bloody gorgeous Hiatt speedcuffs that just clicked in place, not like his rigid ones. There was the CS gas and a radio in the cupboard too. Again, why have double of everything? He should have them with him now. He wondered where he had actually gone. Was he away working or not? *Interesting question*, he thought.

Sarah led Jazz over to the wardrobe and gestured for him to open it. It was truly a treasure trove of S&M. There were whips, a gimlet, a studded black leather collar which made Jazz laugh. Sarah was not amused and she told him.

"This is fucking serious to me, Jazz. Don't laugh, it's my life here."

Jazz controlled himself and apologised. He found a black leather all-in-one suit hanging up. He did wonder what the fucking attraction was to this type of play. There was an outfit that surprised him even more: a red basque with fishnet black tights hanging up as well. Looking down he spotted on the floor of the wardrobe a size 10 pair of black high heels. Now that was a bit of a shock. How could Mr Fabulous who looked so macho be a transvestite? This sight made Sarah start to cry. She just didn't know the person her husband was any more. There were other play things; he didn't quite understand what they did and nor apparently did Sarah but they knew they were used. There was speculation that some were nipple clamps and something nasty that could have gone on a penis. It all felt too painful for Jazz to contemplate and he asked, in all seriousness, what had spooked her particularly and made her contact him. She gave him a look of 'what the fuck do you think I felt about this stuff?'. But realised she had to get to the point.

"I got frightened by what look like threats to me on his computer."

The atmosphere changed and feeling coldly serious Jazz put an arm around Sarah and gave a squeeze. He could see the fear in her eyes as she continued.

"It was a weird message I found screwed up in his wastepaper bin up here that freaked me out even more."

She had put it on the desk and with shaky hands gave it to Jazz. The message read *Enjoy Sherbourne House but don't forget what we agreed.* Jazz read it and looked at Sarah asking what was wrong with that. Sarah, now close to tears again, told Jazz.

"He never ever told me where he was going. It was not allowed. Everything he did was secret for security reasons, obviously. So how did this person know where he was going?"

Jazz nodded and then had a thought.

"But this might have been sent from a colleague who would have known what he was doing. It doesn't have to be anything suspicious. So why do you think it is?"

Jazz was feeling this was going nowhere until Sarah showed him her final piece of paper.

"Look at this, Jazz. He had torn the paper up and the bit that goes with this message has kisses on it and something else… the words look threatening to me."

Jazz read it and the words were quite simple: *remember who we can hurt.* It did look a bit like that, he had to agree. After a few seconds' thought, Jazz asked to look at the computer.

Now the computer had messages on it that Sarah had found mentioning her name and car accidents. A woman called Scarlett sent him a few messages. Again, could they be S&M games? He didn't know what he was looking for. The computer had a diary that was used and he noted that at least a few times per month there was a time and date with a Mrs M. There were a few with a Scarlett. He asked Sarah if he knew who this Mrs M was or a Scarlett but she just shook her head. It all seemed too much for her. In sharing this with Jazz it had all suddenly become real and the man she thought was a standard, ordinary protection officer and husband suddenly looked like Mata Hari in drag!

She made an excuse to put the kettle on and left Jazz to flick through different screens to see what he could find. To be quite honest, computers were not his thing but he saw enough to unplug the computer to take back to Ash Kumar, his moaning but brilliant sidekick. Ash knew everything there was to know about computers and if there was anything to find he would find it. In the meantime, a cup of coffee and a cigarette with Sarah was needed to calm her down. Jazz did wonder if Scarlett had visited Derek here because of all the S&M paraphernalia he had in his cupboard. He still didn't know if there was anything worth pursuing here; it could all be to do with an S&M game. The fucker was obviously hooked on this sort of stuff but he would see what transpired. It beat being a sodding lollipop man. With a smile he took himself downstairs to talk with Sarah.

Over a cup of coffee, he asked Sarah, "So how often is Derek at home when you are at work?"

She picked up his inference and testily stated, "I don't know. What are you asking me?"

Jazz tried to calm the situation. He just needed to know if it was a regular thing. Sarah said he was away often and he would have tranches of time off. She said he worked different shifts. Sometimes he was away for a week but sometimes up to a month and then he would have a week off at home. She hadn't got a clue what he did with his days. He never said. It seemed to Jazz that the pair didn't talk much to each other. He decided not to ask the question of whether they were happily married but he was assuming they were not. Those questions would need to be asked at some point, he thought.

Sarah looked at him and blurted out, "I am kinda scared by the messages. No, I am bloody scared."

Jazz looked into Sarah's face and saw the distress, worry and huge embarrassment that this ballsy girl was going through. She was always the one in the office to *fix* problems. She was the go-to girl for answers and now she was needing help. He felt sorry for her and wanted to set down rules for her safety, and for her standing in the office.

"Look, Sarah," Jazz started hesitantly. He leaned over the chair and took her hand which surprised her.

"Go stay at your parents for the time being. Don't be alone at night. This is confidential between you and me for the time being. If, and I say if, I find problems I might have to bring in someone else to help."

He saw her sit up startled at this and before she could throw in all the 'buts' to anything he said, he added, "First of all, I am including Ashiv to look at the computer. He will do this in confidence and will not talk to anyone but me. He has a history of being a pain in the arse but he never talks out of place." She nodded at this.

"Then, if necessary, I will include Boomer because he is absolutely ace to work with and he won't say anything either. He hates, in his words 'fucking rules' and he will keep quiet too."

She laughed nervously adding, "When has Boomer ever done anything quietly?"

Jazz laughed at this. He added quietly, looking into Sarah's eyes, "If there is anything to find, I will find it. I will keep you updated and I know there is a timescale for his return so we will get on this now. It might turn out to be just an S&M game, in which case you can deal with this as you wish."

Sarah got up and spontaneously kissed Jazz on the cheek and in a fluster thanked him for helping her. As she said, Jazz was the only one she could turn to without causing an almighty problem for her husband if he was just playing an S&M game. She added, "The filthy, lying, two-faced bastard that he is!"

Jazz nodded, thinking *well, that about sums up Mr Gorgeous.*

They returned to Ilford and Jazz sat quietly thinking on the journey. There were a few things he wanted to get done back at the office and he wanted to see Mad Pete. It felt like there could be something worth getting his teeth into. The tingle of anticipation ran up his spine.

CHAPTER FOUR

THE SET-UP

Jazz found Ashiv Kumar, his team member and reluctant friend, sitting at his desk with his head almost in his computer looking at what looked like figures. He never understood how Ash, as he called him, could do such boring, mundane and, to be quite honest, stupidly useless work and love it. Mind you, Jazz conceded his life would be worse if it wasn't for Ash's love of boring. Jazz never had to worry about such mundane tasks as he gave them to Ash who gratefully received them. Okay, he moaned at times, usually because he was a stickler for correct protocol and all that shit, but he was worth his weight in gold.

He put Mr Gorgeous's computer on Ash's desk with a thump. Ash jumped up and started. "Oh my god! You put that computer on vital paperwork I am dealing with. It moved everything. Why did you have to do that?"

Exasperated and seriously put out by this invasion of his quiet contemplation of computer analysis work, Ash's calm control had been destroyed. Jazz always managed to upset his OCD (obsessive compulsive disorder) to detail and tidiness. With a friendly hug, which was not wanted by Ash, Jazz asked him very nicely to look at the computer. He explained what was happening and what was needed. He swore Ash to secrecy and told him how utterly valuable he was in helping to identify a potential problem. In answer to this Ash raised his eyes to the ceiling, sighed, and responded.

"Don't get me fucking nearly killed this time. Your little forays have nearly finished me many times."

Jazz, putting on a hurt face, said, "How could you think I would do anything to such a valuable friend like you?"

With that he ruffled Ash's head and moved swiftly away shouting as he went. "Can I have any info by tomorrow morning latest? No pressure."

He swiftly moved out of the office missing an abusive, nigh on impossible to do, response from Ash.

Jazz, on a roll now, went quickly to Boomer's office. He watched carefully as he strode down the corridors that DCI Radley wasn't going to jump out at him with one of those lollipop sticks to take to the nearest school. He didn't want to say too much to Boomer today. He thought it better to get a bit more info first. What he did tell a bored Boomer who was thirsting for something interesting to investigate was, "Just know this, my friend, by tomorrow I might have the start of something with a bit of meat to it that you will love. The game's afoot, Watson, and tomorrow could be an exciting day."

Boomer made that noise that started in his belly and gradually rose to his throat and came out as something close to a laugh.

"Think you are bloody Sherlock Holmes now, do you? You are a bell-end, Singh!"

With a lightness of step, Jazz, now feeling much better, made his way to the Gascoigne Estate in Barking first stopping at a McDonald's in Barking. It was afternoon now so Mad Pete was going to be out and about. He called him on his mobile and arranged to meet him at his flat. He got to Mad Pete's flat. The lift wasn't working again so he climbed the concrete steps to the third floor of the ten-floor high-rise block. The smell was always the same. Everyone must be cooking cabbage because the stairwell and the hallways reeked of it. He knew that wasn't true. No one could cook in these flats. The nearest to cooking any of them did was microwaving a dinner from Aldi or pouring hot water into a Pot Noodle.

Jazz found the filthy door that was meant to be green at some time in its history but was now covered in dirt. Mad Pete must have pissed off a few people over the years judging by the boot prints on the door. They were obviously tough doors to withstand such a kicking. He banged hard and long on the door, calling out Pete's name. After a while he could hear the muffled voice telling him to 'bloody wait a minute'. The locks and chains being unbolted seemed to take an hour.

"How many bloody locks have you got in there, you bastard?" shouted Jazz, impatient now and wanting to get in. Eventually the door opened a crack and Mad Pete peered out.

"Oh it's you, Mr Singh," he called.

"Who the fuck did you think it was? The Ku Klux Klan or something with all those fucking locks."

Mad Pete stood with hunched shoulders and, looking very put out by the mention of the Ku Klux Klan, started to make moaning noises which were brushed aside by Jazz who barged past Mad Pete to get in.

"This hallway is bloody freezing and I need to talk to you pronto and I brought McDonald's with me and it's getting cold."

Mad Pete closed the door behind him and reconnected all the bolts.

"I have thirteen bolts now, Mr Singh, because there are some very nasty people about these days and you can't be too careful."

Actually, Jazz understood his worry. There were so many gangs, drug dealers and druggies all clamouring to be arsehole of the year no one felt safe. Jazz could see Mad Pete was a bit put out by his visit. Mad Pete nervously kept touching his long greasy hair which hung across his face, a sign he was not happy. Jazz noted this; he needed to keep him calm. Mad Pete when too nervous or excited was prone to a druggy fit which meant nothing sensible could be got out of him. He had been on a cocktail of drugs for a good bit of his thirty years and it must have fucked up his system.

Mad Pete was a local star to younger gang members and known to most of the criminal element in East London. He fenced stuff, usually mobile phones that were stolen and he was the man who could get anything you needed in the drugs world. Jazz and Mad Pete had an uneasy relationship that worked. Mad Pete was always low profile and could work and walk into most situations and no one thought to look at him. He was a long streak of piss and his clothes hung on his miserable hunched frame. The stuff he provided was good quality and together with his skinny frame and can't-be-arsed way of dressing he was seen just as a useful and snivelling creep. It helped he was also known as a consummate coward so the high-powered gangs used his services and never saw him as a threat. Jazz thought him cleverer than he actually looked. He was more like a rat in the sewer; he could hide and work in full view but was mindful not to trespass on others' territory. This got him work and he was thought of as useful. He overheard things that others wouldn't overhear because no one thought of him as anything other than a working rat who was worth nothing.

Mad Pete was a grass to Jazz and helped him when asked. Jazz protected Mad Pete and he was never arrested for drug offences and for fencing. It was a symbiotic relationship that worked. To say they were friends was a bit strong and both would be disgusted at the thought that they could be called friends, but, nevertheless, they watched each other's back.

"I need some help, Pete. You know everyone but not sure this will make sense to you. I have a bit of a name and I wondered if you knew what it meant," said Jazz politely.

Looking to sit down, Jazz grimaced. "This place is a bloody mess. Do you ever clean up"? he asked as he tossed a selection of T-shirts, shoes, some smelly socks and bits of paper off the settee and sat down. He nearly sat on a crushed McDonald's box that still had a few cold chips in it that got tossed onto the pile on the floor.

"Oy, Mr Singh, that's my stuff you are chucking," said a most put-out Mad Pete.

Jazz needed to be nicer to keep everything calm. "Sorry, Pete. I brought you a Mac and chips and a coffee to scoff while we talk."

Jazz knew this was always a winner. They ate in silence and when finished each lit a cigarette and sipped the still-hot coffee.

Mad Pete was not happy. Mr Singh wanted something from him and it usually caused him a lot of trouble and pain. Mad Pete fidgeted, his eyes darting everywhere but never looking directly at Jazz. He waited nervously sucking heavily on his cigarette.

"So!" started an enthusiastic Jazz. "I have got this bit of a name. You know everyone that needs to be known in London and I reckoned you would know what this means."

Jazz didn't think he had a hope in hell of getting a good answer from Mad Pete, but he was his go-to guy and if anyone knew, he would. He looked up and gave Mad Pete an unnerving smile which instantly put Pete on his guard. Mr Singh never smiled at him. They both drew hard on their cigarettes and savoured the few seconds' silence.

"Does the name Mrs M mean anything to you?"

Mad Pete, stunned, looked at Jazz and for a few seconds said nothing. Then with a smarmy mickey-taking grin he said, "Oh yes, Mr Singh. I can certainly help there." Jazz looked up interested as Mad Pete continued.

"Give me a minute while I get my crystal ball and I am sure I can give you an answer."

Before Jazz could say anything, Mad Pete added, "What the bloody hell do you think I can do with being asked about a Mrs M? There are about a million of them in Barking alone. You fucking stupid or what?"

Now that was a tad too much for Jazz and he got up and clipped Mad Pete round the ear for his cheek.

"Let me finish, you stupid fucking idiot, there is more to this."

In pain, and apologetic, Mad Pete held his ear and waited to hear more from Mr Singh.

"This Mrs M is to do with I think an S&M club in London somewhere. Does that help?"

Mad Pete smiled to himself. He knew who it was. Now he wanted to know what was in it for him with this information. In his most smarmy and sickly style he asked, "So, Mr Singh, what's in it for me if I fucking know who this person is?"

Jazz felt that buzz of excitement in knowing things were moving forward but he had to keep a poker face, there were negotiations in progress here.

"Well, Pete, how about twenty quid for your troubles?"

Mad Pete pondered and looked disdainfully at Jazz.

"I reckon it's worth more than that, Mr Singh. No one else would have the information I have about Mrs M. She ain't on anyone's books in the police."

Jazz nodded thoughtfully and came up with his last offer.

"I ain't lying to you, Pete. I need this information and I am prepared to offer a last and final sum of money for what is just a few words from you. I will give you fifty quid and you know I never pay that much out for any information from you. Take it or leave it."

Fifty quid did it, but Mad Pete wanted the money up front and then he would tell Jazz everything he knew. Jazz took out of his wallet five crisp ten pound notes and laid them on the settee for Mad Pete to see. He didn't trust Mad Pete so the standoff was information first and money after.

"Don't touch until I have the information from you, Pete. I want to know who, where and why."

With a nod, Mad Pete, his eyes on the five ten pound notes, told Jazz what he knew.

"Mrs M stands for Mrs Marilyn Manson. She is one spooky woman, Mr Singh. It's not her real name but she likes Marilyn Manson. She likes the singer and in a freaky way kinda admires Charles Manson too, so keep away from her, Mr Singh. She runs an S&M club in Hackney and she is one mean woman."

Jazz sat back and was gobsmacked, in awe of this filthy lowlife. After a few seconds he uttered with total respect, "How the fuck do you seem to know everyone in this town?"

Mad Pete smirked with pleasure at this unexpected compliment and modestly replied,

"Well, Mr Singh, I just do a bit of business here and there, you know."

Again, in awe, Jazz said, "Well you must be fucking rich by now to have all these expensive clients."

Worried now, because he didn't want to look as if he had lots of money, certainly not in Barking (it was dangerous to look to be worth anything in this town) he said hastily, "No, no, Mr Singh, not rich at all. Mrs Manson is not one of my clients full time. It's just when she needs something for one of her clients quickly and her usual supplier can't help so she calls me." With pride he added, "I can always help and have a reputation that I can get any stuff needed pretty quickly."

"Geez, Pete, you are something else. So, what do you supply?" In haste Jazz added, "This is in confidence, of course." He didn't want to spook Mad Pete.

Mad Pete was a man who had skipped most of school in his younger years and found writing difficult. His maths was non-existent and if you mentioned geometry to him, he thought it sounded like Geronimo, one of those Indians in the Wild West films he used to watch. But strangely enough he could spell all the words of the drugs he sold and he could tot up complicated sums of money when buying and selling drugs. It never failed to amaze Jazz. Feeling like he was on *Mastermind*, Mad Pete shifted in his seat and with a look of total disdain proceeded to impress this stupid detective with his vast knowledge of drugs on the street.

"Well, Mr Singh. I had better start with the more common ones, I suppose." Jazz, sensing he was getting a bit above himself and this was going to take ages, stopped him.

"Look, Magnus Magnusson, just tell me the drugs. I don't need a bleeding lecture on it."

A bit miffed at being put down, Mad Pete got on with it.

"Well, first there is blunt (marijuana), boom (hashish), smack (heroin), big O (opium), blow (cocaine), bennies (amphetamine), ice (methamphetamine), for starters, Mr Singh."

Jazz thought that was it but Mad Pete took a deep breath and continued.

"Then there is molly which is ecstasy (MDMA), Georgia home boy (GHB), Special K (Ketamine)."

Jazz stopped him there. "For God's sake, Pete!! You sell more than Boots Chemist."

Mad Pete took that as a massive compliment and smirked. Trying to be modest, he added, "I sell much more than that, Mr Singh, including acid (LSD) and roids (steroids) as well. I can get any gear. Mrs Manson knows that. I don't ask her what the fuck she is doing with it though and she likes that."

Jazz sat and thought. Some of the drugs weren't all happy drugs. Seemed a strange concoction for an S&M club to have. Now for the crunch-time question.

"So, I need to meet Mrs Manson as soon as possible. Can you introduce me to her?"

Mad Pete jumped out of his seat and protested loudly that he couldn't, wouldn't and shouldn't. He stuttered that she was a client and no pig... He apologised quickly for the police slur and corrected his words with he couldn't introduce a police officer to her. It would kill his trade. Jazz, determined that that was not a no, said that he needn't be a police officer, he could be a punter wanting to meet her. Mad Pete was not convinced of this.

"You ain't into whips and chains, are you, Mr Singh?"

Jazz was taken aback by the question and nearly laughed out loud but realised it would destroy the negotiations, so he inferred to Mad Pete that it was something he was interested in. Mad Pete, interested now, was feeling more amenable. He saw an opportunity and slyly told Jazz that he thought he might be able to help him. Jazz said he wanted to see Mrs Manson tomorrow morning and he was bringing a friend, too, who was also interested. Mad Pete did what he always did when accommodating punters, he was helpful and willing and busy sorting out what he could make out of this bit of information. Mrs Manson would pay him for the introductions and Mr Singh and his friend would need his help in some way in the future if they were going down this route. It was a very satisfactory meeting.

Jazz left with Mad Pete promising to ring him first thing in the morning with a time to meet Mrs Manson. He went home with the thrill of expectation that a case was underway; *God and the blessed Guru, I love yah!* he thought ecstatically. Nevertheless, he stopped for a moment and felt the goosebumps on his arms pricking and a shiver ran down his spine. He realised that every time he took on a mysterious and potentially dangerous rogue undercover role it had nearly cost him his or someone on his team's life. The sense of foreboding with a frisson of fear at what was to come overtook him for the moment. With a deep breath and a renewed spring in his step he headed for home. God! He hadn't felt this good for a long, long time.

CHAPTER FIVE

I SPY

Jazz woke early feeling good with a high expectation of a case unfolding and growing into something magnificent. With a rare enthusiasm he was showered and nattily dressed by 7.30 a.m. Today he would wear his best suit; he needed *the look* for Mrs M. He always shaved his head and the smooth, perfectly shaped dome seemed to accentuate his dark eyes and his high cheekbones. He knew he was good looking and it was very useful at times. Women with information always talked to the good-looking hunk called DS Singh; the brooding faces with the looks-could-kill daggers that surrounded him when other CID officers watched as he got all the information they had unsuccessfully worked for hours to get. Mind you, the smug 'I'm fantastic' look he gave them behind the informants' back didn't help either. Everyone loves a good-looking person, Jazz realised. He figured good looking equalled trustworthy in a lot of people's minds. His looks had served him well over the years. He glanced in the mirror at the tall and slim Adonis before him to survey the result. With a smile and a wink, he acknowledged his expensive and oh-so-gorgeous look; he figured he would need it today.

He rang Boomer on his mobile phone. They arranged to meet in McDonald's at 8.15 a.m. to discuss the potential case. Boomer was up for it. Bored with the lack of interesting cases and with too much time on his hands he was thirsting for a 'Jazz case' as he called them. Jazz always found the most dangerous and fantastically and unbelievably juicy crimes that he had ever encountered. He hoped today would bring another one. Pleased with the enthusiastic 'Fucking A Singh, I can't wait to see what you have dredged up' Jazz went on to ring Ash to see what he had found on the computer. Ash had gone through the computer, and after moaning about the long hours he had spent on it, and how long the report took to type out and how he had missed his wife's excellent dinner last night, he informed Jazz that there was quite a bit of worrying information on the computer. Excited now, and barely able to contain it, Jazz yelled down the phone.

"This is fantastic. It's going to be the best day ever. You are a genius, Ash. I love you more than cheese and farts."

Ash didn't appreciate such talk and tutted. Calming a fraction, Jazz asked Ash to meet him and Boomer in McDonald's at 9 a.m. with the information. It should be quite empty in there by then. It was usually quiet between 9 a.m. and 10 a.m. before the crowds swarmed in there again. Ash wanted to meet in the police station where the computer was but Jazz reminded him that this was a bit of covert work at the moment so it had to be outside. With a bit more moaning, Ash finally agreed and Jazz put the phone down feeling an excitement he hadn't felt for a long time. This was going to be immense! He could feel it. He strode out of Mrs Chodda's guest house with a spring in his step and an optimism that would be needed in the days ahead.

He told Boomer everything he knew at the moment. What Boomer immediately noted was that Derek, the husband, must have left the country. Jazz asked why he said that. Boomer, serious and in work mode, said, "He left all his equipment, guns, vest and all the paraphernalia he uses for his job."

Jazz thought he had spares of everything and that's what he found. Boomer laughed.

"Nah! It doesn't work like that. He must have left the country on private work or a holiday or something and he couldn't take his guns, etc. through an airport or anywhere actually. They are so freaking hot about everything."

That made sense to Jazz, he hadn't thought of that. He looked and nodded to Boomer with respect.

"Puts a different flavour in the bowl. Gees! When Ash gets here perhaps he has found something that makes sense on Derek's computer."

But Boomer being the pragmatist added, "Perhaps our Derek is just on a jolly with a pretty girl. It doesn't mean it's anything other than an affair."

That depressed Jazz. He didn't want it to be that but he had to agree, he might have blown the evidence out of all proportion.

"The talk sounds menacing from what you say but if you are into S&M the threats might be a turn-on."

God! thought Jazz, how could he be so stupid. He was seriously fed up now and ordered another burger and coffee for them both to pass a bit of time and think of something else.

"Still," Boomer added, "will be interesting to see if he went with the S&M girl. And looking forward to meeting this Mrs Manson. Been a long time since I have visited such a place."

He saw the look from Jazz and laughed. "Nah, raided a place years ago. Not my bag."

Ash arrived with an armful of paperwork in neat files. Jazz loved him and was irritated by him in equally large, massive dollops. Ash was anally meticulous in what he did but oh boy, he loved to moan and make a song and dance about everything. He spent five minutes fussing about and moaning about everything including his wife's distress at how long he worked last night on the computer and how his dinner was burnt when he got home, even the dog wasn't happy to see him that late, etc., etc. Stopping to take breath and a sip of the coffee, he added it was bloody hot and was Jazz trying to burn his tongue with the bloody coffee. Exasperated and holding his temper, Jazz swore quietly through gritted teeth but managed to ask politely if Ash would give them the update.

Boomer looked on at this fiasco and didn't know whether to laugh or cry. It was fucking ridiculous and if Ash had been on his team, he would have been booted off pretty sharpish.

Ash, now settled, checked to see if Boomer and Jazz were waiting and began. He didn't mince his words. He told them that there were a few veiled threats on the computer alluding to Sarah, his wife; the *be careful of car accidents* and the noxious thought that *your wife could be kidnapped/tortured/cut.* Even Ash wondered if this was just S&M talk but he added with a certain flourish of his hands and head that he had looked at all the deleted postings on the computer. Jazz raised his eyebrows and Ash explained he was trained to do this and said that nothing on a computer was irretrievable. For dramatic effect he took a deep breath, waited a second and said, "I found many more incriminating texts on the deleted files and copied pages of it for you."

Jazz and Boomer sat upright and were very interested.

"We will read it, and bloody good work, Ash," Jazz said enthusiastically. He added, "But for the time being, can you give us an overview of what you found?"

Ash, excited now, pulled the paperwork out of the file he had brought and handed copies to Boomer and Jazz. "First of all," Ash started, "Derek is into something not very nice and I don't mean S&M exactly. It appears he has a sado-sexual relationship with the girl called Scarlett. Judging by the texts, she told him what to do and when to meet (I know, very S&M) but in between offering bizarre and painful sex."

Ash, noting he had their full attention, took a deep breath and added, "He seemed to be into bondage and domination which seemed to keep him well and truly under her thumb and high heels but at the same time she constantly threatened him with his job and his life and his wife. The latest message deleted stated she was sending him to Romania and he would be picked up from the airport. This message was deleted two weeks ago. This woman called Scarlett reminded him that he was to tell no one and not to worry about his family because someone would be watching his wife, his mother and his two sisters to make sure they stayed safe and out of harm's way. Also, looking at the writing of her texts, I think she is foreign because of the way she says things."

Jazz and Boomer took a deep breath and simultaneously said "Bloody hell!!" Neither knew what anything meant except it just wasn't right.

Ash, feeling pretty good, smiled at each of them and asked what the next step was but Jazz at that moment had no idea what the hell was going on and what the fuck he was going to do.

Ash was sent back to the station while Boomer and Jazz plotted their next move. They got another coffee and read through the paperwork. It confirmed what Ash had said and basically it was messages of erotic sex setting out little games to play with Derek always tied up and Scarlett astride him with nipple clamps, a gag tight across his mouth and she would tease him by gently caressing him until her hands reached his balls and she would squeeze hard until he begged for mercy. They read through it both with many a raised eyebrow at the content. But amongst the erotic messages many messages contained threats towards his family and his job prospects. They had to work out what this woman wanted from Derek.

CHAPTER SIX

HOUSEWORK

They stopped reading when Mad Pete came into McDonald's looking for them. Jazz got him a coffee and when he moaned it was fucking early and he hadn't had time for breakfast, Jazz got him a McDonald's breakfast.

"So?" Jazz asked as he put the breakfast in front of Mad Pete.

"So what, Mr Singh?" was the answer.

Mad Pete was asking for a slap. He knew darn well what was wanted. As he took a big bite into his Mcbreakfast Mad Pete looked up at Jazz and saw the warning look in his eyes. It was a disgusting sight watching Mad Pete devouring the Mcbreakfast with a mouth full of egg, sausage and bun while trying to talk at the same time. Jazz was busy dodging the aerodynamic crumbs hurdling out of Mad Pete's mouth while waiting for an answer from Mad Pete he could understand. With a gulp as the last piece slid down his throat, Mad Pete rubbed his hands and sat up straight to start business.

"I spoke to Mrs Manson this morning and she said she can't see you today because she is house cleaning."

"What?" shouted Jazz, incredulous and angry that an S&M club was closed to new people because of house cleaning.

"That's what she said, Mr Singh. She can see you tomorrow and I will take you there," added Pete, a little frightened. He didn't like upsetting Mr Singh who could, in the blink of an eye, give him a painful smack in the head.

"No, we go today, Pete. You will take us. We will wing it when we get there. No time to lose."

"Bloody 'ell, Mr Singh, you are keen," snorted Mad Pete who thought this was very funny. He tried to duck but Jazz caught him round the ears with a stinging slap.

It had been a while since Jazz had gone to Hackney. Some of the streets had been tarted up and houses that used to look tired and ready for demolition had been woken up with lots of money and skills thrown at them. The house Pete told them to stop at was quite fabulous. A two-storey Georgian-looking place with a basement too. Most of these types of houses in other areas had been converted to zillions of flats but this one stood alone as a single-occupancy house. The decor didn't look like an S&M club but more like Number 10 Downing Street with the black door and the fancy railings out front. He supposed it was done up for rich clients. There was no front garden, but it had steps up to the front door. Jazz was highly impressed. He gathered Boomer and Mad Pete around him and pressed the highly ornate buzzer by the side of the door. He couldn't hear it ring inside and wondered after a short while if he should ring again.

Just as he was about to ring the buzzer again the door was thrown open and a vision of a flying Valkyrie stood in front of him. She had spotted Mad Pete who she knew so her welcome was quite rich for her.

"What do you fucking cunts want? Can't you see I am busy?" Jazz looked in awe at this amazing woman who managed to keep a cigarette between her ruby-red lips whilst spitting insults at them. At what was five foot ten inches tall in seven-inch stilettos, with a curvaceous and muscular body, she stood magnificently at the door. Her flowing black hair spread in curls and ringlets around her shoulders and was kept from covering her face by the winged helmet. Her arms, muscular and bronzed, were covered in tattoos of various colours and designs. But it was the circular tit shields on the body armour she was wearing that mesmerized him. He had never seen anything like it before.

This woman was the scariest thing he had ever seen and the look in her big, bold green eyes that were accentuated by the black eye make-up and the thick black eyelashes looked like they could scratch you if you got too close; they had seen everything and she loved it. She saw Jazz transfixed and before anything could be said she gestured angrily at them to come in. Once the door was closed, she started.

"What the fuck do you cunts want? I told you, Pete, not today. I am a fucking flying Valkyrie today and I don't have time to see new people."

Mad Pete, obviously frightened, started to stutter an apology. Jazz interceded and asked why she had a whip and not a shield in her hand. He had learned about the Norse mythology at school.

"It's fucking housework day today, that's why, you stupid cunt," she answered.

With that she threw her cigarette on the floor and put it out by stamping on it with one of her seven-inch stilettos and screwing it into the wooden floor. With a look of disgust at the mess, she shouted at the top of her voice, "No.1 cunt, get here now and clean this mess up!"

From what seemed like nowhere, a man with what looked like a leather black face mask covering his face, wearing just his underpants, scuttled into the room obediently waiting to be directed by Mrs Manson.

"What do you say?" she said threateningly.

"Thank you, Mrs Manson, it will be my greatest pleasure to clean up your shit," was the timid answer.

With that Mrs Manson flicked the whip in her hand and Jazz and Boomer winced as it hit this little man's back. Again, she asked menacingly, "What do you say, you pathetic little cunt?"

"Thank you, Mrs Manson, it will be my greatest pleasure to clean up your shit."

Satisfied now, Mrs Manson led the bemused and quite honestly scared Jazz and Boomer with Mad Pete into another room.

The room must have been Mrs Manson's private rooms because it was tastefully set out with big comfy settees and cushions. She gestured for them to sit down and as they made themselves comfortable Mrs Manson walked towards a door in the corner of the room and shouted, "Cunt No.2, get here now."

In rushed a six-foot tall and nearly as wide muscle man in his underpants and wearing a leather black balaclava with slits for eyes and mouth. He knelt before her. She looked up at Jazz and Boomer and asked in a deceptively sweet voice, "Would you like a tea or coffee?"

They all nodded in unison, scared to upset this mother of Satan's fury. When sorted she looked down at the kneeling man and brought her pointed stiletto up to his face stabbing his cheek viciously with the toecap. Each word had venom in it and she pushed the toecap hard into his face as she uttered, "Get the drinks now, Cunt No.2, and be quick about it."

Jazz winced as he watched this huge man cowering before her and then trying to scramble away as she flexed the whip which cracked in the air as she brought it down on his back. God, he could feel that stinging pain.

The drinks were brought and try as he might, Jazz was wound up so tight he thought his head might explode and swallowing tea was impossible. The venom, the fear, the control was palpable. Jazz could feel it like a knot in his throat. This woman promoted evil like an evangelistic priest, full of promise of no hope, full of retribution and no saviour. This place felt like hell. What he couldn't understand was that people paid for this. He really wanted to leave.

Again, as they held their drinks, each too frightened to make a sound, they watched as Mrs Manson, whip in hand, was telling Cunt No.2 to go back to cleaning her toilet.

"I hope you haven't damaged my toothbrush cleaning the toilet," she shouted at him.

He murmured something ingratiating that Jazz couldn't hear, but the whip again flicked in the air and the tentacles hit the man's back with a piercing sound that tore at his flesh. The whimper from him was soft as he scurried away to do her bidding.

Mrs Manson, now satisfied her minions were working hard at their chores, sat down with a sigh and with a malevolent smile stared at them, just waiting. Jazz pulled himself together and put his game face on; he had to be convincing. He could see that Mrs Manson was no fool. The look in her eyes told him she had seen it all and knew the vagaries of human nature. They had given themselves away with their discomfort at seeing S&M role play. Now was the time for his Oscar-winning performance.

He started with a rueful smile. "Mrs Manson, thank you for seeing us today. Pete had told me you were busy but I had to come today. I have waited a long time to see you. Please let me explain. Tom," and he pointed to Boomer, "has come with me as a friend. He isn't that interested in my own predilection for shall we say a little pain and pleasure."

At this point, Mrs Manson interrupted.

"But the look of horror on your face doesn't make me think you enjoy our skills here, Mr Singh." She looked at Mad Pete and nodding towards Jazz said, "Peteee darling, why did you bring them here? You know how important confidentiality is to us all."

Peteee? thought Jazz, *for God's sake!* But he smiled at Mad Pete in a far too sweet way and continued, "But Mrs Manson, what you saw on my face, and I am sorry, was that it offended me. I do not want to be involved in that type of S&M. I want the exclusivity of one-on-one where we design and work together. I want a sexual partner who understands my needs, Mrs Manson, and I believe you have such a person here."

That answer pleased Mrs Manson. She still wasn't that happy; Mad Pete had broken a bond with her by bringing two strangers to her club especially on housework day when her two minions, one a West End fashion designer and the other a director in a pharmaceutical company, were busy role-playing. Their anonymity was protected by the face masks but even so, it was not the way she liked to work. She would talk to Peteee later.

"So, who are you, Mr Singh? Why are you here and who told you about me?"

She wasn't going to waste any more time. She was busy and her clients were usually top notch and Mr Singh didn't look that wonderful and his companion seemed a bit ordinary to her. She had a reputation to protect and she certainly wasn't cheap either. What she offered, and she offered a lot, was expensive.

Jazz knew he had to get this right. He looked at Mrs Manson. He had to say she was a beautiful woman in her late forties, he reckoned, and the look in her eyes told him she had experienced a lifetime of situations and people. She was not going to be easily fooled.

"Do you know Derek Philips? He was a work colleague and he used to tell me about Scarlett who he visited here. Well, I liked what he told me and as I was a little hesitant because I have never indulged before, I didn't say anything to Derek. Unfortunately, I got moved and I haven't seen Derek for many months and I wanted to know more about Scarlett." Jazz, feeling embarrassed, smiled shyly at Mrs Manson.

"I was fantasising about this Scarlett and now I am obsessed by her."

Mrs Manson understood. "So how did you find me?" she asked.

"Well, I know Pete. What I mean is, Pete has in the past helped me find certain items and supplied them to me so I wondered if he could help. He seems to know everyone."

Mrs Manson smiled at Mad Pete. "He sure is a sweetie, isn't he?" she concurred.

Mad Pete was switching between fear with Mr Singh telling such lies and he was scared he was going to get into trouble, and bathing in the compliments from Mrs Manson. He was feeling ill.

"I am now ready and can't wait to meet Scarlett. Is that possible, Mrs Manson?" Jazz asked.

"What about your friend?" Mrs Manson asked.

"Oh, he is just here to support me, Mrs Manson," Jazz stated glibly. "This is not something I have taken on board lightly and I was a little scared. Considering my job, it's stupid to say that." Jazz laughed self-consciously at that.

"And what is your job, Jazz?" she asked seductively.

"Oh, erm, I am something in the civil service assisting others," was his fudged answer. Mrs Manson was having none of it.

"If you are coming here, you have to be honest. I work with full discretion and everyone here is safe. I have managing directors, senior members of every organisation you can think of. Discretion is our name and that is why we have been here undetected for many, many years."

"Well, if you put it like that, Mrs Manson, did Derek tell you what he did?" Jazz watched in awe as she changed from the hard-edged woman she was, and Mrs Manson shifted seductively her position and changed stance. She looked and gave him a beautiful smile that Jazz thought was only meant for him and he bathed in its brilliance.

"Oh yes, we knew exactly what he did. He had a very important and stressful job. That is what we excel in here, Jazz, we work through your stress and make you feel relaxed again."

Jazz felt goosebumps. The way she said it made him feel safe and scared at the same time. She was very good at what she did. Her words were said with a sensuality that soothed you deeply and made you feel good but the edge was there and you were never quite sure what she would do. God! She was exciting.

Boomer was watching in anxious silence and wondered what the hell Singh was going to do now. He looked peculiar and totally transfixed by this she-devil. He wanted to shout out 'get a room'. The two of them looked like they were flirting with serious intent. He hoped Singh had a cast-iron story to tell her. Boomer could see she would not be fooled easily. This was one hard-edged bitch and he had no intention of crossing swords with her. He shuddered at the thought.

Mad Pete was scared beyond belief. He realised Mr Singh was play-acting and it was his fault. He had brought him here. Mrs Manson would kill him slowly if she found out who he was. He sat transfixed by the spectacle of Mrs Manson and Mr Singh engrossed in each other.

The atmosphere in the room was heightened by the anxiety of Boomer and Mad Pete who seemed to hold their breath while watching the exquisite sexual intensity of Mrs Manson and Jazz's verbal exchange. Mrs Manson moved closer to Jazz and he willed her forward. He wanted to feel her breath on his face and smell the perfume in her hair. Mesmerised by her soft yielding voice he forgot anyone else was in the room. There was only him and Mrs Manson and, my god, he wanted her now!

She moved slowly forward and just within inches of his face, her mouth close to his, her breath slow and she sighed with a longing so sensual Jazz craved more but the moment was broken when suddenly she pulled back and slapped him hard around the face. Seeing his shocked look, she moved in closer and very slowly licked his stinging bright red cheek.

"Does that feel better?" she purred. "Now tell me who you are, darling, so I can help you."

For some reason the tension evaporated. It all seemed normal again. Boomer shifted position and Mad Pete stopped shaking. The story was a good one. Jazz was, of course, as she would have expected if he had known Derek Philips, a protection officer. He said he protected ambassadors and embassies mainly and he had just been promoted to protecting low level royals. Obviously, he couldn't mention names and Mrs Manson totally agreed.

"Darling, I don't need specifics, just type of job so I know what you need," she whispered.

Her voice sent shivers down to his dick and he thought he wanted to stay and talk for as long as she would have him. Again, he asked about Scarlett. Mrs Manson, now stroking his red cheek, told him she was very expensive and only worked occasionally. In fact, she told Jazz that Scarlett had, in the end, only come into work to see Derek. Apparently, most of the girls worked part-time. 'They were engaged in other areas as well', was the way Mrs Manson put it. Money was talked about and it appeared it was bloody expensive to be tortured. Jazz agreed that he was happy to pay the £1,000 up front required to register and further it would be £500 for a two-hour session. Scarlett would be contacted and Mrs

Manson said she would contact Jazz when everything was set up. With a pat of his cheek, she let Jazz go. She nodded at Boomer who was of no consequence to her and she smiled at Mad Pete and cooed,

"Darling Peteee, I will contact you soon for some bits and pieces."

Mad Pete nodded far too much and left behind Jazz and Boomer almost tripping over his untied trainers in his rush to get out.

CHAPTER SEVEN

CATCH UP

They drove for a while and stopped at a pub near Hackney Marshes. No one knew them there and they all needed a drink. The tension was palpable and sitting with a pint of beer each, they all exhaled and visibly relaxed. The questions started. Boomer looked at Jazz and quite mystified by what happened asked incredulously, "You fucking enjoyed that, didn't you, Singh?"

Jazz, still not sure what had happened, brazened it out and unconvincingly said, "It was all an act. Just trying to get her to think I was a punter."

Jazz looked sideways at Boomer to see if he believed that statement. Boomer didn't.

"So, what do we do with that bit of info, Singh? It just doesn't go anywhere. The cost to go undercover is enormous and can't come out of the tea money, you know," he added sarcastically.

Jazz didn't have a clue what to do or where to go with this. For a bit of distraction, he turned on Mad Pete.

"Oy Peteee, what the fuck is she?" Before Mad Pete could answer Jazz, he added, "What the fuck was up with those pair of twats cleaning? I thought they liked to do things like that but I could see they hated it and were in pain."

Mad Pete snorted a laugh and felt quite important. He had information that they didn't.

"There was a reason for that look, Mr Singh."

"What, for Christ's sake?"

"Well," started Mad Pete; he waited a few seconds to just get their full attention and continued.

"They like figging too."

"What the fuck is figging?" both Boomer and Jazz said in unison.

Again, Mad Pete, enjoying their full attention, smiled and waited a few seconds too long because Jazz gave him a look that meant trouble so he hurriedly explained.

"You take a piece of ginger and skin it so the inner bit is showing and it's bloody hot when it is in warm, damp places. They shape it and stick it up their arses."

A moment's silence, an intake of breath, and both Jazz and Boomer looked intently at Mad Pete and then burst into laughter.

"Fuck off," was their response.

"No, it's true. Mrs Manson would have put it there herself. She likes to make sure everything is correctly done and the maximum of pain is felt. It bloody hurts. She used to put hot chillies up there but she found it was too painful and they couldn't do her housework."

They laughed so much they had to wipe the tears streaming down their faces. Every time Jazz and Boomer looked up at each other they started again. It took ten minutes before they were composed enough to ask any more questions. Now it was Mad Pete's turn.

"Mr Singh, you lied to me. Mrs Manson relies on my discretion and you messed it up. I don't want to get on the wrong side of her. She is evil and she knows evil people who would sort me out. I do business with her. Don't do anything to get me in trouble, Mr Singh."

Jazz felt sorry for Mad Pete. It was true he had used him but he was after all a piece of shit so didn't feel too bad. But he needed to keep him calm and with him. He still didn't know what he would need from Mad Pete regarding Mrs Manson. He seemed to have this knack of people trusting him and then telling him things. Jazz reckoned because he was useful and a snivelling coward everyone thought he was of no consequence.

"No, don't worry, Pete. I ain't gonna do anything that will come back on you. I'm just doing a recce. She loves you, I could tell, so you are safe."

Mad Pete almost blushed at that and before he could answer Jazz added, "But that woman's fucking mouth is awful. I hate it when a woman swears like she does." Boomer nodded at that.

"My girlfriend can give it some but never as bad as that woman," Boomer said.

It went quiet for a moment as they both digested such an unbelievable comment.

"You got a girlfriend?" asked a very astonished Jazz.

Boomer with a girlfriend wasn't possible. He hated most women for a start and his lack of charm kept all decent women well off his radar.

"Yeah, well, she's a good sort," muttered Boomer, regretting ever mentioning Sally.

Jazz thought she had to be deaf, blind and dumb; he would delve into this at a later date. For now, they had to discuss the way forward and what the fuck they had made of the visit.

Jazz said he would talk to Sarah and update her. He was worried about the money. *I can't go undercover if I haven't come up with the money she is talking about and I can't take this to DCI Radley. I have nothing to tell him yet and it's more like bloody spy work than police work.* He didn't want to have anything to do with S&M, but was he going to have to go through with it? He worried about what he was getting himself into. What was he hoping to get from a session with this Scarlett? His usual optimistic recklessness had packed its bags and gone on holiday.

DI Tom Black (Boomer) was going to set out what they knew and didn't know for Jazz. He was an experienced DI with years of knowledge. Okay, he worked a little off the wall and that's why he liked working with Jazz. *All those candy-arsed detectives being so PC and wasting time thumbing through the rule books so they don't get told off by the headmaster! made him sick.* Police work didn't happen like that. He was held in high regard simply because he knew the boundaries that Jazz had never found. So, it was down to him to put this all in perspective and find a way forward.

They dropped Mad Pete off at the local Barking McDonald's; he had a meeting booked there, so he told Jazz. Jazz tried not to laugh; *a fucking meeting, you candy-arsed socialite.* He knew it was a drug drop or some such thing but he had too much to consider to worry about that.

Boomer and Jazz took themselves off to the Cranbrook pub for a quiet chat. Boomer had it sussed out for Jazz and they needed to discuss the way forward. Pat the barman was on duty again and knew exactly what Jazz wanted. After a suitable drink was organised, Boomer a shandy (he was working) and Jazz a quadruple vodka and tonic (he was working too), sat down and Boomer gave his views on what to do next.

"So, the money is too much and cannot be found so a way round this is as follows…"

Jazz was listening intently. Boomer always came up with the best results.

"You contact Mrs Manson and tell her in absolute confidence that your job is highly secretive and sensitive. You look after high-profile politicians and you can't be compromised. The only reason you are talking to Mrs Manson is because of Derek. Derek trusts Mrs Manson so you do too but you haven't met Scarlett so before negotiations start you need a meeting with her just to put your mind at rest. In your meeting with Scarlett you give her a lot of bollocks about your confidential work, throw in a few big names if you must and see if she takes the bait. Let it all ferment for a while and see what it brings. It's a start and no money has changed hands although, on second thoughts, you may have to pay Scarlett for her time but better than the big payout."

Jazz, impressed beyond impressed with Boomer, just slapped him on the back and almost gave him a hug.

"Brilliant, it will bide us some time. I will talk to Sarah and see if she wants to fund this visit."

Satisfied that it was a start, they enjoyed their drink in relative silence. Just when they were going to leave Jazz looked up and asked, "So, who is this girlfriend you have? Is she that blow-up doll we bought you the other Christmas?"

Boomer, caught between laughing and growling, just looked at Jazz and uttered under his breath, "Bollocks to you and fuck off."

Jazz laughed and they made their way back to the station.

Jazz phoned Sarah on route and arranged to meet her in the Cranbrook at 5 p.m. to update her. Boomer was right, he didn't need to get too far into these S&M bollocks. He would ring Mrs Manson tomorrow. Things were moving okay and Jazz was feeling a little lighter.

Ilford Station was busy as usual. A drunk was in custody and there had been a few known shoplifters arrested. A pickpocket was chased by a mob of shoppers who spotted him and he was grateful to be arrested by the police. Jazz slipped through the door and made his way to his office watching out for DCI Radley and anyone else who might want to waylay him. He needed to talk to Ash, his one and only detective working with him. Ash, anally awkward in wanting everything to be above board and kosher, was something Jazz just had to cope with, but Ash was the absolute nuts on finding anything worth knowing on the computer. The Police Aware system was pretty good and Jazz would, of course, have used it if he had the time, temperament and knowledge to do so but he had Ash who knew how to find everything. Sometimes if pushed, he could find stuff above his pay grade he shouldn't have access to, so a problem was sorted even if it meant he had to listen to incessant whining about protocols and shit like that.

He found Ash sitting at his desk intently working on his computer. He had been asked to look at statistics by DCI Radley, something Ash loved to do. Jazz crept up behind him to make him jump, something Ash hated. Jazz, always joking and messing around, was an absolute pain. Ash sighed, saved his work and closed his computer. He tried to look offended by this interruption to his work but Jazz was Jazz and for his sins, he loved the guy. Jazz had that look and Ash knew it was going to be trouble. He looked quizzically in silence at Jazz and waited for what he knew was going to be an awkward and possibly illegal use of his computer again.

Putting on his serious face, not hard to do at this moment, Jazz asked Ash to confidentially look into Mrs Manson's business and those that worked for her. He thought that there might be nothing to detect but with a pained look he tentatively asked if Ash was able to search the databases of other agencies like MI5 or MI6. He knew it was illegal, he knew Ash wouldn't want to do it but he needed to find something about Mrs M and her organisation. He gave her address to Ash and made him promise to 'keep it all under his hat'. Ash retorted that he would be a fucking idiot to advertise he was doing treasonable work. Jazz left suitably pleased that if there was something to find, Ash would find it. Feeling good and a little too blasé, Jazz strutted out of the hot-desking office and walked straight into DCI Radley.

With no excuse (he knew he was done for), and with a sigh, he gave in and stood respectfully while DCI Radley, who looked pissed off beyond belief, struggled to keep a semblance of control. His words spitting out over Jazz in a tight-lipped stance which didn't allow for shouting and use of intemperate language, DCI Radley stated "Tomorrow morning at 7.45 a.m. sharp you will report to the secretary's office of Henry Green Primary School,

Green Lane, Dagenham. They will give you the jacket and stop sign. It's a busy road and they need someone who can stop traffic."

Jazz went to open his mouth to say for how long but the piercing 'don't go there' look from DCI Radley stopped him in his tracks. Instead, he just nodded and said, "Yes, sir, I will be there at 7.45 a.m."

With a sharp nod of acknowledgement DCI Radley turned and smartly walked off to his office. Jazz watched him go and as soon as his office door closed, Jazz, who felt he had held his breath for ages, let out a forceful "FUCK!!"

The evening went okay with Sarah. He thought she looked a little bit worn down and she was quiet for her. Usually she was bouncy and full of life and ready to take anyone on. She agreed that if there was a cost to see this Scarlett woman she would pay. She was staying with family at the moment and said she felt as safe as she could. She reckoned, with a rueful smile, it was all S&M talk about hurting her. Even so, she really didn't want anyone else to know about this yet and Jazz, without thinking, took her hand and squeezed it. He reassured her that unless it took a turn for the worse and someone needed to know, he would not involve anyone at the station. She hurriedly and with embarrassment kissed Jazz as she left, grateful for his help and confidence. He liked the kiss but was worried about her. She looked so small and lost.

"Derek, you are a bastard!" he whispered under his breath.

Mr Wonderful didn't deserve Sarah who he thought was perfect. He liked his women to be a bit ballsy and the fact she was a leggy, slim blonde helped too. He smiled to himself, finished his vodka and said an unsteady goodnight to the barman. He had to be up early tomorrow, for fuck's sake!!

CHAPTER EIGHT

SCHOOLBELL

Jazz, up early, reluctantly made his way to Henry Green Primary School not far from the busy junction of Green Lane and Valance Avenue. At 7.45 a.m. in the morning the traffic was fierce and uncompromising. The lights at the junction would change and the cars would put their foot down and race towards him. *This is going to be fucking mad* he thought. He reported to the secretary's office where a very nice smiley lady showed him where to find his stop sign and the bloody awful yellow jacket he had to wear. Dejected and looking around for a candid camera team, Jazz, humiliated beyond humiliation put the jacket on. The smiley secretary cheerfully reminded him that the children would be arriving soon for the breakfast club so *chop chop* he had better get out there, and then as he was about to leave she shouted cheerfully.

"Coo-eee, don't forget your cap."

With a heavy heart and feet that felt like lead, Jazz snatched up the hat and went to take up his position outside.

The first rush of children and mothers appeared far too quickly for him. He had never seen so many pushchairs all in one go. Standing in the middle of the road with the lollipop stick stating STOP on it, didn't stop some mothers catching his feet, his shins and his legs with parts of pushchairs. He felt bruised and belligerent and took it out on the cars steaming towards him. The traffic lights on the corner of Green Lane and Valence Avenue would turn green and it seemed the cars waiting and revving up were going to accelerate faster than any car on a racetrack would dare, towards Jazz standing in the middle of the road armed just with a STOP sign. He thought it a fucking stupid, suicidal job and couldn't understand why anyone wanted to be a lollipop man/woman.

After the third car he had waved down and advised none to pleasantly that he was reporting them for dangerous driving, he was told by the fed-up mothers with fidgeting children on the sides of the road to 'bleeding do your job, we ain't standing here for ever and need to get our kids to school!' He realised he wasn't cut out for this job. After waves of children and mothers and bloody pushchairs it suddenly seemed to go quiet. He looked over at the playground and saw it was empty. *Thank sodding God for that!!!* he thought and was just about to take his sign and coat back to the school and go home when he saw coming around the corner at the rate of knots what looked like a mess that turned out to be a half-dressed boy with a bag.

"You're late," said Jazz, fed up with waiting.

The boy, with a shirt wrongly done up and trying to tuck his shirt into his trousers, just looked contemptuously at Jazz as he crossed the road. Niggled by the look Jazz shouted, "Oy you, did you hear what I said? You're late."

Again, the boy eyed up Jazz and said with feeling, "Fuck Off."

Jazz watched him run into school busy trying to fix his tie and tuck his shirt in. The kid was asking for a clip round the ear (not allowed under PC fucking rules) and he didn't know why, but he actually felt sorry for the poor bastard.

He took his coat and lollipop back to the secretary's office. She looked at him and without a word pointed to a cupboard and he put his stuff in there. He hated this job. Before he left, he went to the secretary and using what charm he could muster smiled and introduced himself in his most sultry of voices.

"Hi, I'm Jazz and it looks like I will be here for a few days. What time do you want me next?"

She smiled up at him and thought she could want him most times of the day but instead she said she was Betty. This was looking good, he thought. He hoped next time he might get a cup of coffee or something but he could wait.

"You have to be here for the lunchtime babies and then the older school so be here by 11.30 a.m. for the 11.45 exit for the nursery. The juniors sometimes go home for lunch and the seniors too and they come out at 12.15. School starts again at 1.30 p.m. Then you are back at 3.30 p.m. for school closing."

She smiled brightly at him but he was pissed off. *Christ,* he thought, *this will take over my life.* He hated his boss, DCI fucking Radley, he hated the children, he hated everyone. He was going to go the station to make phone calls and catch up but it wasn't worth it because in a few minutes he would have to be bloody back here again. But before he left, he asked Betty, "So, who was that lad who came in late?"

Betty was busy with lots to do but this officer was rather lovely and she absent-mindedly pushed an imaginary strand of hair off her face. Jazz was well aware he had her attention and gave her a smile that was normally reserved for those very special in his life. She blushed and stammered a little. Betty was a woman of a certain age; her dress style was something that could have made her forty-five years old. He thought the cardigan gave her an older look, but when he looked into her brown eyes, he saw a much younger woman. Her hair was mousey and unkempt with a natural wave that struggled in all the wrong directions around her shoulders. He noted she had a chubby face that created dimples when she smiled. Betty was an unappreciated little woman that you would not remember as you passed by her.

"Well, actually…"

She felt at a loss for words for the moment. She wasn't used to such attention and Jazz had leaned forward, with his elbows on the counter and his hands cupping his chin looking at her. Blushing fiercely now, she continued, trying hard to concentrate.

"That would be young Master William Winder."

She could see the interest in Jazz and wanted to add more to stop him going.

"Actually, he has a rough time here. The lads call him Willie Wonker on good days and Willie Wanker on bad days."

The smile on Jazz's face came and went in seconds. *Poor sod* he thought.

"He arrived late and looked a mess. What's his story?" asked Jazz.

Betty leaned further forward, feeling more comfortable talking to this gorgeous man. She could smell his aftershave and drank it in. With a crook of her finger, she beckoned him closer which was such a treat and whispered.

"I shouldn't really talk about him. It's not protocol but you are the police after all so I suppose it's okay."

She looked into his beautiful eyes waiting for reassurance. Jazz nodded and winked at her to affirm it was okay. The wink stirred her and she nearly started giggling, but managed to hold back. She looked around with sweeping movements of her head and shoulders in a very theatrical way, to check no one was loitering near them and could listen. Jazz watched her and kept back the giggle threatening to erupt from his belly. He was enjoying this. She leaned further forward towards the hunk of a man in front of her. She was having a great time. Having the attention of a gorgeous man just didn't happen to her and she was going to take as long as she could to keep him so close.

"Well…" she said, looking into Jazz's gorgeously large brown eyes with eyelashes a woman would die for.

"His parents are druggies. I know that is not the correct term, but you know what I mean," she said with a smile and waited for Jazz's reassuring nod and smile.

They were so close she inhaled his breath as if it was hers to take. He could see the look of pleasure on her face and wondered what the fuck was going on.

"He lives in Bennetts Castle Lane," she continued accentuating each word as if it was special.

"Where is Bennetts Castle Lane?" he asked. The spell was broken and she seemed to pull herself together and abruptly said, "Oh, it's down Green Lane on the left after the sex shop."

He was going to laugh but knew he shouldn't. This was just madness and this woman was something else. A femme fatale in a cardigan. He dumped his coat and gear in the room behind the secretary's office and with a smile, said he would see her at 11.15 a.m. She blushed and nodded, adding suggestively as he went out, "I will have a hot coffee waiting for you."

He was glad to get out in the fresh air. He wondered what the hell was going on. His time with Mrs Manson must have set something off, like pheromones. The thought of her made him feel something he hadn't felt for a long time. He sighed at the thought and wondered what the fuck he was getting into. He thought he must be careful in women's company for a while, he was obviously a babe magnet. The thought made him laugh out loud as he made his way back to De Vere Gardens and the safety of his room. He laughed again at the thought. He had calls to make.

This job was a fucking joke and he had to get out of it. He couldn't face Mrs Manson knowing he was a fucking lollipop man!! And he wanted to see her again. She had definitely stirred something up in him. He wanted to know her first name, he wanted to see her alone without his merry men laughing at him. He wondered if she did 'normal' or was it always S&M. In a split second he heard himself and got scared. No woman had made him feel like this for a very long time. Women had always caused him a heap of trouble, but okay, he conceded, it was true he had always been interested in them, it's just he put women on the back burner and concentrated on work; it was safer that way. He smirked at the thought. But this Mrs Manson had stoked a fire that had been simmering for a long time and now it felt ready to explode into a furnace. *What the fuck have I got myself into?* he asked himself.

CHAPTER NINE

THE PACT

Jazz got back to Mrs Chodda's in no time. The traffic was lighter by now and he could put his foot down. He was going to have a mid-morning drink of orange with a little vodka in it perhaps, he thought, and he would call Boomer and discuss strategies but he got waylaid as he got in the door. Mrs Chodda was surprised and delighted Jazz was home. He explained he was back for a couple of hours and out again. He sensed Mrs Chodda was up to something by the almost giggly way she spoke to him. Anxious to get away, Jazz made the excuse that he had to make a phone call before he went out again. Mrs Chodda quickly interrupted his moving away.

"I was just about to send Amrit up to your room to change your sheets. It's time they were washed and any other washing you might have," she sweetly informed him.

Oh God! he thought, *not again!* He didn't want to have to cope with Mrs Chodda pushing Amrit and him together again. It seemed she took every sodding opportunity to get Amrit round to her house and send her up to Jazz's room when he was in using every stupid and useless excuse she could think up. It was getting tiresome. He didn't have time for women; although Amrit was kinda nice, it was all too much.

"Okay, Mrs Chodda, if she wants to come up now, I can make my call afterwards."

Jazz had a soft spot for Mrs Chodda and gave her one of his flash smiles and made his way up the stairs to his room. He thought his relaxing drink would have to wait. He hoped Amrit would be quick and leave him alone; he had a lot to think about and to plan.

The knock on his door was soft and he shouted, "Come in."

Amrit looked rather lovely today. She had a green silk salwar kameez (loose trousers, narrow at the ankles, and matching top) and she looked good. Her long black hair had been brushed and straightened to an inch of its life and had a sheen that mirrored the silk clothing. He knew she would have a dupatta (a matching long scarf) to go with the outfit, women always did, but she was here supposedly to work so that must be downstairs. His eyes flicked over her and moved away quickly but she saw the look of appreciation and she was annoyed with herself that she found it so pleasing. She closed the door behind her gently and for a moment hesitated. Jazz looked and raised his eyebrows quizzically. She normally blustered into his room when she had to and busied herself looking embarrassed and moved off. Now she was just standing there.

"Can we talk just for a moment?" she asked hesitantly.

He didn't like the sound of this and hoped to God she wasn't going to say anything embarrassing, he really didn't need this now. He felt that scratchy irritation that normally made him curt and off-hand, but he tried to look interested and civil even producing a weak smile.

"Go for it," was his answer.

Taking this as a good signal she moved quickly and sat on the edge of his bed facing him as he now sat uncomfortably in his armchair beside her thinking *what the fuck is she doing sitting down?*

With a deep breath she began. It was quite a ramble but he listened carefully.

"So, Auntie is trying to match us up." She looked at Jazz to see if he agreed and he nodded.

"It's becoming a bit of a pain for me and you, don't you think?" Again, she looked at Jazz and he nodded in agreement.

"So, I think we should have a pact between us that we play her game so she feels she is getting her way but we know what's going on." Again, she looked at Jazz and he nodded.

Feeling more relieved, they both relaxed a little. Amrit continued faster now and feeling so much more at ease. She laughed a little and added, "I don't know about you but I was feeling really embarrassed about this. Auntie is really lovely but she keeps pushing me into you and making me ask you silly things. I hated it."

Jazz laughed. "I dreaded coming home a lot of the time thinking you would be on the doorstep waiting to trap me."

He laughed again at his comment. Amrit, slightly put out by the comment, raised her eyebrows and tried to laugh too.

"So now we don't have to worry, we don't want to get to know each other so we can just pretend to play Auntie's game," Amrit added.

They agreed the air was clear now between them and it would make life oh so much easier. Amrit changed the bed and took the washing. As she left, she smiled at Jazz and thanked him for agreeing to this subterfuge. They both laughed but actually neither felt that happy about the situation and neither of them knew why.

It had all taken more time than Jazz thought and he was mindful he had to be back at the school at bloody 11.30 a.m. and it was now 10.30 a.m. and no time for a bloody drink and a bloody conversation with Boomer. He poured a quick orange and spilt a drop of vodka into it, just to give him a bit of a boost. It had been a funny morning.

He rang Boomer and arranged to meet him in the Cranbrook that evening for a strategy talk. Five o'clock was decided as a good time to meet. Jazz asked, no, he pleaded, even begged Boomer to see what he could do to get him out of being a lollipop man as soon as possible. He told him the hours in the day he had to do the sodding work and after Boomer stopped laughing, he pulled himself together and said he would do what he could.

He savoured his orange juice for a little while, putting his feet up on his clean, newly made bed and enjoyed the comfort of his drink. He thought Amrit was a feisty woman. Not many Sikh women would have the balls to talk to a man like she did. He sort of admired that. She might not have a husband or father to listen to but she kept herself very nice and did things her way. Again, he liked that.

In no time at all he had to get going back to the sodding school. He hated his job and he hated all the mothers and the children and the prams and the cars but most of all he hated the bloody hat, yellow coat and lollipop stick.

Lunchtime went well. Betty, as promised, had a mug of coffee waiting for him when he arrived. She added a few biscuits to the tray too. She smiled and said, "These are my very special biscuits which I keep hidden and I only share with nice people."

She blushed as she said this. Jazz thanked her and gave her one of his eye-contact special smiles which she drank in. This was the only fun part of his day; Betty was definitely a femme fatale. The pushchair brigade bashed his shins again but he was beginning to see them coming and dodged out of the way.

When the lunch brigade had gone home, he had an hour to waste before they all came back for afternoon school. He asked Betty if Willy (the late kid) went home for lunch as he hadn't seen him. She told him he had free school dinners and she reckoned it was probably the only meal he had during the day. Jazz felt sorry for the kid. He thought he would take a walk and see where he lived. He got the full address from Betty who inferred he could have anything he asked for. At that point he needed to get out of her way. *Geez* he thought, *she is going to be hard to handle if she goes on like this.* He left with her shouting in that sing-song sort of voice that she would see him later and couldn't wait.

It wasn't far to walk. He found the flat. Well, it was a maisonette and most in the block looked quite good and looked after. He knew which one was Willy's home. It had nicotine-stained nets that looked so old the nicotine was holding them together. The front door was splintered as if someone had kicked it in once but a new lock had obviously been put on. The curtains were still closed but if they were druggies, Jazz didn't think they would bother with such niceties. Now he was here, he wasn't sure what he was going to do. He was a police officer so he could knock and just wing it from there.

It took a long time of knocking before the door was opened. A tall, stringy woman with scabs on her face, and hair hanging in greasy lengths around her face and shoulders stood a little unevenly and asked, "Yeah, what do you want?"

Jazz could see she was totally spaced out and reckoned he was lucky she had the energy to open the door. She didn't smile. *Thank God,* he thought, because as she talked, he could see her black teeth poking out of her scabby mouth.

"I am here to talk about Willy, your son," he said officiously.

"So?" she said, not caring and wanting to get back to her bed.

"I am very concerned about his well-being. He looks underfed and to be frank with you he seems to be having problems with children at school."

He was getting no response and added quickly, "I wonder if you are aware of this."

She looked at him blankly and there was a pregnant pause and then with more energy than he thought she could muster she took a deep breath and bellowed, "Jaaaason come 'ere naaw!!!"

Jazz was not sure what was going to happen and it all felt wrong. Too late now but he reckoned he should never have come here. It wasn't his business and they could complain. *Mind you*, he thought, *I never do what I should so why make a difference now?* He nearly smiled at the thought but she was staring hard at him and it was most disconcerting. The opposite of her in every way appeared, a huge, fat man who had never used a razor, with an obvious paranoia problem by the way he looked at the scum in front of him. He pushed the woman out of the way and bore menacingly down on Jazz. He must have been six-foot five inches tall and at least thirty stone; Jazz at a mere five-foot ten felt very small in front of him. Jason pulled himself together and took a deep breath. Both Jazz and the woman waited for words of wisdom.

"What?" was all he said.

Feeling totally on the back foot and not sure what to do, Jazz did his best to bring a sense of propriety to the occasion.

"I was saying to your good wife," he started.

"She ain't my wife," he replied curtly.

"Your, erm, girlfriend, then." This seemed to work.

"I am worried about Willy. He appears underfed, not well dressed and he is being bullied by others at school. I wondered if you were aware of this and if you need any help." Jazz was not doing very well with these two. He gave a smile and waited for their reply. It was swift and to the point. They both stepped back and the front door was slammed shut in Jazz's face. He rang the bell again and could hear Jason's voice shouting, "Fuck off!"

Standing looking at the filthy door and feeling a total tool, he was left wondering what the fuck he was doing. With a sigh, Jazz turned around and without looking at the neighbours, who by the twitching curtains had watched the display, made his way back to the school. *They were a scumbag couple* he told himself. He would talk to the school and see what they could do. He looked at his watch and saw there was a bit of time to spare before the horde would return for the afternoon and he wondered if they had any food spare in the school kitchen. He felt hungry and it spurred him on to get back quickly.

The dining room was full of noise and chatter as the children sat eating their lunches chosen from a buffet area Jazz spotted in the far corner. It seemed to be guarded by a cheery-looking forty-something woman in a white coat and white cap. He watched as he approached her as she tried continuously to hold back the dyed blonde hair that kept poking out from under the cap rim. A cheeky rogue strand of the brightest yellow hair he had ever seen, kept getting in her eye and she absentmindedly kept pushing it away. The food looked good to his hungry eyes and he walked a little faster, with an amiable grin, up to the woman.

He introduced himself as Jazz and she breathlessly answered that she was Patricia but coyly added he could call her Tricia. She liked him very much. It wasn't often a handsome stranger frequented her dining room. He had a smouldering look that quite made her feel giggly. She gave him a plate and told him rather suggestively to pick anything that took his fancy and she would put it on the plate for him. He did his best to stop the giggle that so wanted to show itself. Instead, he smiled and thanked her. He filled his plate and walked over to an empty table and was a little put out to see the lovely Tricia was following him. *I just want five minutes of bloody peace and quiet and something to eat* he told himself.

Tricia plonked herself down opposite Jazz and was ready for a bit of gossip.

"You bin talking with Betty?" Jazz, with his mouth full nodded.

"You'd better watch yourself, darlin', she is dangerous." Jazz swallowed, nearly choking at such a preposterous statement.

"Why?" he asked.

"Cos she is a whatdoyoucallit." At this point Tricia became quite confused and agitated. "You know, one of those creatures that are in children's story books."

Jazz could see she was having trouble so threw in, "You mean a fairy?"

Tricia looked at him like he was mad and said with disgust, "No, that's wrong but I like it."

"A gnome?" he added.

"No, that's not it," she muttered.

After a few seconds of thinking Jazz threw in, "A nymph?"

The deep relief and joy was written all over Tricia's face and she was now animated.

"Oh yes, yes, that's it!!" she exclaimed. "She is a nymphomaniac."

Jazz gulped down a giggle. "Why do you say that? Betty seems a nice, friendly lady."

The dinner lady laughed. "You should talk to George, our usual lollipop man. He is seventy years old with piles and a hiatus hernia and she can't keep her 'ands off 'im."

Jazz, teasing, said, "Well, I am upset that I am not special any more. I thought I was her one and only."

This comment was taken very seriously by Tricia and she leaned forward and whispered conspiratorially.

"You should bleedin' well think you are lucky cos it caused poor George a very nasty pain in his you know what!"

Jazz leaned forward and their noses almost touched and he asked in a whisper, "What 'you know what' was that?"

Tricia not wishing to say the words mouthed silently 'his bum'. She added, "Can you imagine how painful that is to have someone pat and pinch your bum if you have piles? George is such a gentleman, I told him to report her but he wouldn't. So, you watch her. She can't keep her mitts to herself. She'll be pinching your bum before the day's out."

In near hysteria now, Jazz thanked her, got up, and left. The conversation was too much for him. He got outside and let out a howl of laughter. You just couldn't pay for lines like that. *So, Betty, the femme fatale in a cardigan may strike again.* The thought made him laugh even more.

Back on duty, his mortification continued from the return from lunch to the finish of school. Betty seemed busy so his bum was safe. The joke was getting tired now but it still made him laugh. The kids left school at 3.30 p.m. and again his feet and legs were run over by the pushchair brigade. The traffic wasn't as bad and cars seemed to be better behaved. He just wanted to go home. He hated this job with a passion. The last boy out was again Willy Winder. Jazz thought that funny; last in in the morning and last out at night. As the boy crossed the road Jazz nodded and said, "Alright?"

The boy looked at him for a second and then replied, "Fuck off."

Jazz shrugged and thought at least they were communicating. There was something about the boy that reminded Jazz of himself. He didn't know what that was.

CHAPTER TEN

PLAN OF ACTION

Jazz phoned Boomer on his way home and asked to meet him in the Cranbrook that evening. He didn't want to go to the station and have the mickey taken out of him. Too many officers were enjoying his humiliation of being a lollipop man. He was anxious to get home and phone Mrs Manson and arrange a meeting with Scarlett. He needed to get this rolling. *Darling dubious Derek is home in a few days* he thought and he needed to find out what the hell was going on.

Getting home was quick and a deserved glass of vodka and orange was going to be his reward for a shitty day. Then a call to Mrs Manson and an update with Boomer. He felt relaxed and organised. The knock on his door stopped him pouring the drink and annoyed him. On opening the door, Amrit stood there with a tray of Asian tea (stewed for a day and the colour of thunder) and a plate of pakoras (his absolute favourite). She smiled apologetically, and Jazz invited her in with a sweeping hand gesture. She giggled and he liked that.

"Auntie sent me up with this," she said pushing the tray at Jazz. She saw the bottle of vodka and a glass on the table and realised he was about to have a drink and she apologised.

They spent a few minutes excusing each other and smiling and laughing. He hadn't smiled so much for a very long time. She wanted to stay but was waiting for an invitation. He wanted her to sit down but thought it not appropriate, and she might say no. So, after a few moments of hands flailing a little awkwardly, Amrit, embarrassed now, said goodbye and left. Jazz watched the door, hoping she might come back but he heard her going down the stairs so with a sigh returned to the table with the tray and poured his drink. While he thought about his call to Mrs Manson, he ate the pakoras and drank the vodka. He refilled his glass and pulled out his mobile to make the call. He had to pitch this right and he knew it was important.

Jazz got through quite quickly and after introducing himself he got the terse response of, "What do you want?"

Mrs Manson did not sound in a good mood and he didn't want to mess this up.

"I have a request, Mrs Manson." He hesitated for a moment and asked, "Do you have a first name?"

She replied, "Yes, its Mrs, but you can call me Mrs Manson." Now she had put him in his place, he assumed a more deferential tone.

"My request is that before I join your club, could I please meet with Scarlett?" Before she could answer Jazz went on to explain.

"I have just been told I will be protection officer for a

certain dignitary who will be attending a certain meeting to be held soon."

He knew there was an armaments' meeting coming up with world leaders attending at Chequers in the next few months because it had been on the news and everyone attending would be high profile.

"So," he went on, "I would like to meet Scarlett just to check I feel okay with her first." He hoped this sounded good.

"Of course," he added quickly, "I have met you and I am more than happy to be part of your club. I am actually very excited to start but I need to be prudent."

Mrs Manson understood, which was a relief to Jazz. She did add that Scarlett was not available until next week but she would set up a meeting for him and added there would be a cost of £500 which Jazz agreed to immediately. The call ended and Jazz gave a huge sigh of relief. This was all feeling very difficult and he didn't know where it would lead. *Darling Derek,* the lovely Sarah's husband, was back next week so Jazz wondered if Scarlett went with him to where ever he went abroad. He had hoped to get this cleared up before Derek came back but *that ain't gonna happen* he realised.

The meeting with Boomer in the Cranbrook was a moan fest. Jazz moaned and whined about the lollipop-man job and Boomer after listening for nearly five minutes told him to 'shut the fuck up'. There was nothing they could do about it at the moment. The Derek thing looked messy and Boomer wasn't happy at all about it. Where the hell were they going with this and what were they trying to prove? All questions that neither could answer. After a few drinks Boomer left, Jazz waved him goodbye and stayed until closing time. Neither of them knew they were, again, going to embark on a dangerous and life-threatening journey. They were naïve idiots and would need the luck of the stupid to survive.

Jazz made his way slowly home. After two attempts at putting the key in the lock and missing, the front door opened swiftly and Amrit stood angrily at the sight of Jazz drunk and swaying.

"Hello, darling," he said none too clearly and far to amiably for his own good.

"Get the fuck up those stairs before my auntie sees you," she whispered.

Jazz looked surprised, not knowing what was going on. Amrit followed him up the stairs and told him quickly and quietly that Auntie had a very prominent family in her best room and they were waiting for him to come home. *Another bloody arranged marriage proposal* Jazz thought glumly. Amrit knew what he was thinking and whispered, "There was no young girl there, just three very important looking men. None was Asian but Auntie is beside herself with good manners and hospitality encouraging them to eat and drink, and fussing."

Jazz raised his eyebrows in surprise and opened his mouth to say something but Amrit, with a look of anger and disdain added quickly, "They wanted to see you and if they are important, well, you are in a disgraceful state."

Jazz could hear her contempt and he felt ashamed. He didn't know why but he started to brush imaginary fluff off his jacket and thus avoided looking at her. He felt like a little boy and all he wanted was a hug of forgiveness. She looked at him, drunk and swaying in front of her; she almost felt sorry for him but not quite. With a final flourish, she said, "You had better stay in your room until you sober up which I bet won't be until tomorrow. I'll make excuses and say you had to work through the night."

She was thinking on her feet and even through his drunken haze, he admired her and listened.

"So, text me you are working through the night and I can show them that."

She took Jazz's mobile phone and sent the text herself. She didn't trust him to be able to do it properly. When done, she told him to be quiet and go to bed and she would sort it all out. He thought she was wonderful and told her so. Her reply was a dismissive "Huh!!!" but Jazz could see she liked the compliment.

After she had gone, he plonked down on the bed and wondered who the fuck was downstairs asking for him. Was it the police? He didn't think he rated a visit from three important suited men, he told himself. But there again, they had made him a poxy lollipop man; they could be finding a way to get rid of him. His mind was muddled, he couldn't concentrate and he was too tired to even feel depressed at the thought. It was a mystery he would untangle in the morning. For now he must sleep. He lay down, fully clothed and shoes on, and in seconds he started snoring.

CHAPTER ELEVEN

LOLLIPOP MAN

The alarm woke him. His mouth felt dry and disgusting. He didn't want to get up. *Fuck the job and fuck everyone* was an unhelpful thought as Jazz got up and staggered towards his fridge. He had a few Fanta tins of drink that usually sorted him out. He had thirty minutes to get washed and dressed and out of the door. He muttered more obscenities than he thought he knew in those thirty minutes as he got ready. His head felt better after the drink. He walked out of the door with a mouthful of pakoras he had left from Mrs Chodda's plate she had sent up the other day. The fresh air helped him and the bus was on time so the day was starting well.

It was quiet when he arrived at the school. *The calm before the storm* he thought. Betty suddenly appeared and brought a steaming cup of tea and biscuits. She put them on the table and provocatively said, "Come and get it, big boy." Jazz stifled a giggle. This woman couldn't look less sexy if she tried. Her dress, floral and a tad bright for the time of day, was covered badly with another styled cardigan that looked like it had given up any attempt to look fitted. It strained across her arms and shoulders and obviously couldn't be buttoned up across the heaving, untamed bosom that looked as if it was trying to escape. He reckoned she was wearing a size 14 cardigan for a size 20 lady. Jazz was quite fascinated to watch as she tried to pull the cardigan together as she talked to him but failed miserably. He thanked her for the tea and biscuits and with a cursory smile mumbled that he wanted a cigarette and left to go outside.

He wasn't in the mood to cope with Miss Femme Fatale today. He needed to find out who the men were who visited Mrs Chodda yesterday and what the fuck they wanted. He reckoned DCI fucking Radley was trying to get rid of him and wondered if he sent the disciplinary squad to his home to get some dirt on him. He would talk to Mrs Chodda tonight and find out what was asked before he took it any further.

After finishing his tea and cigarette Jazz checked the time and realised it was getting late and rushed to get his bloody coat and lollipop stick. The morning herd of gossiping women, unfettered children and spiteful prams went as usual. The traffic seemed calmer so Jazz didn't have to take details of cars driving manically this morning. They remembered him from yesterday, he smirked. He heard the bell signifying school had started and just as he was about to hand in his coat and lollipop stick, he saw Master William Winder running down the road towards him, his shoelaces flying as he ran and his jacket half on. In that moment Jazz felt sorry for him.

As William reached Jazz, he could see how agitated the boy was.

"You okay, Wills?" asked Jazz showing a bit of concern.

William looked at him in utter contempt. Jazz didn't know what he had done to deserve such a look. Without looking, William took a step into the road to cross and Jazz grabbed his arm and pulled him back as a blue BMW whizzed past just missing William. The boy winced as he was pulled back and Jazz saw the start of tears in his eyes as William cradled his arm. Suspicious now, Jazz asked, "You been in a fight, William?" He added, "And is that why you haven't got your arm in your jacket?"

William turned to Jazz and bitterly told him that he was a fucking busybody that had caused him nothing but trouble. He told him to fuck off and leave him alone. With that, he said he was late for school and Jazz, realising the time, took him across the road. But it wasn't going to stop there.

Determined to sort this, Jazz strode into reception and called out to Betty to get the school nurse for him. After explanations and an insistence that William needed to be examined, the nurse called William out of his class and in a procession led by Betty, Jazz, the nurse and a reluctant William marched to the first aid room. After a few words Betty was dismissed by the nurse and a put-out Betty, who argued passionately the point of staying and overseeing, finally lost the argument and was seen muttering as she made her way back to reception.

Jazz was allowed to attend because the nurse needed a witness and Jazz was a police officer. She muttered under her breath that Betty was a nosey cow and it was none of her business. William had been seated in a corner waiting for all the melee to settle. Now the nurse briskly asked William to strip to his underwear, please. He at first said

91

no but the nurse, used to children, would not take no for an answer and finally William stripped slowly. His arm was obviously a problem.

The bruises looked fierce and deep. They had gone a deep reddish blue colour. Jazz was shocked. William's arm was covered in never-ending bruises that had all met up leaving his arm black and blue and swollen. The nurse was very professional and after a few painful movements of the arm decided William needed to go to hospital for an X-ray. She thought it could be broken. He couldn't move his arm. The rest of his body was also bruised and she wondered if maybe he had a fractured rib too because of the bruising and the difficulty William had to move his torso without being in pain. His legs were full of bruises too. Nothing on his face, though. Jazz knew why. All the bruises couldn't be seen when covered in clothing but bruises to the face would be noticed. He knew who did this but he had to ask William.

"Who the fuck did this to you, Wills?"

William shifted from one foot to the other. He didn't want to say. He would pay for telling but Jazz, as gently as possible, said he wouldn't let anyone hurt him like that again. Not used to kind words, William, trying to hold back huge tears that were coursing down his face, said it was his dad. He was flaming mad that a bloody police officer had knocked on his door about William and he had always told William not to ever speak to anyone about his home life, it was private and no one else's fucking business. It seemed Dad had worked himself up into a frenzy about the visit and when William got home, he spent the evening making William pay.

This was a wake-up call for Jazz. It was his fucking fault this poor lad had been beaten up. 'He had only tried

92

to help' was a lousy excuse. Mad now, he would get this pair arrested and he would call social services for the boy. The nurse calmed the situation down and said she would call social services but for now the boy needed to go to hospital. Jazz said he would take him. He wanted to help, to make amends in some way. He rang someone at the police station and asked for a car to be brought asap to the school stating it was an enquiry he was working on.

The time at the hospital meant he wouldn't be back in time for lunchtime lollipop work but the police station sent a newbie to cover it for Jazz. So, the wait for the triage nurse at the hospital took time, then getting X-rays and then waiting for an examination meant Jazz and William had a long time together. They bonded. Jazz found out William had eaten nothing since school lunch the day before so he got a sandwich, a KitKat and a drink to tide him over. They talked about the West Ham football team and how they could manage them better than their manager and where the best fish and chip shop was in Dagenham. William asked if they could go back in the police car with the blue light on and the sirens. Jazz laughed and said he would see what he could do. William laughed at this but stopped and grimaced as the pain in his chest stabbed at him.

Finally, the doctor saw William and Jazz. The arm was fractured and two ribs were fractured too. The arm was to go into plaster and the ribs would heal themselves. Nothing tight around the ribs, and paracetamol for the pain. A cold compress on severe bruising areas was suggested. With a new white plaster cast from shoulder to wrist and all the information on pain killers, etc., singing in their ears they left to find the police car waiting outside.

As promised, the siren was put on and the blue light flashed as they sped back to the school to find out what was going to happen now with Master William Winder.

The nurse told them that social services would be there soon. They were very busy, she was told. Jazz took Wills to the canteen to see if a dinner could be rustled up for both of them. It was now 3 p.m. and the canteen was quiet and clean. Jazz looked in the big fridge and found a dinner covered in there. He reckoned it was being saved for someone but it was now Wills'. He put it in the microwave and Wills ate it with his good right hand. Jazz had made his mind up. Wills would come home with him.

Luckily, the local police officer who did the lunchtime lollipop man was there for the 3.30 p.m. finish of school. When Wills had finished what looked like lasagne, Jazz took him to the nurse's station and gave her his home number and address. He told her he was taking Wills to his home and let the poor boy settle. He whispered out of ear shot of Wills that he would send the local police to pick up the parents and interview them. The boy needed to rest. It was going to be a busy evening with police interviewing him and social services visiting. He checked on his way out if the police officer would do the lollipop-man run tomorrow as he would be busy interviewing. This was agreed with his station. Jazz smiled. At least he didn't have to come here tomorrow. He had lots to sort out including who the hell the three men were talking to Mrs Chodda last night about him. He knew it must be DCI Radley; the man hated him!

They had to catch the bus home much to Wills' dismay. He reckoned it would be great to go through Ilford with flashing blue lights and the siren. Mrs

Chodda took one look at Wills and was overcome. She bustled him into her kitchen and made him sit down. She tempted him with pakoras (always Jazz's favourite) and then some coconut sweets, and she poured him a cup of sweet lassi (an Indian drink made with yogurt, sugar and cardamom seeds).

"I have just made a pot of this," she said pointing to her stove.

Jazz loved sweet lassi and she poured him a cup too. Wills looked at it not knowing what it was. Mrs Chodda nodded at him and said, "Try it, you will love it if I say so myself." He loved the fuss and smiled and sipped the sweet drink. Jazz looked at Mrs Chodda bustling around Wills making him comfortable. She hadn't asked why he was there, she just seemed to instinctively know he needed help. He loved that woman!

Mrs Chodda had one small spare room for Wills and she went off to make up the bed for him. She had found some clean and ironed pyjamas that were her nephew's and would fit him. By 6 p.m. Wills was fighting sleep and Jazz sent him off to bed. It had been a difficult day and Jazz reckoned Wills wouldn't have had much sleep the previous night either. The pyjamas were nice and clean. Wills always wore his underwear in bed. He had never slept in such a soft and warm bed that had been specially made for him. He luxuriated in its cleanness and warmth and in moments he was asleep.

First the police arrived and Jazz informed them, showed them the photos he had taken on his phone of the bruising and gave them the copies of the X-rays the doctor had given him for evidence. At ten years old this young lad had been through the mill and those parents would not get him back. Jazz was determined to get them charged. The officers took the photos and said they would talk to Wills the next day. They let him sleep.

Jazz had a private call to make and went to his room and closed the door. He rang Boomer. Boomer, still at work, listened to the urgent questions; *Did DCI fucking Radley send the disciplinary squad to speak to Mrs Chodda? Could he find out if any police had called to find out what he was doing?* Boomer knew everything that was going on in his station, a skill he had picked up over the years and a skill that had saved his department many times when he flew close to the edge on his cases. He said he would check for Jazz but as far as he knew there was nothing at all. He reckoned if there was an investigation he would have been hauled in and questioned because of their work association so it was highly unlikely. He added that DCI Radley was definitely more amenable and happier these days and everyone knew it was because Jazz was up shit creek. The laugh that always started in his belly and rose loudly deafened Jazz and he held the phone away from his ear.

"Fuck off, Boomer, I've got to find out who these men were."

Jazz felt uneasy and irritated. "There's a lot going on at the moment and I am full on with a few things. I need to sort out who these men were. I will get Amrit here to talk me through it. Mrs Chodda will just give me a Mrs Chodda version and I need to know exactly what was said."

Boomer, quiet now, said he would check his end just in case it was police. He had a few contacts around and would know by tomorrow. Boomer was always on top of everything going on and said, "I hear you have a young lad with you. I have also heard the local plods are taking over the lollipop-man job from you so that's a bit of good news."

"It's permanent?" asked a relieved Jazz.

"Yup! Don't know why yet, but I don't know what DCI Radley will say when he hears about it." Boomer was going to laugh again but thought better of it.

"So, to round it all up, my fine young man," said a sarcastic Boomer, "you are into something with S&M that could be of interest or could just mean you will be broke in both ways, money and physically." Boomer had to laugh at that one.

"There could be something nasty going on with threats to Sarah's wellbeing and you are jumping into the hornet's nest as usual. That one is worrying and I think you have to watch your back. You are no Errol Flynn."

Jazz asked, "Who is he?"

Realising how old he was, Boomer just told him to shut up.

"You now have a young lad under your wing and parents to get charged. You have three unknowns making enquiries about you and we haven't a clue who sent them – are they friends or foe? Knowing you, obviously foe."

Boomer would have laughed again but realised how stupidly uneasy it all felt. But on a lighter note, he added, "And the cherry on the fucking cake is DCI Radley is gonna have your gonads barbecued when he finds out you are not a lollipop man anymore."

After a brief silence Boomer said, "That sounds about right for you. It all sounds dodgy and you deffo need to watch your back. These three men sound ominous."

There was a silence while they both took in just what a mess it all sounded. With a deep sigh, Boomer said quietly, "I will find out tomorrow about the men, just keep an eye out for trouble." With that, he put the phone down.

Jazz blinked, took a deep breath and uttered quietly, "Oh fuck."

At 8 p.m. a harassed woman arrived from social services and introduced herself as Mary Hardy. She said how busy she was and that she had no one to look after Wills at the moment. He thought this frayed grey-looking woman who kept pushing strands of long, lanky hair out of her eyes was about ready for the nut house. He swore she was muttering more to herself than to him. Trying to take the sensible line, Jazz explained calmly he would look after Wills and that Mrs Chodda and Amrit were the women of the house who would also look after him. Mary Hardy gave a cursory look through the bedroom door at Wills and saw he was comfortable and asleep. Although not regular, she conceded that Jazz was a police officer and Mrs Chodda was a responsible woman and said until something could be arranged, Wills could stay with them. Jazz sighed with relief. He was getting fond of the kid but he would have to work on the boy's bad language. He laughed at the thought.

It was now 9.30 p.m. and he was hungry. He phoned the local Chinese takeaway and ordered chow mein, rice and other bits which they said would arrive in half an hour. He poured a generous vodka with a little orange and settled down for a few minutes. It had been a full-on day but he felt it was going well. Amrit had been out all evening but he heard her come in and hoped he could speak to her before she went to bed. He just needed a few sips of his drink and a five-minute chill before going to find her. He could have asked Mrs Chodda about the three men but Amrit would give him a more down-to-earth version. Mrs Chodda got carried away and embellished things. He loved her to pieces and hoped she would never change. He raised a silent glass to Mrs Chodda and thought *bugger sipping* and downed the remainder of the glass in one. It felt good.

He went to find Amrit, hoping to have the conversation before his Chinese arrived. She was sitting in the kitchen with Mrs Chodda. Mrs Chodda assumed romance was in the air and left her beloved kitchen, something she rarely did, to check on her husband in the lounge. She gave them both a knowing smile as she left. Both Amrit and Jazz laughed after she left, more from embarrassment than mirth. She told him quickly what had happened in the day and Amrit had Mrs Chodda's version which was far more heroic than Jazz's version. Amrit smiled and teased.

"I thought you had saved the young man's life and taken on the brutes of parents that he had."

Jazz smiled and said, "Not quite." But he liked the idea that he was a hero in Amrit's eyes, he didn't see the teasing. He was anxious to know who the heck the three men were that came and spoke to Mrs Chodda last night.

Amrit made Jazz a cup of tea from the urn that had been standing all day. Indian tea was hot and very strong with lots of sugar. Jazz loved it. When they were comfortable Amrit regaled what had happened yesterday. The three men were very smart and very polite. Auntie, as Amrit, and now Jazz, called Mrs Chodda (Auntie is a familiar female title for anyone who you are fond of or close to who is older than you) was overwhelmed by such gentlemen. They said they wished to discuss Jaswinder Singh with her. They said it was a delicate matter to do with his possible promotion in the police force. Amrit giggled here. She said Auntie was beside herself with excitement and so very proud to be asked about him. They asked questions about his habits which was why she had had to get him away from the kitchen. "I don't think they would have been impressed to see you drunk," she added.

Jazz nodded and smiled. Amrit could see he was quite touched by her concern. Embarrassed now she got sassy and added, "You should be ashamed of yourself. Someone in your job should be prouder of themselves."

Again, Jazz nodded and smiled although a little more ruefully. She nodded, accepting he had been told off, and with a deep breath continued.

"So, Auntie started to get a bit carried away, Jazz."

She was embarrassed to tell him exactly what Auntie said but knew she must.

"She very much gave the impression she was your mother and had helped shape the man you have become. She took credit for your cleverness, and how you had risen in the ranks."

Amrit blushed; this was very awkward to say.

"Obviously, she hadn't a clue as to what you do except you were in the police force or somewhere like that. Auntie told them, when they asked her whether she knew exactly what you did for a living, that she hadn't a clue because you were very discreet."

Amrit laughed at this.

"Auntie didn't want to tell them she didn't understand what you did."

She now started to stutter a little because the next bit was so, so embarrassing she really didn't want to tell him but she had to.

"I think Auntie was sure you were heading for promotion and she wanted to help you so she exaggerated lots of things."

Jazz could see she was embarrassed and urged her on.

"Like what did she say?" He could see the hesitation and added, "I won't laugh or get cross, I promise."

"Well, Auntie actually did say she was your mother and how proud of you she was. She didn't hint, she came out and just said it, with a straight face too – I just couldn't believe it myself."

She looked at Jazz's face and he was actually smiling. After his own mother, he would love to have Auntie as his mother. Buoyed on by his acceptance so far, she added, "I had my back to Auntie and the men, I was at the stove making them tea, and I heard Auntie say I was your wife." Now Jazz did laugh.

Indignant now, Amrit almost shouted. "There! You said you wouldn't laugh; you liar!!"

Jazz stopped laughing at once and shamefully apologised. He had laughed more from embarrassment than anything else.

"I think she said that because in her eyes a man being promoted needs a wife." Amrit now looked down at the tiled floor, too embarrassed to look Jazz in the eye.

Jazz felt awful for her. He was a bloody idiot to laugh. He gently stretched out and took her hand and squeezed it.

"Thank you, Amrit, you are amazing and I am so grateful to you for helping me and for telling me what was said."

She looked up at him and with half a smile nodded. He still had hold of her hand and she didn't know what to do. They were locked in a moment that neither wanted to end. It was ended with a loud clearing of the throat from the hallway as Auntie advertised her entrance into the kitchen.

"Mr Chodda needs his cup of cocoa now so excuse me both of you," said a very smiley and self-satisfied Mrs Chodda. Amrit and Jazz had sprung apart just as Mrs Chodda came in but they were not quick enough and Mrs Chodda saw them hand in hand. In her mind she saw Jazz with a high up position in the police and him married to Amrit. Oh, she would celebrate with a cup of cocoa with Mr Chodda and maybe a biscuit too. It was then she started humming a tuneless melody as she worked her magic at the stove. She shouted a happy, sing-song goodnight to Amrit and Jazz as they left the kitchen.

Jazz whispered to Amrit if she would like to finish the conversation in his room. His Chinese had just arrived and he was really hungry now but wanted more time with Amrit. She came to his room and he got two plates out, one for him and one for Amrit. She tried to refuse but he insisted and she had to admit it all looked wonderful. Chow mein, special fried rice, barbecue ribs and beef in oyster sauce.

"Were you going to eat all of this yourself?" she asked incredulously. He looked at it and surprised and feeling the need to justify such a tasty banquet said with a boyish smile, "Well, yes, I would have eaten most of it, I am a growing lad you know. I haven't eaten much all day but I am not so hungry now so happy to share with you."

He thought that went down well; he was obviously charming her, he could tell by the smile on her face. With a self-satisfied smile he tried to hide from her, he laid out the containers on the table. *This is going well* he thought smugly.

They ate in an affable silence but once the food was finished Jazz, serious now, asked that Amrit just keep what he was to tell her to herself. She could see he was serious and nodded impatiently wanting to hear what he had to say.

"Those men, the ones who came to the house and asked about me. Well, I don't think they were from the police."

He could see she was confused and added quickly, "I do a bit of *off the road* police work."

She wanted to help and added, "Do you mean like James Bond does?"

He liked that and so wanted to say yes but he had to be honest.

"No. Look, Amrit, I am a pain in the arse to the police. Yes, I'm a good officer and I have solved more crimes than anyone else but I do it my way and it's not the police way. They put up with me because they haven't got a good enough reason to get rid of me. It would cause a fuss if they tried because I have contacts in newspapers and they wouldn't let them do that to me." Actually, that statement made him a bit depressed. He could see she was interested and a tad sorry for him. He liked that; it made a change to have a woman sorry for him. He nearly laughed at that thought.

"So," he continued, "it wouldn't have been the police here talking to Auntie about promotion." He hesitated and licked his lips.

"I haven't a clue who they were and it's a bit of a worry. So, I need you to tell me from the beginning what was said and how they looked. Between us we can solve this."

Amrit nodded. Actually, there wasn't very much that Amrit could say and nothing rang bells with Jazz as to who they were. The one big bit of information he got out of it was they were good at what they did. They gave away nothing but got every bit of information from Mrs Chodda about Jazz, even down to his bathing habits which he thought was a bit rich to talk about.

At the end of the evening, he was a little drunker, a bit more flirty, but none the wiser about these men. Amrit, seeing how the evening was going, got up and with the excuse of helping Mrs Chodda prepare the kitchen for the morning and tidy up, she said goodnight. She could see he wanted to kiss her, and for a second, she wanted to stay that bit longer, but on second thoughts, she mumbled more excuses and rushed out of the door.

Disappointed, he sighed a drunken sigh and poured another drink. *Things to think about tomorrow* he thought as he finished the drink and made his way unsteadily to bed. It had been one hell of a day and he had no idea what tomorrow would bring. He was far too drunk to think about it now. Tomorrow would be what it would be.

Closing his eyes, he smiled. The day had got better, he was off being a lollipop man, thank goodness, he rescued the boy, and he nearly got a kiss from Amrit. Life had moved up a notch today, and he felt good.

Jazz woke the next morning to someone pushing him in the back. It was the kid; he had got up and come looking for him. His head wasn't too bad but his mouth felt like the Sahara Desert. He had obviously slept with his mouth open all night. His tongue was stuck to the roof of his mouth and sounding like the Hunchback of Notre Dame tried to ask, "What the fuck are you doing?"

He looked at the clock and it was only 6 a.m. Before he could say anything, an excited William told Jazz that he was going to school today and Amrit was taking him. He was going to go downstairs now for breakfast. He said this with an excitement that took away the bad temper Jazz was feeling. Of course, this kid wasn't used to someone making him breakfast or taking him to school. At this time of day all he could muster was, "That's great, Wills. See you downstairs soon."

Wills went off happily and Jazz got himself up. He checked his phone and saw the message from DCI fucking Radley telling him to be in his office at 9 a.m. sharp this morning. With a groan, he knew this was going to happen, he sluggishly got out of bed and went to get washed and dressed muttering, "It's going to be fucking hell today."

Now dressed and feeling a bit more together, he joined Wills in Auntie's kitchen. Amrit was there too and he gave her a nod and a smile. Auntie saw this and smiled happily to herself. Things were going well. He noted Wills was tucking into a bowl of cereal that Auntie had. He marvelled that her kitchen always had everything you would ever want to eat. She laid an omelette before him without the chillies that made him sick. *She is wonderful* he thought. Before Wills left and whilst Auntie and Amrit were sorting something out in a corner, Jazz whispered to Wills to behave and treat

Amrit well and to not swear. As Wills got up from the table, he looked at Jazz and whispered, "Fuck off." Jazz held back the smile as best he could. Now he had to leave and meet with DCI fucking Radley. He reckoned his day was going to be torture.

CHAPTER TWELVE

SHAKEN, NOT STIRRED

He strode down De Vere Gardens on his way to Ilford Police Station. On his mobile, he spoke to Boomer and told him he was being summoned to the DCI's office. He asked if Boomer had found out about anyone sniffing around his home but the answer was no. He was worried about the three men invading his privacy and who the hell they were. He hadn't spoken to Sarah for a few days so he asked Boomer to give the heads up to Sarah that he was on the case of Devious Derek, her husband, and in a few days' time he would be meeting with Scarlett. In response to Boomer saying he wasn't his fucking secretary, Jazz apologised but said he was on his way to see DCI Radley as ordered and he didn't know what he had in store for him. He added for effect that he could be sent to Coventry. They both laughed at that feeble joke.

He wasn't sure what his DCI would have to say or what he would make him do but, *it won't be good, that's for sure!* he thought, so today had to be written off; the day would be pants. He asked Boomer to meet him tomorrow evening in the Cranbrook pub for a catch-up. Satisfied he had got things organised he put his phone in his pocket and with a sense of purpose walked towards Ilford Police Station.

He hadn't got far, just past the railings for Valentines Park, when a shiny black Mercedes car stopped beside him. He couldn't see the driver through the blacked-out windows. Jazz looked on with interest as a well-built man who had obviously been working out regularly jumped lithely out of the passenger's side of the car and cheerfully called to Jazz. He didn't know him and intrigued, Jazz looked over and waited for the stranger to reach him. With a deferential smile and almost a bow the young man cheerfully said, "We are being watched and I am here to take you to meet my boss. Please just look as if it's work as usual and get in the back of the car."

Equally deferential and smiling Jazz said, "And what if I don't want to?"

The smile still on the Adonis's lips, the stranger added ominously, "Fucking get in the car or those watching could do something nasty like shoot you!"

Jazz nodded thoughtfully and said, "Well, if you put it so nicely, fucking lead the way."

Once Jazz got in the back seat of the car, it sped away at what seemed like warp speed, throwing him backwards into the seat. For a moment the situation had taken his breath away. Now he wondered who the hell they were and what they wanted.

They wouldn't answer his questions; they just ignored him. It struck him forcibly that he was actually a prisoner and had no choice but to stay put. Jazz felt that chill through his body that made him shiver as he remembered how he felt last time. The memory of being bundled into a car by the MI5 mob and not knowing what was going to happen, or even who they were, flooded his brain and left him momentarily struck dumb and tensely immobile. His brain was momentarily scrambled and his tongue twisted and beads of sweat ran down his forehead and stung his eyes. He pulled himself together and tried to reason who they might be; could it be anything to do with Mrs Manson? Had he opened a viper's nest and they knew who he was, a fucking lollipop man with the police? Silently he cursed his stupidity at getting himself into this situation, thinking *you fucking stupid man, what have you done?* He looked out of the window to see where they were going and all he knew was they were travelling up Romford Road towards Stratford at an illegal speed. He hoped a police car might spot them and stop this madness.

They eventually turned off Romford Road around the Stratford area, Jazz thought; he was trying to remember where they were going. He hoped he could get a message to his station at some point and tell them where he was. It all seemed mad and stupid and like a film on the TV but this was for real. They stopped eventually at a small industrial estate. It looked clean but not very busy. The buildings were single storey and Jazz reckoned they were all in reasonable condition from what he could see. They were in a built-up area but this plot stood alone with about four long buildings in it. They nodded to him to get out of the car. Neither the driver nor the Adonis said a word, they just shoved him to move towards one of the low grey buildings. Jazz wondered what the hell was going to happen. He was scared and concentrated on making his breathing sound normal; his pounding heart was making him breathe in panicking short breaths. He wasn't going to give these bastards the satisfaction of seeing he was shit scared.

He was manhandled into a long bleak-looking room that had well-used desks and chairs set out like a classroom. His eyes swept the room and he saw a blackboard, *for Christ's sake*, a flip chart and some sort of projector. It felt weird and disorientating. *Who would have a place like this? Villains don't* he surmised. He didn't have long to find out. The door opened and the two men who had driven Jazz here nodded at the incoming older man and left.

The older man, with a very cultured accent, introduced himself as David and gestured for Jazz to sit down at one of the desks. He looked like one of those non people you could never describe; bland face, flat and uninterestingly plain with a sandy-coloured short-back-and-sides hairstyle with a quiff hanging lazily to one side. He wore an anonymous but obviously expensive-looking grey suit and one of those ties that said old school which made Jazz feel this man was important in some way. Jazz, scared but edgy, and with more bravado than he was feeling, looked at this David and reminded him that he was a detective with the Metropolitan Police and that they would be searching for him very soon.

He asked, "What the hell is going on? This is ridiculous and unnecessary. Who are you and what do you want?" He added rather pompously, "My time is precious and I have a very important meeting with my superior this morning and the alarm bells will go off when I do not appear."

David smiled and nodded, sat himself down and gestured again for Jazz to sit as well. After a moment of adjustment and making himself comfortable, David looked at Jazz and in a quiet, almost threatening way said, "Shut the fuck up, Singh. You have caused us immense problems and interference in some, shall we say, delicate work we are doing."

Jazz's back stiffened as he was now on high alert, and his mind racing. He realised these were not villains. David had a well-spoken accent and departments like MI5/6/7 or whatever, seemed more likely. It didn't help. MI5 had been a nasty piece of work when he came to their notice when he was working on the paedophile ring case. He didn't want to upset them again. David could see he had Jazz's full attention. He noted he was sitting up straight and waiting.

"I prefer to work with you on a need-to-know basis, Singh, but unfortunately you have stuck your big fucking feet into a hornet's nest."

Jazz opened his mouth to say something and David shut him up and said, "Just fucking listen for a change."

There was a knock at the door and a man brought in two mugs of tea. When he had left, Jazz tasted his tea and said, "How did you know how many sugars I take?"

David smiled and rummaged in his pocket and took out a packet of cigarettes offering one to Jazz. David lit both. In the silence, they drew on their cigarettes and blew out the smoke and both relaxed for a moment. David's first comment was, "We know everything: what you have done, where you have been and how many sugars you take."

He looked at Jazz and added, "And you are a fucking stupid idiot that has got in our way and caused problems that could cost lives."

This shook Jazz and he thought of Devious Derek. As if he could read his mind, David said, "Yes, that's right. You have put Derek and his family in grave danger."

Jazz thought *Christ, he can read minds, too.* This was getting scary and he didn't know where it would go.

David, calm and collected and in a quiet, seductive voice, continued.

"So, what do we know?

1. Sarah contacted you about Derek.
2. Mad Pete, as you so quaintly call him, helped you find Mrs Manson.
3. You visited Mrs Manson's establishment and booked Scarlett.
4. You have involved DI Tom Black into this and I believe Detective Ashiv Kumar."
   Sarcastically David added, "Golly, good work, you prick! You've endangered all of them."

Again, Jazz almost jumped up from his seat and wanted to answer this sardonic heap of shit! David put up his hand to silence him.

"I know you want to know who we are. Well, I can't tell you except we are a government body."

Jazz stated, "You're fucking MI5 or 6. I had a run-in with you before."

David smiled a condescending smile. "You were a fucking arsehole then."

Jazz was getting angry now. He wasn't sure why he felt so angry. This bastard was making him angry, but the thought he might have caused any danger to his friends had scared him. What had he got into?

"So, the three men that visited Mrs Chodda, your landlady, were to do with Scarlett and Derek. They were sussing you out."

Jazz moaned at the thought. For fuck's sake, what had he done? They had come to his home and now knew Auntie and Amrit. He was beside himself with worry and looked at David now hoping he was going to help put this right. David could see the effect of his comments and was pleased to have a more receptive Singh in front of him.

"So, our problem with you is we know you have told Mrs Manson you were a protection officer and we couldn't allow you to continue being a bloody school-crossing patrol officer or as you call it, lollipop man. For Christ's sake! Who puts a detective sergeant on school-crossing duty? It's laughable." Jazz nodded in total agreement.

"As you are aware, Derek appears to be working with whoever these people are (we know who they are but you do not need to know). We are monitoring him and want to see what is happening. Then you, as usual, just interfere without checking anything, conferring with anyone, or just doing your job in a more professional way." Jazz now looked down and was embarrassed. What he said was true.

Jazz said, "But I wanted to protect Sarah as well."

David sighed. "We know exactly what is happening with Sarah. We have eyes on her so she is safe. That's when we saw you getting involved."

Jazz asked, "Why am I here?"

David grimaced and said, "There's the rub. We had everything organised, we are a well-oiled team you know, and then you messed it up. We have two days before

Derek and Scarlett return, and in that time, we need to build you a credible storyline. We took you immediately off school-crossing work – how pathetic was that job? We have squared everything with your commander and DCI. Just know, we can do what the fuck we like so be confident we have your back too. Now we need to give you an identity as a protection officer because they are looking at all your details and they have far too good an access to confidential information. This is something we have been monitoring for a while and we do not want you to mess it up. My boss has made it abundantly clear you are in on this. We are now forced to use you and get you involved – God help us!"

David was not happy to use such an unpredictable, untrained officer but they were forced to realise that Singh was honest, brave, resourceful and very successful in what he did. They noted he had the intelligence of a fox and could manage situations, however uncomfortable or dangerous and always seemed to find a way out of them. That was just the qualities they needed but he was also a rogue officer so a worry to them.

Jazz, in a state of regret, excitement and to be honest, satisfaction that he would not be working alone, thought *so, they knew about Derek.* Derek's career was now over. He would be done for treason, Jazz reckoned, even though by the sounds of it he had no choice if they were threatening his wife. He felt sorry for Sarah. But who were these people that this David wouldn't talk about? There was lots more to find out, he was sure of that. He felt unexpectantly on a high. He was going to do undercover work! Wow! Who would have believed that? Certainly not DCI fucking Radley. That made him smile.

David told him they were going to have some lunch and then the work would start. "What work?" Jazz asked.

"For fuck's sake, Singh! Your new identity, how to use a gun because we know you have never been allowed to use one and what happens next. This is not a game. This is for real with real consequences if it goes wrong."

David wasn't messing around and he walked off wondering if this was going to work.

Jazz was taken to another building by someone called Angela. She said he would be more comfortable there. It was rather nice in comparison. It had armchairs and tables and the smell of coffee came from behind a partition. Angela, who was very easy on the eye, was, he reckoned, about twenty-seven years old. She smiled a lot and flicked her long blonde hair as a way of finishing sentences which was very appealing. She got him a coffee and he watched as she walked purposely to what he thought was a kitchen. She was gorgeous with a well-honed figure. Her fitted trousers made her legs look like they went on for ever, she was very fit and he reckoned she could look after herself. His eyes were everywhere in this room; he saw the armchairs were old and worn but classy and comfortable, all the tables and chairs didn't match but had a style to them. The framed photos on the walls were pretty standard stuff of London in days gone by with streets of olde-worlde shops and people Jazz had never seen in his lifetime. He wasn't sure, but it felt like there were cameras watching him; he looked for the tell-tale signs but couldn't see a camera anywhere. This was all very weird and he was trying to make sense of it.

Angela seemed to be very accommodating and answered most of his questions. She explained that this was just an outpost of their organisation. The room he had been in was the ops room used by undercover police and her organisation when they worked together. Apparently, there were such places around the country. He thought his training, if that is what he was going to have, would have been in one of those places out in the countryside where training goes on. She laughed at this and told him he watched too much television, but declined to answer him. He asked if she was MI6 which was all about foreign powers. She again smiled and declined to answer. The lunch came and it was really nice. It was his favourite roast dinner, lamb roast. They really did seem to know everything about him. He looked at Angela as she sat opposite him at the table and said with amazement, "Now you are just bloody well showing off! How the hell did you know roast lamb was my favourite?"

Angela raised her eyebrows. "It's the day of the week when we always have a lamb roast. Glad it's your favourite." She smirked and tucked into her plate.

He wasn't sure if they knew or it was just luck. He felt like they were playing mind games with him and he needed to stay sharp and in control. They obviously needed him to play his part in all of this but, by the same token, he promised Sarah he would do his best to sort this out. A part of him hoped, for Sarah's sake, he could save Devious Derek from the sack if he got involved.

They had a very cosy lunch with Angela talking and laughing and listening to him for a couple of warm and relaxing hours. He reckoned she was flirting with him and her eyes sparkled when he flirted back. They goaded each other with little suggestive references, they laughed a lot and she held his hand as he told her about his mother.

He told her about DCI fucking Radley putting him on lollipop duty and how he lived his life and how Manchester had been. He had never spoken for so long about himself. She really understood and cared how he felt.

He realised afterwards that he knew very little about her but she had found out a lot about him without even asking directly. He was in the company of a very slick and professional organisation and he felt very alarmed at how easy it was to tell her everything and anything about his life but, strangely, as uneasy as he felt, he admired her and the organisation. She was not the 'flirty girly' she portrayed herself to be, she was a very skilled interrogator. *So, what the fuck comes next?* he wondered. It wasn't long before he found out the next bit of this surreal day.

David returned and thanked Angela. Jazz watched closely as she walked with a catwalk skill and grace out through the door. He was sorry to see her go. He had questions, the first being how come the only people he had seen in this place were Angela and him and the two who brought him there.

"Is this place empty?" he asked. All David would say was, "It serves a purpose."

Jazz, feeling quite edgy, wondered why he never got a fucking straight answer to anything.

David gestured towards the soft, well-used, old leather brown armchairs and some faceless person brought them a mug of tea each. Jazz wondered what the hell was with all the tea. He felt uneasy and unsure of this surreal day. What did they want from him? Well, he was just about to find out.

After a few sips of tea, David fidgeted in his chair and the old leather squeaked and creaked as he made himself comfortable. He cleared his throat and proceeded to tell Jazz just what was going to happen. He said that tomorrow all the pertinent information and his alias would be ready but for now he wanted to explain what Jazz's part in all of this was. They had been watching Derek for a while. There was a very important conference being held in Essex in three weeks' time and Derek was the protection officer for a high-level civil servant who was attending. There were grave concerns about Derek. It would seem Derek was helping the said people and he was being watched very closely by them and the British. Everything was going well until Jazz poked his nose into it. David again stopped for another sip of tea and carried on and emphatically stated, "It is imperative you continue with your cockeyed interference as planned. I don't want anyone to suspect anything. That includes your accomplices Tom Black, Ash Kumar and Mad Pete as you call him. You will not be involved in anything to do with the operation, you will see Scarlett as arranged and become a member as you were going to. You will not get involved; you will not interfere. Is that clear?"

Jazz nodded. Now it was his turn.

"So if I am not involved in anything further, why did the men come to my home and ask Mrs Chodda about me?"

David smiled and condescendingly stated, "My dear chap, this is standard practice. You have admitted you know Derek and you are associated with him so they will check you are legitimate. They are not playing games, DS Singh. They are deadly serious."

Again, Jazz asked, "So what do they want Derek to do?"

David, with creased brow, thought what to say and nonchalantly said, "That's none of your concern. You play the part you started and that's all. We have to bring your cohorts into this because I don't want them checked out and found to be something other than the storyline we have constructed for them. You will all be here tomorrow. You are the key player so we need more time with you."

"So, who is going to pay for all this playing about? It's going to cost a fucking fortune," Jazz added.

"We will pay, of course." David was getting ready to leave.

Jazz, now a little desperate to keep him a bit longer, asked, "So am I in danger? Is Mrs Manson in on it too?"

David, already on his feet, looked down on Jazz and said, "We will look out for you but you are just a punter as far as Mrs Manson is concerned and that's all you are. You are not 007, DS Singh; we just want you to join the club as a member as you intended to do and as Mrs Manson expects you to do. You are here because we don't want you compromising our mission, so we will leave it at that."

With those words, David turned and left the room. The two drivers who had brought him here came in and gestured for Jazz to follow them. Once in the car, the blonde, fit one said, "We will pick you up from your home tomorrow at 8.30 a.m. Please be ready. Do not talk about today to anyone."

Jazz nodded in agreement and spent the journey back to Ilford in thoughtful silence.

CHAPTER THIRTEEN

WE ARE FAMILY

Jazz was home by 4.30 p.m. and it sounded like Wills had just arrived home too. The noise in the kitchen was deafening with Wills shouting playfully and Mrs Chodda laughing at something. Respectfully Jazz knocked on the kitchen door and waited to be asked in. The door was flung open by Wills. His eyes were sparkling and his face was red with excitement and he was smiling. Apparently, Mrs Chodda had bought Wills some iced buns for when he came home from school and made him a glass of sweet lassi which he really liked. Jazz was amazed how quickly children recover and enjoy life again.

"Auntie, you are spoiling him," said Jazz as he led Wills back to a seat at the table so he could finish his feast.

He smiled at Auntie and suddenly feeling a great warmth for this wonderful woman, he walked around the large kitchen table and kissed her on the cheek. He whispered, "Thank you, Auntie, for being so kind."

Both were surprised by this act of affection but each

pleased and embarrassed at the same time. They were instantly distracted by Wills asking what was for dinner as he bit into a large chunk of iced bun. Jazz ruffled his hair and called him a *greedy bugger* and left to get himself a drink. He had a bottle of vodka and some orange in his fridge calling him.

He sat in his room, taking a deep breath and feeling relaxed for the first time today. He needed time to think about today but as he sipped his nicely chilled vodka and orange, he realised he hadn't seen Amrit tonight and wondered where she was. He hadn't seen her in the kitchen and she must have brought Wills home. After he finished his drink and feeling more at ease, he went back to the kitchen and asked, trying to sound disinterested.

"Aunt, where is Amrit tonight?" He qualified his asking with, "Who brought Wills home?"

Mrs Chodda perked up at the question and smiling far too much said Amrit had to go to her home that evening. Something to do with her son who was in India with her ex-husband. Jazz remembered she had a son and felt bad he had never asked after him.

"So why is her son in India with her ex-husband?" he asked, to which Mrs Chodda shrugged her shoulders and shook her head.

"A father can take his son on holiday which he did."

Jazz nodded and checked that Wills who had homework was doing it and not getting under Auntie's feet. Satisfied all was well he went back to his room, poured another vodka and orange and rang for a Kentucky Fried Chicken to be delivered in an hour. Now he wanted to sit and think.

The next morning started as chaotically as the day before with Wills waking him at bloody six in the morning! The lad was still excited at all the attention and nice living which he wasn't used to. Jazz roused himself and after getting ready for the day went down to share breakfast with Wills. Auntie again made him an omelette for breakfast. This was unusual. He didn't usually have breakfast in her kitchen but he enjoyed the domestic feel of it all. Amrit was there too and she smiled hesitantly at Jazz. She was a lovely warm girl and he found it hard to dismiss her and smiled for a tad too long in her direction. Auntie was bustling about with eyes in the back of her head watching the pair of them and she started that tuneless self-satisfied humming again.

Before he left for school, Jazz took Wills to one side and told him to behave and have manners at school. No swearing and do as he was told. He tried to explain that life was like a mirror; if you smile and nod and behave then this is reflected back to you. Teachers would treat him better if he didn't tell them to fuck off and he might learn something instead of sitting outside the headmaster's door most of the day. With these gems of information, Wills looked at Jazz disparagingly and told him to fuck off and left with Amrit for the school.

At 8.30 a.m. precisely, the car arrived to take him to MI6; Jazz had decided that was who they were. He wasn't a complete idiot and could work it out. Auntie saw the big car with blacked-out windows and the lovely man who seemed like a chauffeur and was opening the door for Jazz. She was mightily impressed and would remember to tell Amrit how important Jazz was with such a fine car to take him to work. She waved Jazz off and looked around to see if the neighbours had seen this fine display of grandeur. She would tell them all at the Gurdwara today while she worked voluntarily in helping cook the curry and rice for the worshippers and anyone who entered the Gurdwara and needed a meal. This was something she did every week as part of her *Sewa* (service to others as part of the Sikh religion).

Mrs Chodda was very religious and liked to quote the guru often. Her saying for today was by Guru Nanak: *Those who have loved are those that have found God.* She liked to quote these to Jazz in the hope it helped him. She could see he was often troubled. She was a good woman and never knew the problems and dangerous situations that Jazz got himself into.

CHAPTER FOURTEEN

SECRETS

Jazz arrived at what was called Area 10. He presumed there were many such units around the country. The place still looked quite empty but he noted a few more cars parked there. He was shown to the first grey hut where he had started yesterday. There was a screen pulled down now and it looked like a computer on the table was going to be used to project whatever. He was asked to sit down by the fit one who now said Jazz could call him Harry. Jazz didn't think that was his name but at least he had a name he could use. As Harry left, Jazz looked around the characterless room. It was bleak and just full of old chairs and small tables neatly arranged in rows. He reckoned this building would hold about forty people. He wondered if anyone else was going to join them.

David entered looking a bit distracted with a bunch of papers in his hand. He sat down beside Jazz and nodded curtly. Jazz could see it was going to be a busy day. There was going to be no messing around today, thought Jazz grimly, as he watched David sort the paperwork out and then look up at Jazz with a sigh and get ready to start the instructions.

"You can stop right there," said Jazz sharply and firmly which made David stop what he was doing and listen. Jazz had considered everything to do with Devious Derek, Mrs Manson and MI6 because that was who they must be, during an evening of vodka and orange, and had come to a conclusion about all of this. Jazz had had enough of this and after much thought decided he wasn't going to take any more of this bullshit. He came to the decision that whatever was going on, they obviously knew about Derek and what he was doing, so it wasn't his fight. He had promised to help Sarah but now it was out of his hands. To be honest, he felt relieved. All this BDSM and playing at spying was a bit rich for him. Having just got over the paedophile case and all that had entailed, he wanted a quieter life.

"What is this all about? I just wanted to help Sarah. I don't want to be involved with any MI6 crap that is not in my remit. It sounds like Derek was blackmailed into something and I wanted to help. But now you know about Derek it's too late for me to do anything. If you want to catch Derek, fine! That's nothing to do with me. I want to go back to my police station and work as trained. I am not an *airy-fairy nancy-boy* farting around with Glocks and fancy handcuffs and wanting women to whip me and tweak my nipples. I don't need to meet up with Scarlett now as you are on the case. I will let you get on with whatever you have planned and good luck with that!"

Jazz watched as David shifted in his chair and started to go red in the face. The deluge that followed put Jazz right back in the frame. With a restrained anger that kept his face bright red, David, in a tight, measured tone, spat out the words.

"Shut the fuck up and listen. I have no choice and you have no choice. My boss, who is extremely high up in the government, says you are to continue. I suggest you do not upset him. He has the power to hire, fire and eliminate. Need I say more?"

It was going to take the rest of the morning explaining everything and Jazz, chastened by the big boss's dictate, had no choice but to sit and listen as David set out everything necessary for Jazz to be aware of on a need-to-know basis.

Overall, Jazz was told that he had put himself in the frame because he had told Mrs Manson he was part of Derek's team. At the moment they were watching Derek to see what was happening and who was interested in him. David told Jazz, to date, they didn't know who was orchestrating this. They knew locally who was using Derek but not the masters of this or necessarily why. At this point David nearly lost his temper in telling Jazz that it was his bloody interference in a very delicate surveillance that nearly ruined the operation and could have put many lives in danger and there was still the possibility they could be discovered. He added they were dealing with some very professional, clever, murderous bastards. David gave himself a few moments to collect himself and continued.

David went on, more controlled now, that whoever was behind this was very powerful and had access to highly confidential information, almost throwing away the comment that it was another matter and was being looked into. For the moment, as Jazz had put himself in the frame, they needed to give him a new identity so that he didn't alert the enemy (as David wished to call them) that they had been rumbled. He added that they had taken him immediately off school crossings which still disgusted David, and Jazz was definitely with him on that. Again, David needed to say that he had never heard of a DS being put in such a role before. He also told Jazz that money had been put into his account for expenses including paying Scarlett. His work place at the moment would be here and that DI Tom Black and DC Ashiv Kumar would work here too. He added that Jazz had involved DI Tom Black in his little escapade with Mrs Manson so he needed to look like he was on the same team and DC Kumar because his name had cropped up somewhere as having worked with Jazz.

Almost in a whisper David stated, "The people we are dealing with seem to have access to all our records and we needed to build new files for the three of you for them to find. And before you ask," he added, "we know we have a mole in our organisation and we are working on that." David growled.

"It's been a bloody nuisance and a lot of work that was totally unnecessary if you had kept your fucking nose out of something that was nothing to do with you!"

Again, David took a few moments to calm himself down before he continued.

In the meantime, Jazz's brain was going into overdrive wondering if Derek was the mole. Perhaps the blackmail had made him give over lots of information. His lack of respect for Devious Derek dropped even lower. What a scummy traitor he was. He reckoned at some point there was going to be bad trouble. He felt sorry for Sarah who would have to live with this. He looked up as David cleared his throat to speak.

"We think we know what this is all about," continued David. "The reason why Derek was blackmailed into helping them and where this will be happening. At the moment we think that it's to do with a highly confidential secret meeting to be held near Stansted Airport in three weeks' time. This event will bring together various high-level people to discuss a new weapon that could affect the world and needs to be managed. I can say no more on that. We chose a mansion we have access to because it's close to the airport into which everyone involved will fly and the journey to the mansion will be very short. We know one of the visitors is targeted for assassination but we don't know who at the moment. Everyone attending the meeting could be the target. This meeting needs to happen and it is highly prestigious that England and our security systems have been chosen to host this meeting. If anything untoward happens it would be a humiliation that our government couldn't handle. It is imperative that this works."

Having outlined roughly what was happening, David needed to tell Jazz exactly what he was doing. Jazz by now was speechless. He sat almost open-mouthed wondering what else there was to know.

"So, you are a qualified security operator for MI6. Yeah, I know, now you do know who we are so keep it to yourself." David smiled ruefully.

"Your file will show you have been with the department for the past six years. Your training was, of course, at Fort Monckton in Portsmouth and I suggest you read the manual I have here for you so you are familiar with it. You are fully trained in all aspects of our work. A second language is a usual pre-requisite and fortunately you have Punjabi." Rather sarcastically David added, "More by luck than judgement, I believe."

Jazz at this point smirked. This man was keen to bollock him when ever he could. It would be wrong to say that Jazz was not interested in all of this. He could feel that prickly sense of an adventure and although he shouldn't have, he was feeling quite excited at the prospect.

"So," continued David, "you will be shown how to handle a Glock so you don't look like a prize prick."

Jazz asked if he was going to carry live ammunition and got told in horror, "Good God no, we value our lives and I don't want any friendly fire."

Jazz still didn't know what was expected of him and why he had to learn to handle a Glock which, quite honestly, he had always wanted to do. He thought he was just going to see Scarlett to start visits there; why would he need to learn how to handle a Glock?

The answer, he felt, would need to be dragged out of David who didn't want to tell him too much at this time. Jazz thought the bloody Secret Service kept far too much secret. Apparently, he would be expected to attend this meeting because he was part of Derek's team and it would seem strange if he wasn't there. Jazz, quite interested now, asked who he would be minding. David with a look of disgust told him in no uncertain terms that there was no way he would be looking after anyone's safety at the meeting. He reminded him that he wasn't trained, didn't understand protocols, needed to be able to conduct himself in a polite and deferential manner and was a total dickhead. Jazz nodded. He understood that.

"So, what the fuck am I going to do then, be a kitchen helper or some such fuckwit?"

His role would be one of security on the gate into the mansion. David said he couldn't do much harm there and all he had to do was look at the IDs of cars that came into the grounds and phone through to security in the mansion. Feeling a bit dejected, Jazz asked why he was going to be there at all.

"Because you know Derek, you stupid fucking idiot. We have to place you there. Don't think we want to. You are the last person we would want messing around on a highly sophisticated security surveillance job. It's the only place we could think to put you out of the fucking way so we can do our work."

Jazz, quiet now, realised he had walked into this mess. He asked if his family was safe, Mrs Chodda in particular. David smiled and said no worries. "You are a lowly cog in this wheel. No one would be interested in blackmailing you. You don't have access to anyone." Jazz nodded. He then asked if Derek was under investigation and how would that work because he would be there in the mansion. David again smiled and said that everything was under control and his people were watching what was happening. He added that after the meeting had finished and all had returned safely, it would then be time to sort out Derek and his involvement. He added that it was nothing to do with Jazz and he must not interfere, this was MI6 work.

It was a tremendous amount of stuff to take in and David called for coffee and biscuits to be brought to them.

He said he would give Jazz time to digest everything and they would carry on in twenty minutes. They had the visit to see Scarlett to discuss. With that, David left the room. Jazz had a headache starting and rubbed his temple. What the fuck had he got himself into here?

CHAPTER FIFTEEN

DISCIPLINE

Jazz wondered what the next piece of instruction was going to be. He was looking forward to handling a Glock. A wonderful piece of work, light but effective and used by most experts in the world. He had always wanted to fire such a gun but was never allowed by the Met. He had applied for training many times but they said he was not a suitable candidate. He thought that was fucking stupid but he was going to have the opportunity and looked forward to that.

The twenty minutes passed and the coffee break was over. To the minute, David came back into the room and sat down. He first informed Jazz that Derek and Scarlett would be returning to England in two days' time and Jazz would be meeting with Scarlett possibly the same day they arrived back. Jazz wondered how they could be so specific but they seemed to know everything. They chatted for an hour and after another great roast lunch Jazz was taken by Harry to another hut that had a firing range set up and they spent the afternoon handling a Glock, loading it and firing it. Jazz fancied himself as a crack shot but when the targets were wound back to him from the fifty-yard firing line he realised he was shit. Harry told him with a smirk that it didn't matter how bad a shot he was because he just needed to know how to handle a gun; he was never going to have live bullets to shoot.

By three o'clock, the day was deemed over and Jazz was led to the lunch room where he found Boomer and Ash. Boomer was lounging back in an old leather chair as if he didn't have a care in the world and Ash looked like he would like to curl up in a ball and sit unnoticed in a corner.

Jazz nodded at them both as his eyes darted everywhere to see who was watching. He sauntered over to Boomer and sat down opposite him. Ash instinctively moved closer to them. Ash was desperate to say something. Boomer had told him to stay quiet and listen and look but now Jazz was here too he started babbling in a whisper.

"What the hell is going on?" he asked. "Boomer and I have sat here for quite some time with no information or answers to anything."

He was beginning to sound hysterical and Jazz touched him on the arm to calm him and whispered, "Will explain later, this is not the place to talk about this. I know why you are here but don't know what you are expected to do."

He could see the fear in Ash's face and added, "You are safe, you are only here to protect my story."

Boomer had an idea of what this was about; he always covered himself in a blustering loud attitude but he was an intelligent man; there wasn't much he didn't know about criminals and their mind set and he understood the side of life that lives in the shadows. Quietly, he listened to Jazz and nodded.

Ash told Jazz how both he and Boomer were told to leave the police station and follow these men. Apparently, DCI Radley was aware of this and had agreed. They arrived at Area 10 as they were told it was called and were left to stew for an hour. He understood they were to work from this depot every day for the next few weeks. He said, with a smile, he liked the chauffeur-driven drive but wanted to know why they had to work there and what work were they doing? Boomer jumped in and told Ash to calm down and just wait and see. He reminded Ash he was still paid; he was in no danger and got a free ride to work every day. Boomer laughed and told Jazz, "It sounds fucking wonderful to me and they fed us!"

Harry arrived to take Jazz home and Boomer and Ash were going to be taken separately. David came in and reminded everyone that they could not discuss anything about today with anyone outside of the unit. He looked at Jazz and told him to stay in character as there was a small possibility he could be being watched but not to worry, nothing would happen. He added, as he left, that when Boomer and Jazz met for a drink in the Cranbrook that evening, to ensure they didn't talk about anything to do with this project, as he called it, and to ensure they couldn't be overheard. Dumbstruck for a moment, Jazz worried about being watched but then wondered how the fuck he knew they had arranged to meet. Boomer told him later that their phones must have been bugged and added, "The fucking bastards know everything!"

Ash was bewildered and feeling left out asked if he could join them that evening for a drink and both Jazz and

Boomer, in unison, stated *NO*. They quickly explained that just his face would give away the plans. He looked shit-scared and at the moment, if they were followed, he could be in danger, so going home was his safe option. This sorted out his mind and Ash said he would see them both there again tomorrow.

They took to their respective chauffeur-driven cars and went their own way. Jazz went home and would meet Boomer at the Cranbrook at 8 p.m. that evening as arranged. He asked Harry, as they drove down Romford Road towards Ilford, if he was a chauffeur by profession and whether this was what he always did for a living, knowing it would piss him off. He wanted to see his reaction. It was a curt reply that did nothing to suggest anger or interest.

"Shut the fuck up, Singh, and just do what you are told."

It was a reaction of sorts and that pleased Jazz. When they got to De Vere Gardens, he said he would see Harry tomorrow at 8.30 a.m. as usual and he swanned off towards the house.

He stood outside the front door and waved Harry off and took out a cigarette. He needed a few minutes to think clearly. *What the fuck was today all about?* He was caught up in something very sinister with a potential traitor. He didn't fully blame Derek for what he was doing to protect Sarah, but he couldn't trust him. He would have a Glock which he loved the idea of, but no live rounds! The inference was that these people, whoever they were, were killers or international terrorists, not anyone he had experience of, that was for sure. Now he wondered, was he being watched? He surreptitiously looked around and couldn't see anyone in a car watching him or anyone standing on the street. He hoped Mrs Chodda was safe. David said he wasn't doing anything at the meeting that they would blackmail him for so he hoped that was right. He lit another cigarette; he needed a two-cigarette think! He looked forward to seeing Boomer tonight to share the information he had with him. He knew he wasn't supposed to talk about today with Boomer but *fuck that* he thought.

CHAPTER SIXTEEN

FAMILY STUFF

He went indoors hoping for a few minutes' peace and a drink before sorting out Wills but Mrs Chodda was having none of that. She opened the kitchen door and beckoned him in urgently. He wondered what was going on. Apparently, Wills hadn't told them that it was his open evening at school and someone had to attend to talk to his teachers. Mrs Chodda looked pointedly at Jazz.

"So, Wills, how come you didn't give us notice of an open day tonight? Don't you want me to go there?" Jazz asked pointedly.

Wills, looking non-committal, shrugged his shoulders and didn't answer. Not happy with such a response, Jazz, with all that was going on at the moment and now this, was feeling a little tetchy and reckoned Wills was taking the piss. Seeing the look on his face Wills blurted out, before Jazz could rant at him, "I didn't think it was worth telling you. My mum and dad have never gone to an open evening so I didn't mention it."

Jazz, now feeling bad, gave Wills a friendly punch on the arm and said, "'Course I am going to your open evening tonight. Gotta see what stuff you have been up to." Just adding to the banter, he joked "Hope you spent some time in your classroom and learned something and not just sitting outside the head's office waiting for a bollocking."

Wills murmured, "Fuck off."

Mrs Chodda tutted at such language in her kitchen and in unison Jazz and Wills hung their heads in shame and said sorry to Mrs Chodda.

They had to be at the school at 6 p.m. and Jazz reckoned he would still be in time to meet Boomer at 8 p.m. He got up quickly from Mrs Chodda's huge wooden table and told Wills to be ready by 5.30 p.m. and he would just go up and change. He had half an hour which was time enough for a badly needed drink. But *fuck it*, he thought, only one drink because he would have to drive to the school. Mrs Chodda was dishing up a meal for Wills and Jazz would pick up something after the school. He thought *I fucking don't need this tonight.* He had wanted to just sit and think a bit more. He had to do right by the kid, but he needed a chat with Boomer tonight to help him make some sense of the MI6 stuff.

They arrived at the school a little early and Wills had to show Jazz where to go to see his teacher. Wills was a bit frisky and smiley. Jazz realised this had never happened to him before and he thought how his own parents had attended all his open evenings when he was a kid; sometimes he had wished they hadn't when he was bollocked for not working hard enough.

The school secretary, Betty, saw Jazz coming in and made it her business to go and see him. She still carried a torch for him. He saw her coming and wanted to be polite but how the hell could he get away? He smiled at *Miss Temptress in a cardigan* and with his most apologetic look said they were a bit late and had to get to the classroom. Disappointed but full of optimism, Betty suggested he might like to pass by her office afterwards. Jazz smiled again and with a rueful look said he had to be somewhere at 8 p.m. so couldn't but next time he was here, he would look her up. She smiled hopefully and Jazz made a brief excuse and dashed off with Wills.

Mr Compton, a twenty-two-year-old barely shaving teacher, looked up as Jazz plonked himself down on the tiny school chair opposite Mr Compton's desk. This teacher smiled haughtily and gave off an air of superiority. His suit jacket hung badly on his bony frame and his hand fiddled continuously with his mousey-coloured hair that just kept flopping over his left eye. This spectacle niggled and irritated Jazz, but he just smiled and watched waiting for Mr Compton and his pimply-faced look of concentration to stop writing in his book and address him. He waited for what seemed five minutes and this was not good for Jazz who thought the teacher was taking the mickey and keeping him waiting.

Eventually Mr Compton looked up and smiled apologetically. Apparently, he was new to this and this was his first open evening. He had to write everything down as soon as he had seen a parent otherwise, he said, he would forget. This appeased Jazz somewhat; he realised just because he was a teacher and clever, it didn't mean he couldn't be a fucking stupid ignorant arsehole too. He smiled back and waited.

Mr Compton looked confused and asked, "Who are you here to talk about?" Jazz leaned forward and said William Winder. Looking non-plussed, Mr Compton coughed and asked if Jazz was his father. Jazz by now was rattled. Of course he wasn't the fucking father, they were different skin types. He was Asian and Willy wasn't.

"I am at present the legal guardian of William Winder."

He sounded pompous and wasn't sure if he was actually the legal guardian but he reckoned this streak of piss wouldn't know that. Mr Compton accepted this and clearing his throat and looking through his notes, looked up and told Jazz that William Winder was not doing very well at school up until now. He went on to say that there had been a dramatic and encouraging rise in the work William presented. Jazz smiled; he reckoned it was because he had taken William away from the druggies for parents. Mr Compton had another point of view.

"I believe William has changed his work ethic and produced some stunning and insightful work since I have joined this school in the last few weeks. I am modestly suggesting my new and innovative style has helped progress William and given him the impetus to work well."

Mr Compton looked up at Jazz and smiled and waited for the compliments to come his way. The time was ticking on and Jazz was edgy and put out by this lump of turd taking credit for nothing. Okay, he conceded, he might be working better because of a new teacher but this idiot had obviously not looked at William's background and seen what the lad had had to live with in the past and how his life was now. But not wanting to upset William's relationship with his teacher he decided to be diplomatic.

"I am sure you have helped a great deal, Mr Compton. But may I suggest you do your job and look at this kid's background before you make such sweeping statements on your ability to change him in two weeks. What are you, a fucking magician!?"

Mr Compton, shocked at such language and opinion, sat dumbfounded for a moment. Jazz took the opportunity to jump in quick. He hadn't got time for this.

"So, Mr Compton, is William doing good? Is there something as his legal guardian I can do to improve his work? What can I tell him you have said about him to give him some confidence?"

Mr Compton pulled himself together, adjusted his jacket and looked back on his notes and with a hesitant start told Jazz that all his homework was being done correctly, he was attaining reasonable grades and that his swearing in class was a lot better. He understood that William was often outside the head's office for misdemeanours but he had to say that had not happened since he had been in his class. So, his work and attitude had improved to a good level. This pleased Jazz and he shook Mr Compton's reluctant hand and called William away from a group of lads chatting in the corner and made his exit from what must have been the assembly hall. William looked at Jazz in the car and wanted to ask but didn't know how.

"It's okay, kid," said Jazz. "It was a good review and you are doing well. Mr Compton seems a fair teacher. What do you think?"

Wills replied, "I think he is a fucking idiot."

"Oy there, that's not what you should say about your teacher. Although I think he is a fucking twat, but that's my personal view."

They both nodded and laughed. Feeling it was a successful evening and in a good mood, Jazz added, "You have done good so I think I should get you a McDonald's as a treat to take home. What do you reckon?"

Wills smiled and thanked Jazz. He had never had anyone go to the school on an open evening. Now he got a McDonald's as a treat too. Life felt good.

CHAPTER SEVENTEEN

DUNGEON CHIC

Jazz got to the Cranbrook pub at just turned 8 p.m. and walked in with Boomer. Jazz ordered a quadruple vodka and tonic for himself and a beer for Boomer. They settled themselves down at the corner table at the back of the pub; they had things to discuss in private.

Boomer, who got pulled into this by MI6 with Ash, told Jazz that from his point of view, he hadn't got any fucking idea what they expected of them. Ash was panicking and they found him a sweet job he was enjoying. They were teaching him some new search engines and that was keeping him quiet. Boomer thought he was there because he went to see Mrs Manson with Jazz and was part of the team. At the moment they didn't know what to do with him. He was promised some work with a Glock but nothing much else was said to him apart from Jazz being the front runner in this. The only thing they said for definite was that because Boomer and Ash worked closely with Jazz they had to be removed from their place of work so Jazz wasn't compromised. Jazz nodded, he reckoned it was his fault Boomer and Ash were in this. He told Boomer about his day and what they wanted him to do. They drank their drinks and Jazz had another quadruple vodka and tonic but Boomer said he was alright with his pint of beer.

Jazz added that at least he had backup in this. It had begun to feel very sinister and dangerous. All because fucking Devious Derek did something kinky that made him worth blackmailing. The costs Jazz was going to have to pay were now being paid for by MI6 and they said they had his back too, so that was good he supposed. According to them all he had to do was attend a couple of meetings with Scarlett so there was no suspicion that he was anything other than who he said he was. The job at the mansion was a piss-poor job of being a gateman so no problem there. It all sounded pretty easy.

They sat in silence while they drank their drinks, deep in thought. Jazz finally broke the silence and stated, "I don't trust any of them."

Boomer quickly retorted, "Nor do I. They are fucking liars, Derek is a traitor and the villains are hit men – what the hell are you and maybe me letting ourselves in for?"

"I am off to see Scarlett tomorrow evening apparently. She is going to contact me when she gets back in the country with Devious Derek. I have got to decide what the fuck I am into with this Scarlett. I am not happy."

Boomer made that noise that started in the bottom of his stomach and rose into his throat and came out as a laugh.

"You have gotta take pictures," was all he could say and laughed louder and longer. Jazz had to smile, it all sounded ludicrous, but he did know what he would do. He told Boomer.

"I've got it figured out. David said to go for wanting to be controlled and dominated. I can do that," said a reluctant Jazz.

Jazz needed to go before he got too drunk. He wanted to ring Sarah on the way home and Mad Pete too. He had things to plan. He reassured Sarah that all was well and being worked on and she was to just stay quiet about everything. Sarah thought that was a bit strange but Jazz was slurring his words a little so she thought it was the drink.

He rang Mad Pete and heard, "Fuck!!!! Thank God you rang me back, Mr Singh, I've been trying to get you all day."

Jazz checked his phone and saw he had missed about six calls over the afternoon and evening. He thought he had better take his phone off silence more often.

"What's up?"

"I had Mrs Manson on the phone this morning about you. She's gonna kill me, Mr Singh. She does some bad things in that house and I'm scared."

Jazz thought, *for fuck's sake, what are you on about?* His head started to hurt and the constant whining from Pete was getting on his nerves, but the fact Mrs Manson was making enquiries worried him.

"She asked me how I got to know someone as smart and classy as you."

Jazz nearly laughed. Smart and classy? If she saw him now, she wouldn't think that. He had started to stagger a bit. The fresh air and the drink were having their effect and he couldn't walk in a straight line if his life depended on it. Feeling a bit apprehensive Jazz tentatively asked "So, what did you tell her?"

"The only thing I could think of, Mr Singh. Don't tell me off, gawd knows it was a difficult one. It was the only thing I could think of. She scared me, Mr Singh. You set me up with her, that's not fair. She will kill me slowly if she gets to know you are fucking pigs."

Bloody hell, he was fed up with this snivelling rat.

"Shut up and just tell me what you told her, for fuck's sake!"

Mad Pete started snivelling again and Jazz just shouted "Stop!! Tell me!!" And that seemed to do it.

"I said, Mr Singh, and don't hurt me, that you were into coke, mollies and a little Rohypnol occasionally. And you came to me because I was far away from anything to do with your work and I was safe."

"Bloody hell, Pete! You made me sound a real druggy. I am a sharp person; I am a protection officer so I wouldn't have all these drugs every day would I, you idiot!"

"No, no, Mr Singh. She said that too and I said you liked it when you had days off and you came to me then. I said you weren't a steady user, just a *fun day* user."

"So, bloody hell, I am into cocaine, ecstasy and why a bloody date-rape drug, as well? You made me sound a real sleaze ball."

"Well, Mr Singh, I thought that would look good to Mrs Manson."

Jazz thought about it and reckoned Pete was right. Yes, that sounded good.

"You've done well, Pete, thank you. I will treat you when I see you."

Embarrassed by a compliment, Mad Pete said that he was only doing his best to look out for him. They both knew that wasn't true but that was okay. Tomorrow was going to be an interesting day.

By the time Jazz got home, all he wanted to do was go to sleep. He hoped Auntie and Amrit would leave him alone. It was 10.30 p.m. and all seemed quiet in the house and with a sigh of relief he took himself to bed with a nightcap and settled down.

The next day was as usual. Harry picked him up and took him to Area 10. They did a bit more work on gun training which he loved. They gave him the Hiatt speedcuffs too and he was going to make sure they didn't get those back. They were fucking brilliant. They would get lost after this. He asked if he would have a Heckler & Koch MP5 sub-machine gun too and they told him in no uncertain terms that they didn't want to give him that but sadly he had to be the same as the others in the team. This pleased him no end and a bit of training was arranged. The day was spent kitting him out. He got the comfortable bulletproof vest, much better than the stab vests given to his station, and the CS gas and radio. He reckoned he could lose the lot but they would want the guns back, sadly.

He got the phone call from Mrs Manson at 2 p.m. saying he could meet Scarlett at 5 p.m. that evening at her place. So, Harry took him home at 12 noon in time for him to make his way to Mrs Manson in Hackney. His only words of advice from David were 'Don't fuck it up'.

He explained when he got home to a surprised Mrs Chodda, "Auntie, I am out again at 3 p.m. on duty. I am just here to change and get a bite to eat." Auntie sent Amrit up to his room with a plate of pakoras, his favourite. Amrit could see he was distracted and busy so smiled and said she would speak with him another time. He was grateful for that. He didn't know what the hell was going to happen, or what he should do, but he needed to make it seem genuine.

He parked up and rang Mrs Manson's bell. Mrs Manson opened the door and looked a vision of loveliness. She stood provocatively in a long black silk dress that clung to every curve with a dramatically plunged front that barely held her breasts in place. Her long black hair had been brushed to excess and it shone and fell in waves of beautiful curls nestling on her bare shoulders. She said hello and her lips were bright red and glistened temptingly. He was mesmerised. This woman was a goddess. Her eyes glinted and sparkled and looked so inviting. He stood on the steps unable to move, just drinking in the vision.

At her insistence, he walked in and followed Mrs Manson as she glided into a beautiful room full of settees, antique tables and what looked like original paintings on the walls. It was a very upmarket Victorian room; it dripped riches and opulence. She sat him down on a settee opposite her and she crossed her legs in a very stylish way. He made sure his mouth was closed; she made him feel highly sexual and if she told him to crawl to her over broken glass, he would have done that. She understood the look very well and needed to get the business side done first. She asked him for his bank account details so he could pay the £500 for meeting with Scarlett today. He duly gave her the details and waited.

She asked if he would like a drink before meeting Scarlett and Jazz nodded. He wanted to spend more time with Mrs Manson. She gave him one of her best smiles and he bathed in it. A vodka and orange was brought to him and they sat sipping their drinks and engaged in gentle conversation. His eyes never left hers.

"Gosh, you look tired today, Jazz, if I may call you that," said a demure Mrs Manson.

"I've been busy. There is a lot of work to be done for a conference coming up in the near future. But I have the next few days off so I can relax," Jazz added, hoping this would be helpful to meeting Scarlett.

"Well, if you don't get on with Scarlett, I am sure I can find you someone else," said Mrs Manson provocatively.

"I suppose you don't do what Scarlett does?" asked a hopeful Jazz.

"No, I don't, but I may make the odd exception sometimes."

She looked deep into his eyes when she said that. Jazz tried to keep himself on track and realised he had to see Scarlett, but fuck it, all he really needed to do was to be here to maintain the storyline and not corrupt the work being done to sort the traitor Derek out.

"I think I would rather be with you," he blurted out. This woman was just something he had never experienced before.

"Well, that's settled then, you will have me."

His breath had become laboured, he was feeling a little giddy and wondered if it was the drink. *Bloody stupid,* he thought, a skinny vodka and orange would do nothing to him. This woman had him by the balls and would drag him wherever she wanted to.

"Look, meet Scarlett, she has come in specially to meet you and then make up your mind. I am here if you want me."

Gosh, she made that sound so inviting. Mrs Manson took hold of Jazz's hand and he followed helplessly. They went up the stairs into a huge room. "This is one of our dungeons, my favourite, actually," she said.

Jazz looked around and to him it looked like a torture chamber. In the corner was a chaise longue that looked totally out of place in this scary room. There were ropes and straps hanging from rafters in the ceiling. He saw what looked like work benches made of steel but on closer inspection they had straps, etc. on them. Mrs Manson sat him down on the chaise longue and told him to wait for Scarlett and she left him alone. The ceiling had straps hanging down but the walls were full too. There were mirrors and a long line of hanging things; some were whips, he recognised, and there were belts, paddles and something else that looked like an old-fashioned truncheon. It was spooky and scary and he didn't like them at all. What the fuck had he let himself in for?

Scarlett came in and she was utterly gorgeous. She had a tight-fitting basque outfit in red and her black stockings covered her long legs. Her heels looked seven inches high and she strode determinedly over to him. She must have been about twenty-seven years old, Jazz reckoned. She had her black hair beautifully constructed into a chignon and looked a little oriental with beautiful almond-shaped eyes. She wasn't messing around and grabbed him and pulled him out of his seat. She looked straight at him and pouted her bright red lips. Then raising her chin, she uttered words slowly and with malice he didn't think she would be capable of.

"You will do as I say and not answer me back, is that understood?"

He nodded.

"I will show you our equipment here so you know what I am going to do to you in the future. But first…"

And she took his hand and pulled him to one of the structures in the room. It looked like a short massage table with a bit on the end for your face to go into, so you would lie on it on your stomach. It had hand, foot and arm struts with leather restraints.

"This is the master table which requires extreme obedience from you. But it is the beginner's table. I will show you something more extreme."

Jazz again nodded. It looked fucking awful. He really hated this. She took him to another table and it was the most frightening thing he had ever seen. She talked like a car showroom salesperson.

"This is not a lie-down bench. It's called the extreme punishment bench and it's my favourite. I can restrain you by the neck; it has a strap-on surface that allows me to attach all my toys and dildos and I have a lot," she said in a tone that caused fear in his genitals.

She saw the look in his eyes and smiled. "This will be wonderful for tying you up and spanking you. Oh, there is so much I can do with you on this one." She kissed him slowly on his neck and stroked his arm. She felt him shudder at her touch and that pleased her.

"You have never been to a place like this before?" she asked.

Jazz, in truth, said he had never experienced a place like this. But he took the opportunity to add that he had dreamed of such a place and he was grateful to be here and meet her and experience everything.

"You want to be my slave?"

She asked in an accent that made him feel she didn't know the right words but he agreed by nodding furiously. She smiled and cupped his chin and pulled him over to another table that looked like a gym workout bench that she provocatively said was great with a blindfold.

The hanging straps from the ceiling were everywhere they passed but suddenly she grabbed his hands and before he knew it, she had pulled on the hanging straps and fastened his hands and his arms. She let go of the straps and his hands pulled his arms above his head. It was a shock and it scared him.

"How does that feel?" she asked.

"Wonderful," said a lying Jazz.

With that he felt a sting on his buttocks as she hit him using one of the paddles he had seen on the wall with a force he didn't think a five-foot-ten woman in seven-inch heels could produce. This very sweet and sexy-looking woman put her face into his, nearly kissing him but not and said with a venomous tone he never thought possible from her sweet face, "I can give you more next time. You will do as I tell you and if you are good, I will reward you. If you are bad, I will punish you. You will call me Mistress and you will thank me for beating you."

Jazz nodded quickly and far too many times.

"This is your lesson for today. I will see you tomorrow for a proper lesson in humility and servitude. Be here by 11 a.m. and not a minute later."

With that she brought the paddle down on his back causing a stinging sensation that brought tears to his eyes. She helped him out of the ropes and told him to thank her for her work today. Jazz, glad to be free from the constraints, thanked her again and again and smiled and almost bowed to her and left the room.

He didn't like that at all. He didn't think Mrs Manson would be much better but he preferred her to Scarlett who seemed less kindly, less sensual. He would ring Mrs Manson when he got home. He just wanted to get out of the place and go home. He needed a good drink.

After two tumblers of vodka and orange and twenty minutes of thinking, Jazz realised he wasn't in this for his benefit. So, with a heavy heart he made the decision he would stay with Scarlett. It was what he had asked for, after all, and she was close to Devious Derek and that was the point of all of this. He was fucking fed up with this bloody game. The frisson of an adventure sprinkled with a bit of danger was all dried up now. He was just a pawn for the MI6 bastards and he wasn't going to be involved in any of the interesting bits leading to arrests. It was going to be all pain and no gain for him. At that miserable thought he poured his third tumbler of vodka and orange. He needed it, he told himself darkly.

It was only eight o'clock and Jazz needed to talk. He rang Boomer and asked him to meet him in the Cranbrook in half an hour. He wouldn't talk on the phone because he didn't know who was listening in. It was fucking awful. MI6 seemed to know everything he did and he wasn't sure if Scarlett and whoever she was in with was watching him too. At least the pub was a usual place to visit and Boomer was his usual companion there.

The drinks were bought and it was Boomer's turn to buy the first round. He got Jazz a double vodka and orange. Jazz peered at the glass and with a look of disgust asked, "What the fuck is that?"

"You drink too much," was the glib reply from Boomer who was sipping contentedly on his beer.

"So how was it this evening at the torture house?" said Boomer trying not to laugh.

"It was fucking awful. I am not sure I can go through with this. Tonight was a taster and for what it's worth it wasn't pleasant but I can take it," said a not convincing Jazz.

"I have to go tomorrow at 11 a.m. This Scarlett is beautiful, an absolute vicious woman and I don't fancy her at all. I really don't want to do this, and don't know what she is going to do tomorrow."

He looked at Boomer and a thought horrified him. "I don't want to have sex with her. I don't have to do that, do I?"

Boomer couldn't help it. That rumble in his stomach came out as a raucous laugh that didn't stop. Jazz looked at him in disgust.

"Fuck you! I am in the middle of something sleazy, painful and could be nasty and all you can do is laugh?"

Boomer controlled himself and apologised. It actually was a difficult situation and he sat thinking about what Jazz could do to make it easier.

"I think you can say you want to be controlled but you don't want to have sex. You are used to taking women which is why you use Rohypnol; it's your way of enjoying sex. You don't want Scarlett for that. You want to experience being controlled and to see if ultimately that would lead to you enjoying a different sexual experience."

"Fuck me!! I sound like a true sleaze ball."

"You do but you only have to do this for a month

or so. This big meeting is in two months' time and after that, things will have settled, and you can go back to a normal life, whatever that is." Boomer laughed at that.

CHAPTER EIGHTEEN

NO PAIN, NO GAIN

As usual Wills shocked Jazz awake at 6.30 a.m. by shaking his arm. It was becoming a habit and Jazz quite liked it. No hangover this morning, he obviously hadn't drunk so much last night, but he felt groggy. Wills went downstairs for breakfast and to see Auntie. He now called Mrs Chodda Auntie like everyone else did (auntie is a loving name for a woman who is not necessarily a relative but who you feel close to). With a groan Jazz got up and sat on the side of the bed trying to get his brain in gear. He checked the clock on his bedside table. It was 6.35 a.m. He rubbed his forehead hoping it would make him feel more awake. It didn't. He took a deep breath and this seemed to kickstart his brain. He remembered with a groan that he was seeing Scarlett at 11 a.m. for a beating. He groaned again at the thought. *Fuck, I want out of this,* he thought. Knowing that wasn't going to happen he reluctantly got washed and dressed and joined Wills in Auntie's kitchen.

Amrit saw him come into the kitchen and got a mug full of black coffee for him. She could see his eyes hadn't focussed yet. They smiled hesitantly at each other. Auntie quickly made an omelette for Jazz making sure she left out the chillies. She gave it to Amrit to place before Jazz. She could easily have taken a couple of steps and given it to him herself but as Amrit, Jazz and now Wills knew, Auntie was again pushing them into each other's space: The self-satisfied smile was a big giveaway and this made Amrit blush and Wills and Jazz struggled to hide a giggle.

Because Jazz was working later this morning (well, that was what he told Auntie), it was decided that Jazz would take Wills to school on the bus today. It had now been a while since he had started living with Jazz and Auntie. It was amazing how he had adapted and now it was like he had always lived with them. There had been speculation by Amrit and Auntie that it might be good for Wills to make the journey by himself. He was nearly eleven years old and old enough to try. It was the 169 bus that took him outside his school and he had a short walk to Cranbrook Road to catch the bus. Jazz wasn't sure the time was right just yet. He reckoned he was becoming a fussy, fucking old woman. He smiled at this.

On the journey he asked Wills how he was doing at school. Wills looked at him like he was mad. He didn't want to talk about school on a bus for goodness' sake! You never knew who was listening. "Fuck off."

Jazz nodded and whispered, "Okay, just listen then, you mouthy bugger. Be polite at school, do as the teachers say, and don't tell them to *fuck off*. Do your work and make yourself proud."

Wills looked at him and nearly smiled but worked hard to make sure that wasn't seen. No one had ever been that nice to him before. All he could say was, "Fuck off."

Jazz looked at him and smiled. He knew he understood.

Wills got off at his school and Amrit was collecting him later that afternoon. The bus turned around just up the road at the Merry Fiddlers Dagenham so he stayed on the bus and returned to Ilford an hour later. Now only 9.30 a.m. he had time for another coffee and he needed to find some talcum powder. He reckoned Auntie would have some, she always seemed to find whatever you asked for hidden in the depths of her cupboards.

He knocked on Auntie's kitchen door and she found very quickly the talcum powder and asked for it back when he had finished with it. Amrit followed him out into the hall and Auntie closed the door behind them with another self-satisfied smile.

"Just checking all is okay with you. It's just we haven't spoken for a while and I just wondered." She hesitated a little and then pushed herself to say, "Just worried after the, you know, the men who came here." She looked at him enquiringly, hoping for a satisfactory answer.

"Oh, that's okay, Amrit. Those men are accounted for by my boss. Don't worry. All is well."

She actually didn't believe him but left it there. She knew he had to be out in half an hour and didn't want to take up his time. Embarrassed now, she turned to go back in the kitchen. He touched her arm and she turned quickly to face him.

"Look, thanks for being concerned. I appreciate it very much. You take care of yourself."

They smiled that almost embarrassed but it was an understood smile that seemed to go on for at least ten seconds longer than it should have. The silence was broken by Jazz who looked at his watch and swore under his breath as he ran up the stairs taking two steps at a time. It was getting late and he needed to leave fairly soon. He boiled the kettle, made a coffee and added cold water to the hot so he could drink it quickly. By quarter past ten he was outside the house and ready to go.

It wasn't often he drove his own car but today he was sober and could drive. He loved his BMW, his pride and joy. He spent more time cleaning it than driving it but today he was taking the black, immaculately polished car to Hackney. The traffic at this time of the morning was not too bad and he arrived in Hackney with five minutes to spare. He took out the talc and put a little under his nose and left the container in the car. With a deep breath he headed for the house and rang the bell.

Mrs Manson opened the door. She looked stunning in a long red dress with a plunging V showing her magnificent breasts. She had long black hair and ruby red lips and Jazz was hooked. Every day she was a vision of loveliness and she could see he was smitten. With a smile she beckoned him in.

"Darling, Scarlett is here waiting for you. Let's just confirm the bank details you gave me last night."

She confirmed the account details and looked at him for agreement and he nodded yes.

"Darling, now that is done, whenever you come here, you don't have to think about payment, it will be automatically done. Nothing will interrupt your enjoyment."

The words were said precisely and in his mind with an intimacy that made him hold his breath. This was the sexiest woman he had ever met and to be honest he would have been happy to just sit with her and listen to her.

He was led out of the room by the magnificent Mrs Manson into one of the dungeons upstairs. It was the one he saw yesterday and he tried to look happy but he was fucking not!

"Would you like a little coke to enhance your experience?" Mrs Manson whispered seductively.

"No thanks, I partook before I came in."

She noticed the white smudge under his nose and nodded.

"It will enhance your experience, darling," she said.

No it bloody won't!! he thought. Boomer and he had discussed this last night and it was decided if he was the said sleaze ball, on his day off he would have had some coke. The talcum powder did the trick and he just had to be a bit more talkative and jumpier to enact the effects. He bloody wished he had got something to take. He thanked Mrs Manson and he watched her magnificent, well-defined arse as she wafted towards the door. She turned and defiantly stood watching him, her whole demeanour changing from sexy woman to mistress. Her tone was diamond-sharp and full of contempt.

"Now you fuckin' stay put and don't move, you snivelling cunt!! Your mistress will be here soon and she wants you ready to receive her."

Scared and shocked at the change of tone, he was left alone waiting for Scarlett the Torturer.

It was an interesting hour he later told Boomer over a much-needed vodka. It was 2 p.m. so he felt entitled to a quadruple vodka and a smidgeon of tonic. This time Boomer managed not to laugh or smirk. He informed Boomer, in a matter-of-fact way, the essence of a dominatrix way of working. Scarlett entered the room and was splendid in seven-inch heeled thigh-length shiny boots. She had a see-through black netted body stocking with long sleeves with only a G-string on under it and no bra. He noticed quickly she had perfectly formed breasts that pushed against the netting. She was the dom and he was the sub (dominatrix and submissive). He told Boomer that for the hour he had no control over anything. She handcuffed him and whipped him and spanked him all the while telling him he was dirt and not worth her attention. Then she spent time just caressing him as a reward then she made him crawl to her pleading to be punished again. If he forgot to call her Mistress and beg for her attention, she hurt him. She had something called a wand that was like a cattle prod and she used that a few times. "It fucking hurt," was all Jazz could say. To emphasise what it was like, he lifted his shirt to show the bruises that were developing across his back and chest. The barman with no other customers in, watched them from a distance and saw the bruises and wondered what the hell was going on.

Boomer asked what happened at the end. Jazz told him that she did whatever she wanted with him and fondled him in places he didn't want to be fondled. She stripped him down which made him feel defenceless. He said he was scared for his crown jewels most of the time. Boomer, with immense difficulty, held back the laugh that was going to explode.

"The woman fondled everything but every now and then she would get vicious and punch or squeeze and I was on high alert thinking she could cripple me if she wanted to. At the end she sat me down and said I had five minutes to speak but every sentence had to start with 'If it pleases you, my Mistress…'. It was fucking awful. I explained I didn't want sex with her but I craved the fear she generated in me, that what she was doing was enough for now. I gave her the story about taking defenceless women but wanted to experience the reverse for me. She seemed pleased with that and I am going back next week on my day off. Oh, by the way," Jazz added, "she gave me get-out words if everything got too much and I wanted her to stop. The words were 'God help me'."

Boomer couldn't contain himself any longer and that deep belly laugh exploded in the quiet of the pub causing the barman to jump and nearly drop the glass he was drying. "What a fucking mess! At least it's not for too much longer."

"Do you get that Devious Derek likes that stuff?" asked Jazz.

They both shook their heads. It was a mystery to them. But they needed to think about tomorrow. They had to go back to Roswell (this is what they called the MI6 place, Area 10, because all the people there were weird and like aliens). It didn't feel right there; something was very wrong. Both felt they were being used in whatever game they were playing and it all felt wrong; neither trusted the MI6 bastards but at the moment they had no choice but to go along with it. DI fucking Radley looked like Mother Teresa in comparison to the devious, deadly MI6 mob.

Apparently, Ash was loving every minute of his time at Roswell. He was being shown how to access areas that he had never heard of before. His research projects had a lot more avenues to explore and he spent his time checking them all out.

MI6 liked him and unbeknown to him, they were watching and considering asking him to join their team. They thought he was wasted working for the Met who they viewed with utter disdain as idiots in blue.

CHAPTER NINETEEN

HOW IT WORKS

The day started as usual. Wills now woke him up by jumping on him. It scared the hell out of him at first but now, Jazz put his alarm on so he woke about ten minutes before the 6.30 a.m. wake-up from Wills. Today he put the pillows under the duvet to look like he was sleeping and hid behind the door. It was his turn to jump out at Wills and scare the hell out of him. The shouts and screams from Wills caused Amrit to rush up the stairs in alarm to see what had happened. She was really pissed off when she spotted Jazz and Wills pillow-fighting. One of them wasn't a kid and should have known better, she thought. Jazz, seeing her in the room, looked up and smiled and she just had to laugh. She shook her head and went downstairs. *He really is an idiot!* she told herself unable to stop smiling.

The car arrived to take him to work and the usual *Pinkie and Perkie* (he called them this out of total disrespect) were driving and sitting in the front. Mrs

Chodda saw him to the door and stood waving him goodbye. She felt so proud that he had a chauffeur to take him to work. *He must be so important now* she thought with pride. With one last look around to see if any of the neighbours had noticed the beautiful car leave, she went back to her kitchen.

Jazz arrived at Roswell and was taken immediately to the firing range. He was introduced to Philip who said he was his instructor for the day. Philip obviously loved the Glock 17 and proceeded to show off. The Glock was dismantled and reassembled in the blink of an eye and Jazz was told he didn't need to do any of that, it was just so he knew how great the gun was. A Glock 17 was a semi-automatic weapon and was made of polymer material which meant that a fully loaded Glock 17 with a double stack (magazine of bullets) was light to carry, smooth and very reliable and beat many other guns. The beauty of a Glock, he was told, was its simplicity. He added he wished women were as simple and easy to manage as his Glock 17. He laughed at his joke and Jazz tried to grin at this fuckwit.

Jazz didn't care what it was made of or how great it was to carry and how it could be concealed well in a waistband. All he wanted to do was fire the thing. Eventually, Philip allowed him to hold the gun. He was told to make sure it was held in a safe direction. He was told to get used to holding it, to feel it squarely in his hand. Jazz liked the feel and understood that his hand had to get used to the grip. He struck a pose and felt like *Dirty Harry* and was about to say 'Make my day' when Philip told him to fucking grow up! Jazz realised ruefully this wasn't a game and he needed to take this seriously.

He was told to step forward and face the firing range with a target ahead of him. Philip showed him how to slip the bullet magazine into the handle of the gun, with the flat side of the magazine to the back of the gun then tap the bottom to ensure it was fully in; again making sure Jazz didn't turn around with the gun in his hand. He was told to aim and fire at the target. The magazine contained seventeen rounds of ammunition and Jazz fired them all in quick succession. He felt quite proud of his performance and turned smiling to Philip, expecting to be told he had done great.

"Point that bloody gun at the floor when you turn round," growled Philip.

Jazz asked how he had done, fully expecting to be told how great he was. He had loved the feel and sensation of firing the gun and reckoned he was a natural.

He was told he handled the Glock like a ten-year-old on speed which he thought was a tad unfair. Apparently, he was never going to be trusted with ammunition but had to look like he knew how to handle a Glock. He thought that was fucking wrong and the instructor was a fucking twat!!

The day went fairly well. He was shown how to handcuff using ASP rigid handcuffs. Jazz, feeling a bit aggrieved (he wasn't some snot-nosed newbie for fuck's sake!) was about to say that he used handcuffs daily (not quite true, not every day) so didn't need any help thank you very much until he saw the slick black crème-da-la-crème ASP handcuffs. They were so nice and looked expensive unlike the Viper tactical ones he had to use that were made out of old tin cans in comparison to these beauties.

He kept quiet and respectful while the instructor showed how slick the handcuffs were to snap onto a wrist, however big or small, because they would adjust and fit as necessary. They were made of a unitized stainless-steel frame with polymer over mould. There was a locking bridge in the middle of an ergonomic palm swell. The folding mechanism was easy for carrying. There was an automatic lock open to form a reliable restraint and with that said, in the blink of an eye, Jazz was handcuffed and had nowhere to go. He had to laugh, it was really impressive, no messing about. Jazz thought *I've gotta have a pair of these!* Before he took the handcuffs off, the instructor reminded Jazz that they were an expensive item and to look after them and to return them in good nick. Jazz had other ideas. He reckoned if he was careful, he could constructively lose them for later use. He would be the envy of the station when he got back with a pair of ASP handcuffs. The instructor sighed as he caught sight of the smile and knew they would be lost.

The day passed quickly but at least they fed him, Jazz thought. They served good meals. He went and said hello to Ash who was knee-deep in paper and computer stuff and looking very happy indeed. Ash was usually a miserable moaner, always telling Jazz off for getting himself into problems, but for once he was all smiles and happy which Jazz found quite uncomfortable. He told Jazz he loved the work here, that it was challenging and he was learning so much. He didn't know why, but Jazz felt quite depressed and thought *bollocks to this, Ash has gone over to the dark side.* Apparently, Boomer was somewhere else and he couldn't find him. They were due to meet for a drink in a few days so he would hear everything there was to know then. Soon, they told him, they would sit down and explain his duties and where he was going for the 'event' as they called it. He was driven home feeling a little disturbed. Something didn't feel right. He couldn't put his finger on it but the uneasy feeling wouldn't go away.

Amrit was waiting for him at home. She was anxious to give him the good news. Apparently, Wills had done something right at school and he had been awarded a 'Most Improved Young Person' certificate. Auntie had got very excited and baked a chocolate cake for him. Wills was a bit overawed. It was the first time anything like this had happened to him and to be praised like this was uncomfortably wonderful. So, as Amrit told Jazz in whispers, there was going to be a congratulatory tea tonight and Jazz was to go straight into the kitchen. He tried to look pleased when all he wanted was a bit of quiet and a drink. There were things he needed to think about. But, nevertheless, he felt a bit of pride that Wills had done so well and was taking school seriously. He looked at Amrit and felt something he hadn't felt for a long time. She made him feel special and he wanted to hug her in that moment but of course wouldn't. He put out his hand and tenderly touched her on her shoulder.

"Thank you, Amrit, really kind of you to meet me here and alert me. Nice to be greeted with good news."

She blushed at his words and touch. The few seconds passed as they stood locked in a smile, then, she took a deep breath and told him with authority that he needed to go to the kitchen now and see Wills and Auntie. With a nod he did exactly that. The smile hadn't left his face as he entered the kitchen to congratulate Wills.

The tea was good and Auntie made the best chocolate cake he had eaten for a long time. There were pakoras too, his favourite, and coconut ladoo, very sweet coconut cakes, round in shape, made with milk, sugar, cardamom and ghee. Auntie opened up the tin where she kept her coconut candy which was only brought out for special occasions. It was a real feast and to cap it all, she also brought out her wonderful semolina cake, called baath. It had been a long time since Jazz had seen such a feast of cakes. Wills had never seen the likes of this and the look on his face warmed Jazz's heart. This had turned out to be a good day. He was going to suggest a trip to McDonald's as a treat but this was so much better.

When everything had been tried and eaten, Jazz took Wills up to his room and gave him £10 for him to spend as he wished. He congratulated him again and added that it paid dividends to do your best and succeed using the evening tea and £10 as a good example. Wills smiled, thanked him and told him to "Fuck off" as he went to his room to get ready for bed and do his homework. Jazz poured himself a drink and smugly thought he would make a great father. For a few seconds a feeling of regret at never being a father came over him but a few swigs of the vodka brought him back to reality.

It was now just a week before the meeting was to take place. There had been two more visits to Scarlett and he was getting used to them as he told Boomer who thought it was the best laugh of the year. Scarlett had tried all different things with him including handcuffs, blindfolds, gimps and one thing he flatly refused. Boomer needed to know what he refused and waited to hear. Jazz told Boomer that his last visit had been different.

"Look, it was weird," said Jazz, a bit embarrassed but looking back found it almost funny. "A woman came into the dungeon when we were there and Scarlett introduced her as Peggy. Now she was quite butch-looking and was all in black, in one of those rubber outfits from head to toe. Scarlett did the talking and said this was a treat for me. Apparently, Peggy was what she did."

Boomer hadn't a clue what the fuck that meant. Jazz went quiet for effect and watched Boomer's face trying not to laugh.

"Ever heard of pegging?" Jazz asked a very perplexed Boomer, who shook his head.

"Well, it's when someone has a strap-on and this woman was brought in to service me. Can you believe that?"

Boomer looked at Jazz with raised eyebrows and asked the question, "Did you?"

"No, I fucking didn't! That was beyond the pale for me. Geez, it was bloody frightening."

That did it. Boomer could no longer control himself; his raucous laughter was so loud and so long he was fighting for breath while Jazz, bloody annoyed now, watched with disgust at the spectacle of Boomer flaying his arms around in hysterics, almost sliding off his chair.

CHAPTER TWENTY

ASH

It was now just a few days before Jazz, Boomer and the MI6 mob were going to what they now knew was called Crossley Manor. *The place has a name at last* thought Jazz. All the secrecy was getting on his tits! He was told to wear a suit and tie and he would be staying three nights. The conference was for two days but he would be expected to be there the day before to orientate himself to the building and the team there. He was to be the security on the gate letting in those who were expected to attend; he would receive a list of members attending and he would recognise an MI6 badge when flashed at him. He knew he had to ring through to the manor house when a car arrived with whoever was the expected distinguished passenger. Jazz reckoned miserably that the job was just about one stage up from being a lollipop man.

It was now decided that Boomer wouldn't be required to attend and he would work out of Area 10 (Roswell) while the conference was going on. So, Jazz realised he would be there alone with the arrogant MI6 tosspots and Devious Derek, the traitor. Not happy with this and feeling hard done by, he took the sheet of paper with all the participants' names on and the rooms they would be staying in. He understood that it was top secret, but he needed to be familiar with the layout of the mansion and where he would be sleeping too. He thought it strange he was trusted but everything so far had seemed strange and weird.

He met Boomer at a prearranged time in the Cranbrook Pub. It had become a regular meeting where they could talk in private. It was four days now until he had to go and stay at Crossley Manor. He told Boomer he would be taken there and briefed on roles and timings. Boomer was put out that he wasn't going there now. He wanted to see what was happening. It felt odd that Jazz was going but he wasn't. Before he showed Boomer the list of members and where the conference was being held, Jazz got Boomer his beer and himself a quadruple vodka and tonic. They sat in the corner at the back of the pub where they could talk and not be overheard. The place had very few customers. A man who looked about ninety years old sat by the window at the front watching late-night commuters walking home from Ilford Station. Another middle-aged man in a suit, probably a commuter, sat at the bar having what looked like a whisky before making his way home. He was talking to the barman who nodded every now and then as he polished glasses. Jazz wondered how the place could stay open.

After a few sips of his beer, Boomer asked Jazz how he got on at Mrs Manson's the night before. It always cheered him up to hear of the punishments that Scarlett metered out to Jazz. Jazz, after downing his quadruple vodka a bit quicker than he should have, sat back and in an expansive mood reminded Boomer that it was *a bloody awful way to spend an evening.*

"It was my last night there as far as they are concerned. David said I don't have to go next week as the conference would have happened and everything would be settled. Scarlett thinks I am coming next week at the usual time," explained Jazz.

"Yeah, but you could still go if you want to. I mean you have got used to it now. I reckon you have got a taste for it," uttered Boomer who tried to keep a straight face.

"Fuck off. I went above and beyond the call of duty with that one. It has opened my eyes to many things. For instance, you won't believe what you can do with a banana."

Boomer, bubbling with laughter, asked, "What do you do with a banana?"

"Don't ask," was the glum reply.

It took Boomer five minutes to regain his composure. This was better than any evening at the Comedy Store. He hadn't laughed so much for years and would have stories to tell his team when they met up in the pub in the following months.

Jazz, fed up and not happy with Boomer's mickey taking, told him to get serious and look at the list given to him. He wanted Boomer's opinion. There were going to be about twenty attendees and the list had some pretty high-powered names from countries in Europe. They were Ministry of Defence, scientists, arms specialists, etc. They both thought Mr Edwin Kaloski, whose job title was First Minister to the Head of NATO in Cannerberg, Maastricht, would be a target for any terrorists. The information he could tell together with his contacts would be worth a fortune. Jazz reckoned Devious Derek would be the one to be his bodyguard. But both Jazz and Boomer reckoned MI6 would know this and have it under control.

"To be honest, Boomer, I think I am safer staying on the security gate and letting the MI6 goons do whatever they need to do."

They both nodded profoundly at this statement and finished their drinks. Jazz was just going to suggest another drink for the road when the pub door was flung open and a whirlwind of a man rushed into the pub, stood for seconds looking around gasping for air and when his eyes alerted on Jazz and Boomer in the corner, he rushed over looking covertly from side to side.

"What the fuck are you doing, Ash?" asked Boomer, horrified by such a spectacular and obvious entrance into their hideaway.

Ash, taking no notice, sat himself down and got an enormous amount of paperwork out of his briefcase. Both Jazz and Boomer watched mesmerised as Ash assimilated and put into a neat pile all the paperwork. His heavy breathing settled and when he finished setting up, he looked enquiringly at Jazz and Boomer who were silent and open-mouthed during this process. After a pregnant pause, Boomer again asked, "What the fuck, Ash?"

Taking a deep breath and leaning forward in a very conspiratorial way which pissed both Jazz and Boomer off, he whispered he had some news that may be of interest. They couldn't help themselves; both Jazz and Boomer leaned forward towards Ash and waited. Seeing he had their full attention which was unusual because usually they thought he was a pain in the arse, he tried not to smirk as he told them of his findings.

"Well," he began, "I have had a great time at Area 10 as they call it." He added unnecessarily, "I know you call it Roswell but officially it's Area 10."

They were getting impatient and they could tell he was obviously nervous about something by the way he was messing around but they let him get on and hoped he would settle down and tell them what the fuck he was there for.

"So, I was being shown some interesting sites and how to find them and use them. I think actually they might offer me a job with them. I get that impression." He looked up at Jazz and Boomer and was disappointed to see them just nodding. He would have preferred that they might rush to say 'Oh no, Ash, you can't leave us' but that wasn't going to happen. With a deep breath he started again.

"So, I have been left to work on my own and with the new information I have been given I sort of explored that side of the Internet I didn't know was there and I possibly found MI6 undercover information."

He looked up and happily saw he now had their full attention. Ash was not happy being devious and was scared most of the time when working outside of a police station so this was a big deal for him and his hands shook as he reached for the paperwork in front of him.

"I found a site where there were emails going back and forth. I couldn't find out who they were from but they were from MI6 mainframe and I didn't know where they were going. Most of the emails made little sense to me and didn't say anything very interesting until I found an email buried in an email so to speak." He looked at their quizzical faces and Ash shook his head and said not to worry about that.

"The emails that made me concerned were these." He handed a couple of copies to Jazz and Boomer.

"If you look at the list of rooms and names for Crossley Manor you will see that it is a different list to the one you have. The people attending the conference have been re-settled and the one that looks of interest is the most important person at this conference, the chair of Strategic Global Terrorism. I looked this person up and his group specialises in chemical terrorism."

He saw the quizzical look on Jazz's face and added, "He runs an important group looking into global diseases manufactured around the world and their use as chemical weapons in a war. He has access to a highly confidential and classified list of names of scientists around the world and what they are working on. I delved deeper into his work and it appears that this information hasn't been shared with other countries. Great Britain is the keeper of this information and this man holds the key to where it is kept." He let this information digest a little before adding "They have moved Jacob McHenry, that's his name, into a room that is away from the other rooms and I wonder why. Guess who is his protection officer?"

They nodded at each other, knowing it would be Devious Derek. They all took a deep breath wondering what the hell it all meant. Before questions could be asked, Ash jumped in again.

"There is more to consider and possible worry about."

They looked at him wondering what the fuck he was going to add to the already explosive information.

"Look at the second email. It wasn't very specific about anything. Looked like routine stuff about meals and timetables with meetings. Somewhere in the middle there is a reference to you, Jazz. It says *Security on the gate is arranged.* They added *Please note this security officer is not armed and can be dismissed if necessary.* I think that's a bit strange, don't you?"

"A bloody understatement, Sherlock," said a thoughtful Boomer.

Jazz, feeling the prickle of fear rising up his back and about to hit him on the back of the head, asked Ash to repeat what he had just said. He looked at the email to find those words just in case he had misheard and there they were, in Arial 12 point, staring at him.

"What do you reckon 'dismissed' means?" asked Jazz.

Boomer jumped in with, "It means you fucking don't go there, that's what it means."

Ash, very worried and scared added, "If they knew, whoever *they* are, what I have done, I reckon I will be dismissed."

It wasn't funny. In fact, they were both horrified at what Ash had uncovered, but for some reason, to Ash's dismay, both Jazz and Boomer started giggling uncontrollably at Ash's joke. They coughed and pulled themselves together and apologised profusely saying it was just releasing the tension they felt, which was probably true.

They read through the paperwork again, just to check whether they were viewing the information like it was a le Carré novel and reading meanings that were not there. The room changes were not the same on the list Jazz had but he decided he would wait until tomorrow to see if he was given the new list Ash had found.

Secondly, they had to decide whether stating that gate security was not armed was just a fail-safe, so everyone knew who had weapons and who hadn't. They talked about the word *dismissed* and that it could mean he wouldn't be needed after a certain time.

When all of this had been talked over and broken down into pieces and all the logical ideas had been put forward it was decided unanimously that Jazz was fucked and they would have to work on ways to protect him. Ash was thanked for his genius at finding the information and they told him to be careful. Ash left them still worried but feeling more like James Bond. He had a spring in his step and promised to keep them updated if he found out anything else.

Jazz and Boomer got another drink and sat down to plot what they would do next.

CHAPTER TWENTY-ONE

PLANS

The next morning Jazz was up early and before Wills entered his room to jump on him as was his usual way of saying good morning. He had things to plan and needed to be up and dressed early. He needed to ring Mad Pete. It was going to cause him a lot of trouble as Mad Pete usually didn't get up until 10 a.m. but this was urgent.

It was 6.30 a.m. and Wills crept into the bedroom ready to pounce on Jazz only to find him up, dressed and fully awake. His disappointment at not being able to maim and annoy him was plain to see. This bit of domestic bliss was something Jazz had come to enjoy. He told the kid to fuck off and get dressed and he would see him downstairs in twenty minutes.

He got a Fanta out of his fridge, something that always helped his fuzzy head first thing and dialled Mad Pete. It took three redials and what felt like half the morning before Mad Pete answered belligerently.

"It's the fucking middle of the night, Mr Singh, why you phoning me at this time?"

The whining went on for as long as Jazz could stand it. But keeping calm and polite and with a personable tone, he said, "Look, sorry, Pete, but this is mega urgent. I need to see you tonight at 6 p.m. usual place. Don't want to say any more. I need to use your brain for something to do with a young lad who is staying here."

"Are you mad, Mr Singh? Why the fuck do you need to ring me now about this?"

The personable bit was wearing thin, and pissed off with his moaning, Jazz abruptly said, "Just shut it, Pete! See you at 6 p.m. I'm busy so got to go." With that, Jazz hung up.

He couldn't tell him the phone might be bugged and he didn't want to draw any attention to anything that the bastard MI6 would be interested in. Boomer and he had talked about what they were going to do. They agreed that no one was to be trusted with any information at the moment. They hadn't a clue who was sending these messages. It could have been Devious Derek or his driver or even the canteen cook at Area 10. Who the fuck knew?

Jazz went downstairs and could hear Wills in the kitchen. The bugger had found his confidence and voice and was being cheeky in Auntie's kitchen. He entered the mayhem and rescued Auntie who was having trouble with Wills jumping around her kitchen moving stuff and just messing around and giggling. Although not angry, Auntie looked out of breath and was glad Jazz calmed the boy down. Amrit arrived just behind Jazz and the two of them nodded to each other and almost embarrassed looked away and each got on with breakfast. Auntie knew those looks and starting humming that tuneless tune again as she stirred the big pot on her stove. Again, she made Amrit hand Jazz the plated omelette, something she could have just reached over to give to him. Both Amrit and Jazz knew this game and both blushed a little. Wills was now in on this little game and giggled at them. Jazz told him to shut up and ruffled his hair, something Wills did not like as he took good care of his hair these days. This was an idyllic family breakfast. Jazz felt a contentment he couldn't remember ever feeling before. It was an odd feeling but he liked it.

Before long Amrit told Wills to get his books for school as it was time to go. Jazz, as had become his custom, took Wills to one side and told him to behave at school and not swear at the teachers. Wills, as usual, told him to fuck off and left happily for school with Amrit telling him off for swearing. Wills looked at Jazz as he got to the door and they both smirked.

Pinky and Perky (the name Jazz disrespectfully gave the two who picked him up) arrived and took Jazz to Area 10, or Roswell, as Jazz called it. David was already there and introduced Jazz to someone known as 'the boss'. This guy was particularly polite and apologetic. He went on to thank Jazz for continuing to work in this way. He recognised that this was not the type of work Jazz was used to so his commitment and enthusiasm was noted. Jazz wondered where he got the 'enthusiasm' from but it was a nice change to be spoken to as an asset instead of being a pain in the neck which was what he usually got told. He liked this guy and he was obviously the top boss by the way David acted deferentially to him.

"I want you to know that a good word will be put in to your boss regarding this episode. As you are aware, it is somewhat a strategic and inter-personnel terrorist situation that could have a devastating effect on the country, nay, the world's peace and prosperity."

Jazz thought that a pretty awesome statement to make and that tingle of fear and trepidation surfaced again. He knew it was serious but fuck, world peace and prosperity sounded very ominous. He thought quickly that he was in a situation that couldn't be that more dangerous and he had a gun for protection but with no bullets. The boss carried on with a smile and a pat on Jazz's shoulder with the passing comment.

"I hope it goes well for you. David here says you are doing the entrance security so you should be out of harm's way. I have decided after much discussion with David that your colleague DI Tom Black will come along too. We will put him in the kitchens to watch the back door so to speak. He will also be out of harm's way. DC Kumar will stay here. He is a computer bod so wouldn't be expected to work on security. We don't know who we are dealing with yet so everything must look like a normal event using the team. Stay put on your station and let us do the work necessary to make sure this has a good outcome."

With that the boss walked off with David scurrying behind him. Jazz hadn't realised he had been almost holding his breath while the boss was there. He exhaled loudly and sat down. He understood it would be a dangerous assignment but somehow it felt more dangerous. He was glad Boomer was coming; just to have someone there he trusted made him feel that bit safer.

It wasn't long before David returned. His face was like thunder. Jazz asked what was up.

"I didn't want DI Black to come along. It's bad enough we have you to cope with. This is a professional assignment and my men are highly trained. Now I have two numpties to worry about. I don't want either of you interfering in what transpires and I don't want to have to worry about what you are up to. There is enough going on."

"Well, thank you very much, David. I would prefer not to be going. I am fucking fed up with all of this."

This seemed to calm David down for a moment and he relaxed, smiled and almost laughed.

"I am sorry, Singh. You are professional enough to do what is asked of you. I just worry that I have two untrained men to be concerned about. It will be fine, I am sure."

Jazz took this opportunity to just ask, "So, I have my list of who is in what room and the layout of the mansion. I know where my room is. Have you a room for DI Black? And is my list still relevant?"

David took the list that Jazz was waving around and scrutinised it.

"Yep, this is the right list. Boomer will be in one of the rooms in the north wing where you will be sleeping. It's well away from the event itself so you will both be fine there. My men will have rooms around you too."

That answered the question very well for Jazz and he smiled and thanked David. Now he knew something wasn't right.

"Can I team up with DI Black if we are both going together?" asked a charming Jazz.

"Well, okay, you can, you will have tomorrow to get yourself packed and the following day you will be collected by your drivers and taken to the mansion to orientate yourself on what you are doing and where you are sleeping. Everything will be explained to you when you get there."

With that David left. Jazz could see he wasn't happy about this change of plan. This had really rattled him. Jazz went off to find his drivers. He wanted to get home and think. He had arranged to meet Boomer in the pub at 8 p.m. *That should be interesting* he thought ruefully. His drivers dropped him at home and told him to be ready the day after tomorrow at 10 a.m. when they would be off to the mansion near Stansted.

CHAPTER TWENTY-TWO

PREP WORK

He was home early today and Auntie, hands full of flour, cleaned them quickly and caught jazz's attention before he could get up the stairs. She beckoned him silently and urgently into the kitchen. Worried now, he followed her and wondered what on earth was wrong.

"Thank goodness you are home early, Jazz. I have no one to collect Wills from school. Amrit had an appointment and couldn't collect him. I was going to put my coat on and collect him myself."

He was relieved it was nothing serious. He reckoned with all the stuff going on with MI6, he was now paranoid and saw problems everywhere.

"No problem, Auntie. I will get him. I am out about 5 ish but can bring him home. I will collect him by car so it won't take as long as the bus."

Auntie, grateful for this burden to be lifted, made Jazz a cup of tea from the urn that worked all day containing tea that had stewed for hours, just how he liked it. He couldn't drink now, so a tea would do. He took the time to tell Auntie he was going away for a long weekend which was work. He said tomorrow was packing and getting ready and he was off on Friday morning and back Monday. He hoped it was okay with looking after Wills. Embarrassed, it suddenly dawned on him how he had left most everything to Auntie and Amrit regarding feeding and looking after Wills. Stuttering at this realisation, he promised to make it up to Auntie and would obviously increase his rent a bit more. He paid extra of course for Wills but not enough. Auntie, who took everything in her stride, said, "Remember, Jazz, Guru Granth Sahib says we must remember our three core tenets: Meditation upon and devotion to the Creator, truthful living and service to humanity. I am at peace with everything so don't worry. Just do your work and we will look after Wills."

He loved the woman and gulped his tea and gave her a hasty kiss on the cheek and was off to get Wills. He shouted from the door that she shouldn't worry about Wills' tea because he was getting him a McDonald's. She tutted at this, she didn't approve of such a meal for his tea, but he was gone before she could comment.

Wills liked the idea of being picked up by Jazz and in his BMW, but he liked the idea of a McDonald's even more. They went through the drive-in and parked up eating their Big Mac and large fries and chocolate milkshake. It was silent until both had finished; it was an unwritten rule that you didn't talk while eating McDonald's. Beefburgers and chips got cold very quickly so eating fast was important.

"I am away for work from Friday until Monday so I want you to behave and help Auntie and Amrit over the weekend. Mr Chodda works weekends so you will be the man of the house and I want you to act like a responsible adult and help where needed."

Wills nodded and asked where he was going. Jazz had to tell him that it was top secret and he couldn't say. This caused Wills to become very animated and he whispered urgently, "What, like 007, you know, James Bond?"

Jazz, quite taken with the idea of being James Bond, smiled and proceeded to lie his arse off.

"Well, I suppose I am a little. But you mustn't say anything to anyone otherwise I would have to kill you." He thought that was a bit heavy but the reaction from Wills was great.

"Wow! Don't tell me then but do you have a gun and stuff like that?"

"Of course I do." Jazz was taking this too far now so he just said that he didn't want to talk any more about it for Wills' safety. He nearly giggled at that comment but seeing Wills' face, earnestly believing every word, he kept a straight face. He could see he now had a hero-worshipping fan who looked at him open-mouthed and he would use that.

"So," he added, "you be good to Auntie and Amrit. I am depending on you."

The reply was adamantly yes and confirmed by nodding his head far too much. He took Wills home and arrived in time to see Amrit just taking her coat off. They hadn't spoken for a while now, and for no particular reason. Either Amrit was out or Jazz was home late so seeing each other felt a bit strange and they fidgeted not knowing what to do or say. Auntie, seeing the situation, jumped right in.

"Amrit, why don't you make Jazz a nice cup of tea and give him one of my sweet meats (coconut cake)?"

Amrit nodded and showed Jazz to the kitchen table and chair. She wondered why Auntie didn't just make it herself because the urn was full of tea stewing there but, of course, she knew why. Jazz, seeing what was happening and how uncomfortable Amrit felt, smiled. This could be fun. He teased Amrit.

"So where were you today, Miss Amrit? I collected Wills from school. Did you go somewhere nice?"

He was surprised by her curt reply.

"Mind your own business!"

It took his breath away. *Wow! What's the matter with her!* he thought. He stuttered a little, saying, "Look, I am sorry, I was only teasing. I didn't mean to interfere. Of course it's your business."

He could see she was close to tears and wondered what the hell was going on. Everywhere seemed strange at the moment. The silence was heavy and the pregnant pause uncomfortable. With a theatrical look at his watch and an exclamation of, "Is that the time?" he got up and told anyone listening he had to go to a meeting and was late already. Glad to be out of there, he messed up Wills' hair as he passed and said he would be back later.

He took his prized black BMW with white leather seats to the Gascoigne Estate in Barking. He didn't usually like to leave his pride and joy outside anywhere in Barking. It was the sort of car that joyriders stole, that creeps keyed (scratched) or punctured tyres or just smashed the windows. But he was running out of time and it was quicker to go by car.

He got through the traffic and arrived at the Gascoigne Estate after travelling at a snail's pace because it was still rush hour. He parked up in one of the parking bays and looked around for a loitering yobbo. He spotted one lounging on a corner smoking something illegal and called him over.

"Look, mate, I will be half an hour. Stay here and look after my motor and there is a fiver in it for you."

Jazz wasn't stupid. It was cheaper than a paint job. His car would have lost its tyres, stolen or been keyed if he left his lovely BMW on this estate. The yobbo nodded and leaned against the BMW. Jazz wanted to tell him to fuck of his bonnet but it was better than nothing. He wasn't happy and felt nervous; his car was his pride and joy. He made his way up to Mad Pete's flat. The place still stunk of cabbage, again, and he thought *who the fuck eats cabbage in this place?* They were all on Pot Noodles or having takeaways from the chicken hut. The only greens these fuckers had was cannabis dried and rolled in a fag. He nearly laughed at that but instead kept banging on Mad Pete's door and shouting for him to, "Fucking open the door before I kick it in."

Mad Pete was flustered and mumbling, "Yeah, yeah, nearly there" as he unlocked all the umpteen locks on his door to let Jazz in. As he ushered Jazz in, he whined.

"Mr Singh, I open the door as fast as I can. I can't take a chance with fewer locks in this area."

As he closed the door behind Jazz he whispered ironically.

"This place is full of thieving bastards and they ain't getting any of my stuff for free."

Jazz was now feeling very agitated. Leaving his car with the spaced-out yobbo was worrying him, and standing in the stinking hallway waiting for Mad Pete to open his fucking door and now listening to this whining was making Jazz less than diplomatic.

"For fuck's sake, shut up and listen. I don't have much time; I need something fast."

Scared now, Mad Pete dribbled his, "Sorry, Mr Singh. What do you need?"

"I need a magazine of bullets for a Glock by tomorrow. Is this something you can get for me?"

Mad Pete put on his business hat.

"Yes, yes, Mr Singh, but what magazine do you need. A Glock 17 has a double stack that holds a seventeen-round capacity or a single stack with ten rounds. I can get a single stack tonight for you but a seventeen double stack is quite difficult to get at the moment. I could get you two single stacks if that helps but the cost is £65 each stack."

"That's fucking expensive. How come it costs so much?"

"This is under the counter stuff, Mr Singh. If you ain't worried who knows you are purchasing a magazine of bullets, why come to me?"

"Fair point, Pete, fair point. Can I have two stacks and I can pay you tomorrow? I need it tomorrow morning. I will meet you in Ilford McDonald's at 10.30 a.m. and I will give you the money then." He added, "Oh, by the way, I need a burner phone on the cheap for a young lad. It's my excuse for seeing you. How much will that be?"

"To you, Mr Singh, I have one ready for £20."

"Well, Pete, how about mates' rates for me?"

"Mr Singh, I have given you a cracking price. I charge much more to punters than you. The phone will be a top of the range burner phone that you will be fucking pleased to have."

"Stop with the top salesman speak, arsehole, and I will take that," was Jazz's reply.

But before he left, Jazz had to ask the question.

"Is there anything you can't get? I am fucking amazed at what you are into and who you know."

Mad Pete knew he was good but trying not to smile and doing his best to be modest said, "Well, Mr Singh, I just sort of do the best I can to make a living. I am considered in my circles as *the dog's bollocks* and I am quite proud of that."

Jazz, trying not to laugh, clapped him on the back and left. He needed to check his car was okay and he wanted to pick up fish and chips, go home, park his car and then get to the pub by 8 p.m. to meet Boomer. He was tight for time but things were coming together.

Boomer was sitting in the corner of the Cranbrook pub when Jazz arrived breathless at about 8.10 p.m. He had to wait for his fish and chips and ran and walked fast to the Cranbrook pub. He didn't bring his car as he intended to have a fair few drinks. He nodded to the barman as he walked in and his drink was waiting for him in seconds. A quadruple vodka and small bottle of tonic on a tray. Bliss.

Boomer, who was sipping a pint, watched as Jazz tipped a tiny bit of tonic into his glass of vodka and downed it in one go. The barman was pouring the next one as he finished. This was a routine they both knew.

"What a fucking day it's been," were the first words to Boomer. Boomer nodded.

"Glad I am coming too. Think you will need some backup, don't you?"

Jazz nodded in agreement. He was relieved to have a friendly face with him and someone who would watch his back.

"I have ordered two magazines for the Glock so I won't be naked. Hope I don't have to use the gun but who knows. At least I won't be a sitting target any more. David is a fucking nightmare. He thinks all his men are so great and obviously sees no problems. He thinks you are a problem, though." Jazz laughed at that.

Affronted by such a comment, Boomer retorted, "Bloody cheek, I am taking my own personal firearm to this place as well. I do have bullets for my gun."

Boomer smiled and added, "I haven't a clue what we will encounter but it's bloody exciting nonetheless."

Ash had purloined a couple of small walkie-talkies from Ilford Police Station used for surveillance work. Boomer also got them the latest bulletproof jackets. They were less bulky than the 'officer plod' ones. Boomer had found them in DCI Radley's office. Apparently, they were state-of-the-art prototypes that were not in use yet. Why DCI Radley had three of them Boomer didn't know but now he had one only. They were hanging up next to DCI Radley's ceremonial suit, so he borrowed two of them. Now both Boomer and Jazz had a way of contacting each other but not through mobile phones that could be tracked and they had bulletproof jackets that made them both feel invincible. They could watch Devious Derek between them and watch how everything progressed.

This was going to be dangerous; they were stupidly unaware of what they were dealing with, they had no expertise in this type of work, and there was a good chance of being shot; both were now excited and looking forward to the weekend.

They finished the evening with again, too many vodkas, and Boomer had one or two too many beers. It was a tense time and both justified the need for a stiff drink. Just before leaving, Jazz asked how Boomer's girlfriend was panning out. The big man, usually gruff and loud, seemed to shrink into his seat and go a bit quiet.

"Yeah, thanks, she's a good 'un."

Quite fascinated by such a change in Boomer, Jazz wanted to know more but got the usual curt reply.

"Fuck off, Singh, and mind your own business."

Relieved Boomer was still normal, he raised his now near empty glass in salute. This was not the time for Boomer to go tits up over a woman. They had things to do. Bolstered up by half a bottle of vodka, he felt a bit like Superman, invincible and strong. He was a bloody idiot and there was a heap of trouble looming just around the corner.

The meeting next day in McDonald's went well. Jazz handed over the money and took the mobile phone and the two magazines which were surreptitiously given to Jazz under the table, just in case they were being watched. Mad Pete felt a bit jittery. It was unusual for Mr Singh to act so paranoid and it worried him.

"The phone's a good one, Mr Singh. Tell the kid to look after it otherwise I will be getting it back through my boys."

He laughed at his little joke because all of Mad Pete's phones were stolen and he fenced them for the lads around Barking. Against his better judgement Jazz smiled. He got them both a McDonald's breakfast and coffee and now he had what he needed he felt calmer.

"So, Pete, what's your day going to be today?"

There was nothing in Pete's day he cared to share with a fucking DS in the police force so a bit on edge, he told him the only legal thing that was happening that day.

"I'm going shopping later, Mr Singh. I need some essentials for the flat, like crisps, fag papers, bread, that sort of thing." He hoped he sounded domesticated but by the look on Jazz's face he wasn't sure.

"Any updates to tell me on Mrs Manson and her team by any chance?" Jazz enquired hopefully.

"Nah, Mr Singh, nuffink to say there," Mad Pete lied.

He wasn't going to tell Jazz that he had been given huge orders for various drugs, some of which surprised him. He didn't know why Mrs Manson needed Rohypnol, that was a knock-out drug, but she paid for it so no bother to him.

That evening, Jazz took Wills to one side and gave him the burner phone and he put some money on it and put his mobile number on the contacts list. He told him to ring him if he needed to while he was away. Wills, who had never had such a gift, was very taken with the phone and didn't know what to say to Jazz. He wasn't used to having a present and such a wonderful present at that and Jazz had got it just for him. He was a bit overwhelmed, embarrassed and emotional so he just growled a sort of thank you as he took himself off to his room to look at it in private.

The evening was for packing and he had a few nice suits to choose from and he selected a couple of shirts and ties. His vast collection of aftershaves was sorted through and a nice but not too potent one was selected. Packed now he phoned for a pizza takeaway and opened a new bottle of vodka to enjoy a few quiet, peaceful drinks. Before he got stuck into relishing a smooth vodka and orange, an insistent light tapping on his bedroom door disturbed and irritated him. He reluctantly got up and answered the door to Amrit.

Smiling now, Amrit said she just wanted to wish him well for the weekend. Surprisingly shyly, Jazz smiled back and thanked her. They stood for a few seconds not knowing what to say. Jazz was on the verge of asking her in but she did a clumsy turn towards the stairs and waved a flappy hand in the air goodbye and left. Perplexed at such a strange interruption, Jazz got back to the bottle of vodka and waited patiently for his pizza to arrive.

Friday morning, packed, showered and feeling great, Jazz took his suitcase downstairs. He was wearing his Kevlar vest which wasn't too heavy to wear. *Well, they can stab me and shoot me now and I am protected* he told himself. He silently thanked Boomer for 'borrowing' them from DCI Radley. He giggled at that thought. DCI Radley would be spitting blood when he found they had gone.

Auntie had made him an omelette again and he sat and ate it. Wills was just off to school and Amrit had her coat on ready to go. Wills, full of energy and very excited with his new phone, punched Jazz on the arm and said goodbye as he left for school. Jazz thought they had a great relationship. He reckoned he would make a good father. This made him smile too. Him a father? *No fucking way* he thought but a bit of him wondered. Still, he had a few words with Auntie and said he would be back on Monday and he hoped Wills behaved himself. Apparently, the timing was bad. Mr Chodda was going to be away for the weekend too. The post office was sending him to Manchester of all places to look at their working practices. Auntie, optimistic as usual, said, "Don't worry, Jazz, William will be fine and I will not have to worry about Mr Chodda so will have more time for William." She liked to call Wills William which Jazz thought was kind of sweet.

The knock on the door told Jazz to move himself. He had put a magazine of bullets in his case and one magazine with the Glock in his holdall, just in case he needed to get to it quickly. He should have been scared or at least apprehensive but he was excited and couldn't wait to see what would develop. Now he had Boomer coming along too things would be fine. He was an optimistic idiot.

CHAPTER TWENTY-THREE

HIRED HELP

Jazz had left approximately ten minutes beforehand when there was a knock at the door. Mrs Chodda loved this time to sit and have a cup of tea and her breakfast in peace and quiet. Surprised, Mrs Chodda got up from her kitchen table to see who would be knocking on the door at this time of day.

The two men standing in her doorway smiled and she smiled back. They were in dark suits with ties and looked very smart. She hoped it wasn't the Mormons calling again, they seemed to have a lot of trouble understanding she was a Sikh woman and would never be a Mormon although she liked to offer them a cup of tea for their trouble. These two men were so polite and called her ma'am which she liked very much.

They were at pains to inform her that they had been sent from Jazz's office to help during his absence. Mrs Chodda blushed and felt very honoured and invited the two men into her kitchen. They remarked on how warm and cosy her kitchen was and she blushed again. They sat on one of her solid pine chairs placed around her big farmhouse kitchen table and Mrs Chodda busied herself by pouring them both a cup of tea. She insisted they had a drink even though they refused. With the tea came cakes and biscuits which she encouraged them to eat. You didn't argue with Mrs Chodda; it was her duty, she felt, to feed anyone who came into her kitchen.

When the cakes were eaten and tea drunk one of the men said he would like to explain what was happening. Mrs Chodda, sitting comfortably, hands clasped on the table, nodded while they explained. The slimmer man who Mrs Chodda thought was about thirty years old and Pakistani spoke first. He introduced himself and his companion who was obviously a western man and he was taller and bigger built.

"My name is Manj and my fellow officer is Graham. We have been asked to come here by a national organisation that we cannot mention to protect you and your family. We understand that Mr Chodda is away for the weekend and that Mr J. Singh is also away for the weekend."

Mrs Chodda nodded and asked why they needed to be protected. She suddenly felt a little scared. She had never felt the need to be protected before and from what did she need protection? Manj raised his hand to calm her and smiled.

"Mr Singh's office is very powerful and Mr Singh was concerned about your welfare this weekend while he is away. He is working on some highly confidential projects and he wanted to be sure you were okay. He is our boss so we do as we are told."

Mrs Chodda liked this very much indeed. She knew Jazz was more important than he let on. He was such a modest man, she thought proudly. She looked at Manj and before he could continue, she asked, "Are you a Punjabi Sikh?"

Manj smiled and shook his head.

"I am a Punjabi Muslim. Did my accent give me away?" he asked with a smile.

Mrs Chodda knew all about the area of the Punjab and felt more comfortable that this man was a Pakistani man and they would understand each other better.

"So," continued Manj, "if it is alright with you, we will stay for the weekend. Don't worry about us getting in the way. We will sit in the corner and keep out of your way. We will organise our own food so we won't be any trouble to you. We just want to do our job and ensure all is well for you for the weekend."

Graham, the other man, piped up with a smile.

"Mr Singh is involved in highly important work and he has asked that no one calls him during these very important meetings he is attending. He will be back Monday at some point so not away for long. We would prefer you do not mention anything to anyone until Mr Singh returns, it is highly confidential work and the prime minister is involved so you can see how important this is."

Mrs Chodda positively glowed and promised faithfully not to mention anything to anyone. She hoped that when Jazz returned, she could tell her friends and neighbours and everyone at the Gurdwara just how important her Jazz was. She felt so honoured to know that Jazz was in such company and she needed protection that she looked at the two men wide-eyed and excited, and silently mouthed the words 'Prime Minister?'

The two men nodded gravely in agreement.

At this point Amrit breezed into the kitchen and in the middle of removing her scarf stopped suddenly when she saw the two men. They both smiled and introduced themselves. Amrit, at a loss for words, nodded and shook their hands. It was now Mrs Chodda's chance to tell Amrit the wonderful news.

It all sounded unbelievable to Amrit. She had no idea that Jazz was involved in anything this high-powered. The two men each had little comments to add like 'Mr Singh was well known to the higher echelons of security'. And 'he was the best man for the job'. Amrit, unlike Mrs Chodda, had lots of questions to ask but the two men shut the questions down straight away with, "Everything is top secret and we cannot divulge any more details. Mr Singh will be back Monday and he can tell you what he is allowed to tell you. We are here to protect you and please keep all this to yourselves as state security is involved. No phone calls out to anyone and not to Mr Singh while he is involved in this work over the weekend."

That shut Amrit up. She felt uneasy but she was a simple woman who knew nothing about state security. The men seemed nice and spoke highly of Jazz. Before she could think any further Mrs Chodda, her cheeks red with pride and excitement, started pulling out her big saucepans and said to Amrit, "Right, we need to get to work, Amrit. We have cooking to do for these fine gentlemen. Please get some chicken, and some beef and some lamb out of the freezer. We have curries to make. I will get the lentils for the dahl and the rice, too." Manj asked if he could help and Mrs Chodda said, "No thank you, Manj, I have everything I need here in the kitchen."

He saw her go to a large dustbin in the corner and it was full of rice to be cooked. The other dustbin had lentils in it. He recognised this was a typical Indian kitchen. She was going to make her pakoras too. So another dustbin was full of flour. She was bustling around pulling out giant saucepans, collecting what she needed from each area and humming happily. This was cooking on an industrial level and she was in her element. Neither had any idea who had sent these two men but accepted what they said because they worked for Mr Singh and that was good enough for them. Ignorance is bliss.

Mrs Chodda skilfully carried on cooking, happily thinking of what she would tell those at the Gurdwara next time she was there. She would boast for weeks about how important Jazz was and how important she was in his life. *Who else gets protection from a government department for a whole weekend* she thought? This was going to be one of the best weekends in her life.

CHAPTER TWENTY-FOUR

NOW IT BEGINS

The journey was quite good. Pinky and Perky had very little to say. Jazz asked why they hadn't picked up Boomer as well. He just wanted to irritate them for his pleasure.

"Is this car diesel? Surely with all the eco warriors and climate-change people about it would have been more effective to have both of us in the same car. Do the press know you waste money and energy and run these huge gas-guzzling cars?"

Jazz smirked as they told him to keep quiet and fuck off.

They arrived in silence. The manor house was large and had its own drive up to the house. The place was perfect for a meeting. He passed the security hut he would be working in. It was a stupid little box with a window. He hoped he had a chair to sit on. He wanted to work in the house like Boomer so he could see what was going on, not stuck at the end of the almost mile-long drive up to the house. He felt a bit disappointed but perked up when they reached the house and got the chance to look around inside. He was told he was to report to someone inside and would be taken to his room.

The hall was as big as a church with a huge table that was long, old and looked stupidly small in this massive area. The staircase was one of the grand sweeping staircases that should have had ladies in long ball gowns walking down it. Jazz had never experienced a place like this and he looked around open-mouthed. In a matter of seconds, he was called over to the table and given a badge to wear and someone appeared to take him to his room. An itinerary was shoved in his hand and he was told in two hours to report back to reception, as they called it, for a briefing in the conference room. He wanted to ask if Boomer was here but he was hustled and waved off to his room. He was taken through a doorway off the hallway into a long corridor. This was a fantastic house and the walk to his room took ten fucking minutes. This place was huge.

They went through a door and the style of house changed into something less grand and more practical. He knew he was in the servants' quarters. His room wasn't very big but it had a single bed and a wardrobe so he wasn't bothered. As soon as he was alone, he tried the walkie-talkie Ash had given him and Boomer. Boomer, the lucky fuck, was in his room and it sounded bigger than his. They were only a few doors apart so as soon as his clothes were put away, Jazz walked the corridor to find Boomer.

They checked watches and knew they had at least one and half hours before the briefing in the conference room. They decided to explore and check out the other rooms.

There was a lot going on with people toing and froing. There were contractors, cleaners and all sorts preparing for the weekend. They hoped they wouldn't be noticed if they walked around purposefully.

With a map of the rooms and who was where and with the additional knowledge of where Devious Derek was, they went looking. Jazz spotted a parcel sitting outside a room and grabbed it, hoping to look like he was delivering to someone. They skirted the entrance hall and found some backstairs that took them up to the first floor. This house had wings. Jazz found that odd but as explained by Boomer, all the fucking huge manor houses had wings (areas of rooms subordinate to the main house). They found the west wing where Devious Derek and Jacob McHenry had been moved to. Mr McHenry's room was a suite of rooms and Jazz and Boomer slipped into them quickly before anyone arrived. They checked the rooms and found two bedrooms with en suites, a lounge and a small kitchen. They thought it pretty lucky to find the rooms empty but before they could congratulate themselves, in walked Devious Derek who was beside himself with rage at finding the two of them standing there.

He knew who they were. He said he remembered them from various get-togethers that Sarah had dragged him to. They noted quickly he had no idea they were meant to be involved in this conference. Jazz took the lead as something needed to be said.

"Well hello, Derek. This is very exciting, isn't it? We have been asked to attend and help out. We are very honoured to have been picked and we sort of thought we would look around." He hoped that was working.

"Is this your room?" asked an incredibly stupid Jazz. "Blimey! You have done well for yourself. Ours is a poxy little room in the cellars."

This amiable chat seemed to have stunned Derek for the moment who stood and listened. The silence was deafening. But it wasn't going to last. Through gritted teeth, Derek answered, "Get the fuck out of here now. We have important people arriving tomorrow and the last thing they need is *Morecambe and Wise* waltzing around upsetting the dignitaries. What the fuck are you doing here?"

Jazz, staying amiable and smiley, enthused, "Look, we are sorry to be a nuisance. It's such a great place we just wanted to explore. We've been given overtime to do this brilliant weekend job. It's a really great place here. I am on security checking the people in at the gate and Boomer is watching the kitchens."

Derek looked at Boomer's big belly and almost laughed. "Yes, I can see you will do well in the kitchen, Black."

Boomer was impressed he remembered his name but left the comments to Jazz who seemed to be doing well.

"So why are you here, Derek?" asked Jazz a bit cheekily.

"Never you mind what I am doing. You get the fuck out of here and don't come back. I have work to do and as I know you, I won't report you this time. But if I catch you out of bounds which this area is, then I will get you removed and disciplined. Do you understand me?"

They certainly did fully understand him and with a quiet thank you, they left. They could see on Derek's face that he thought they were just mindless idiots who hadn't a clue about anything.

"Bloody 'ell, Singh, we got away lightly there, I reckon."

Jazz nodded in agreement. Both were a little shaken by the confrontation, not knowing what Derek might be capable of and a little surprised they were not reported by Derek as intruders. Jazz reckoned it might have been because if he was a traitor, he didn't want to draw attention to himself by reporting them. Boomer thought that sounded about right. They needed to watch Derek as closely as they could. Something just didn't feel right.

They took themselves off to the kitchen which was going to be Boomer's area to work in. They hoped to find a tea or coffee going spare in there. They had nearly an hour to waste before going into the conference hall. The kitchen was quite full of various people. Thankfully none of them looked like MI6 people which Jazz and Boomer wanted to avoid if they could which was a ridiculous thought as the place was swarming with them.

The chef, Arthur, was idling in the corner. Apparently, according to Iris, who was his second in command, he wouldn't be cooking much until tomorrow when the big guns arrived. Iris, a chatty middle-aged woman with a middle-aged spread that her apron barely covered, liked the look of Jazz and was very amenable to talking to him. Boomer had seen this before and although pissed off to be ignored by this monumental woman, he kept quiet and listened.

Apparently, the kitchen had six cooks, most of whom were under the direction of Arthur, and the waiters and waitresses who would serve the bigwigs were the cleaners who would double up as waitresses and waiters. In answer to a question from Jazz, she looked in surprise that he asked such a thing, but quickly realised they hadn't been to many of 'these sorts of dos'. She gave them the impression that the staff here today were hand-picked and worked on many such conferences. They were trusted staff who knew what was expected of them. As usual, at these events, everyone working this weekend couldn't go home until the last bigwig had gone. So, all the cleaners and kitchen staff, etc., would stay here. When she heard Jazz and Boomer had a room to themselves, she moaned that she had to share a dormitory with the other women employed here and the men would be in a dormitory too. She wasn't that keen on sleeping with other women, but with a giggle, she cheekily suggested Jazz might like some company. Jazz batted away such a comment with 'sadly, he was most probably working all night anyway'. They both giggled and Iris went off on her merry way to help make lunch for the huge number of staff there today. Boomer, watching this full-on flirtation, retorted with disgust as Iris walked away.

"You are such a tart, Singh!"

"I can't help it; I'm obviously a babe magnet and you are just a jealous prick," was Jazz's smug reply as he searched the cupboards for something to drink.

They found the tea and helped themselves to a handful of biscuits found in a big tin on the table close by. This conference seemed a tried and tested well-oiled machine and a very normal event for people like Arthur and Iris. Jazz and Boomer wondered if this one would be different.

They wandered into the conference room and were amazed at how many people were there. Boomer reckoned at least one hundred. It seemed from the introductions there was a mass of media people dealing with the TV screens and the microphones, etc. Then there were the cleaning, waitress and waiter staff together with an assortment of admin staff too. The security men were quite a small bunch in comparison but again, Boomer reckoned they were not all visible. The meeting was more about agendas and timings and health and safety, pretty mundane stuff that didn't seem to apply to either Jazz or Boomer but it gave them a chance to see how this well-oiled machine would work.

As it finished, David stopped them and ushered both Jazz and Boomer into an adjoining room. It looked empty and quiet. After the heat generated by a stampede of staff rushing to get out, creating mayhem and noise as the conference room emptied, this room felt still and very cold and Jazz shivered. David gestured them to sit down. Apparently, they were only there as token workers to appease whatever was going on with Devious Derek. He told them off for venturing into areas that they shouldn't have gone to. Jazz wondered how he knew that.

All the important people were arriving tomorrow morning and the conference would be held in the afternoon, and the evening was the banquet with Sunday morning being a photo shoot and all would go home early Monday morning. They knew that. They had just sat through it in the conference room so they both wondered why he was telling them again. David, in no uncertain terms, told them why. They were rank amateurs and needed to be out of the way for most of the important stuff. Jazz was not to be trusted on the gate letting important people into the grounds and house so he would be working in the security box when everyone had arrived. This was particularly disappointing and Jazz didn't like the idea of sitting alone with nothing to do in the stupid, sodding pillar box like an idiot all night. Boomer started to smirk but stopped when David told him to sit outside the back door all day and evening. He would get comfort breaks every three hours and that was his job. Jazz was to stay in his room out of the way until he was summoned to work and so was Boomer. With this, David left saying he had lots to do and good luck.

When he left, Jazz and Boomer looked at each other incredulous.

"Fuck!" was all they could say.

They decided to have a short walk around the grounds; a breath of fresh air and some privacy was actually what they were thinking. They went out through the kitchen and a voice shouted that lunch was available in half an hour if they were interested. With a nod Jazz and Boomer walked briskly into a lush green kitchen garden and followed a path leading to God knew where.

"Look," said a placatory Jazz. "I think we just have to let David and his team get on with whatever is happening. I haven't a fucking idea of anything any more."

Boomer nodded and added, "Fuck them! We are just nosey bastards and this is nothing to do with us. I just hope we get paid double time for this weekend."

Jazz laughed at this and agreed. They would just sit it out and see what transpired. David had it sussed and when the shit hit the fan, they both hoped they got to see it. For the time being they went to see what food was on offer in the kitchen and hoped a few beers were not out of the question. Jazz had his bottle of vodka with him just in case so he wasn't that bothered about beer.

Jazz and Boomer took themselves off to the outside kitchen garden for a smoke just to get out of everyone's way. They grabbed a coffee each from the dining room and found a bench to sit on. It was bloody hell in the house and they were glad to be outside. The seat was just behind a privet hedge and they felt cocooned from the chaos in the house. Sitting quietly, enjoying the midday sun, they sipped their coffee and smoked their cigarettes.

The stillness was interrupted by footsteps on the gravel on the other side of the privet. Both extinguished their cigarettes like naughty school boys and held their breath wondering who was after them.

"Keep a good eye on those bastards. Why the hell the other bastard had to come I don't know but I want everything to go smoothly. Make sure nothing goes wrong."

With that, the footsteps continued and moved away. Jazz and Boomer looked at each other.

"Who do you think they were talking about?" asked Jazz.

Boomer shifted uneasily in his seat and replied, "I have a horrible suspicion it's us." He was silent for a moment and then added, "Why are we such a problem? It actually doesn't make sense and now I am feeling fucking nervous and I don't know why."

"If it is you and me they were talking about then we will be watched very closely and on the surface that shouldn't be a problem but I, too, feel something doesn't make me feel good."

They decided that they would keep in contact by the walkie-talkies Boomer had borrowed if they got separated later. They were small enough to hide in a pocket. Each hadn't got any idea if anything was wrong and both wondered if they were just adrenalin junkies seeking danger in everything. Time would tell.

The day went quite quickly. Jazz and Boomer tried to keep out of everyone's way. People were dashing around; checking, cleaning, talking in small groups about what goes where and when and they just felt like spare parts with no real role. The house closed down early at 9 p.m. so everyone would be fresh and ready for the start of the arrivals at 8 a.m. the next day. Jazz was told he wouldn't be needed in the security lodge until 4 p.m. and he would stay there until midnight. He was told that no one was expected to enter or leave the grounds so he should have an easy evening. Boomer would sit just outside the kitchen door at the same time. He was told to keep out of the kitchen staff's way because they were cooking the banquet that evening.

Both Jazz and Boomer went to bed with mixed feelings. On the one hand they were both fucking useless spares who should not be there and on the other hand something felt not right. They hadn't seen Devious Derek since he caught them in his room and they both wondered what was going to happen with McHenry. They both reckoned MI6 Dave, as they called him, seemed to have everything in hand and would make sure Mr McHenry was kept safe and Devious Derek would be apprehended. They both had interrupted sleep wondering what the day would bring.

CHAPTER TWENTY-FIVE

WILLS

It was three o'clock and time for Amrit to collect Wills from school. It was agreed, well actually the men told them, that they couldn't collect Wills alone. One of them must go with Amrit. Graham explained that it was Friday so when he was home all would be safe indoors for the weekend but for now the journey could be compromised and so Graham would drive Amrit to the school and bring Wills home.

Actually, that sounded good to Amrit. A ride to the school was better than waiting for a bus and then waiting outside the school. The days were getting a little chilly. The journey by car was quiet; Graham didn't have much to say. He seemed to grunt in answer to anything Amrit said.

"Shall we stop and get some cakes on the way home?" she asked and Graham said no.

"Can I get some sweets for Wills, then? It's Friday and it's a treat for him." Graham said no.

Amrit was feeling a little uncomfortable. She didn't know why. She felt more like a prisoner than someone being protected. There was nothing she could say. Graham said to pick up Wills and take him straight home. There would be no detours, no arguing and it was for her safety. She couldn't argue with that.

Wills thought it was very exciting. He liked the car and the thought that he had his own 'protection squad' as he called them. He didn't mind if there were no sweets, he had his own stash anyway in his room. He asked if Jazz was like 007 and Graham stifled a smile and said perhaps. This made Wills more excited and the journey home was full of questions that Graham didn't answer and Amrit felt more and more confused by everything. *Why didn't Jazz mention to me anything about having protection? Why didn't Jazz warn me about this?* It didn't seem like him at all.

When they got back to Mrs Chodda's house, Wills rushed in very excited by everything. He asked Manj if he had a gun and was told not to ask such things. He raced around the kitchen being a nuisance to everyone. Amrit could see the two men were getting bored and fed up with Wills. They were not smiling any more. Their eyes had a cold glint in them and this made her quieten down Wills and tell him to go to his room and change out of his school clothes and do his homework.

Mrs Chodda produced four amazing curries for everyone to enjoy with pakoras to start with. Manj enjoyed the curries but Graham went out to buy fish and chips. He said that he was not a curry man. Mrs Chodda was beside herself. She should have asked if he liked curries. Wills had grown into her curries and loved them but when he knew Graham was getting fish and chips he asked if he could come too for some chips. Graham said he was to stay put and he would bring him some back.

They all ate together. Amrit looked at the two men through hooded eyes. She wondered who they were. She could see a look in their eyes that she didn't like. It was a hard look and when not smiling they looked quite nasty. She told herself that as they were protection officers, they wouldn't be sweet and lovely anyway. They had a job to do. This explanation didn't help her unease.

Amrit thought if they couldn't go out, the weekend was going to be a difficult time. She tentatively asked if she could pop to Tesco for some shopping bits in the morning. She was told no. Mrs Chodda said she was due to help in the Gurdwara on Saturday but both were told no one was to go out that weekend. Amrit couldn't wait for Jazz to come back so she could give him a piece of her mind. This was bloody stupid.

That evening Mrs Chodda had found spare blankets and pillows and asked if Manj and Graham would like to sleep on her settees in the other room. Both were grateful and said they would take it in turns to sleep because they were there to guard them. Mrs Chodda wanted to chat with Manj about the Punjab but he was having none of it and said he had his job to do. Mrs Chodda, a little embarrassed, nodded and left. Amrit thought he was incredibly rude and wondered if he had been to the Punjab and perhaps didn't want to talk about somewhere he had never lived.

Mrs Chodda made them all some hot chocolate to take to bed and she offered this to Manj and Graham who politely refused. Amrit took Wills to his room and told him to stay there. She didn't know why but she didn't want Wills to be alone with the men. Again, there was something she didn't like about them.

Mrs Chodda, Amrit and Wills went to bed feeling a little scared, and very confused. Were they in danger? And from what were they in danger? No one had a good night's sleep.

CHAPTER TWENTY-SIX

SATURDAY

Saturday morning at 6 a.m. was hectic. With nothing much to do all day both Jazz and Boomer watched as the kitchen staff rushed around and in no uncertain terms told both the duo to get out of the fucking way. Apparently, in the dining room allocated for staff, was anything they required to eat or drink. They idled over to the room and found eggs and bacon in heaters with a room nearly empty now of staff. The actual conference room was full of what looked like admin staff, security men sweeping electronically the area and cameras and microphones everywhere. They were told by security to get out of the room. The hallway was being hoovered again and someone was polishing the beautiful bannisters.

By 7.30 a.m. they tried to go outside but found the drive full of Coldstream Guards lining up with musical instruments. This was all just a tad too much for Jazz and Boomer who had never experienced anything like this. They were hoping to see the dignitaries arrive and watch how they were escorted to their meeting place and by whom. They still hadn't seen Devious Derek and wondered what he was doing. They found they had their own minders and were strong-armed back into the house and told to get into their fucking rooms now as dignitaries were due to arrive and they wouldn't want to see their sorry arses! Everything felt like an anti-climax but they did as they were told.

Confined to their rooms and now with their meals being brought to them so they didn't get in anyone's way, Jazz and Boomer were left to their own devices. At 4 p.m. Jazz would be taken to the security box by the front gate and told to stay there until midnight and Boomer was to do the same by sitting outside the kitchen back door to ensure no one entered that way. It all seemed stupid but they understood they were only there as a token to help catch Devious Derek and anyone assisting him. In whispered tones they checked with each other that the walkie-talkies worked. Boomer showed Jazz, not wishing to say anything in case they were being bugged, that he had his gun on him. Jazz showed Boomer his Glock and that he now had bullets which made Boomer raise his eyebrows. The modern Kevlar bulletproof vests were put on and they looked pretty good under their suits. They were ahead of the game which quite honestly made them feel a little smug and pretty cool which was a pretty dangerous attitude. They had no idea what would emerge or if they were in real danger but as Boomer said, in the words of Superman – Be prepared. Jazz thought that saying was a Boy Scout saying but Superman sounded good. The pair giggled quietly at the thought. Each was perversely hoping something did happen and that they would be involved.

The knock on the door at 4 p.m. saw Jazz and Boomer ready to go to work. Jazz was taken outside and shown a golf cart which was to be his vehicle to get to and from the security box. Again, he was reminded by some unknown security officer with a hearing piece in his ear, he was to let no one into the property or out of the property without express instructions from the house. Jazz listened intently and then asked,

"Can I have one of those hearing aids you have? They look pretty cool."

"Bugger off, no. You have a phone in the security box and that's all you need. Stop fannying around and just do your job. You are a bloody nuisance on a busy night so get on with it."

With those words ringing in his ears, Jazz gave a sarcastic salute and took off in the golf cart which he found pretty cool.

It was about 10 p.m. when things started to kick off. Jazz, ensconced in the stupid security box and pretty bored by this time, had nipped in and out of the box for a cigarette and the odd tot of vodka he kept in his flask in his jacket. The house was lit up and he could see it in the distance. The drive up to the house was at least a quarter of a mile and he could hear the music faintly and reckoned they were having a pretty good party. It made him giggle to think of all the high and mighty people attending, dancing and drinking the night away.

Boomer was equally as bored sitting outside the kitchen. At least he could get a drink and something to eat when he wanted to but he was still mind-numbingly bored. The conversations with Jazz were very quiet and not too frequent over the walkie-talkies. They had said they were for emergencies only but as Jazz said, boredom was an emergency. They both agreed with this stupid idea but tried not to speak too often.

Sitting in the security box, Jazz was mesmerised by the quietness and almost nodded off when the peace was suddenly disrupted by the phone ringing loudly which made him jump. Excited by something happening, he picked the phone up wondering what he should say.

"Security box speaking," was all he could think of. MI6 Dave, the head man, was on the other end and sounded exasperated.

"For God's sake, man!! Just use your name." Calming down, MI6 Dave said, "Listen carefully. In five minutes, a catering van will arrive at the gates. Let them in immediately. They will only be about ten minutes and then they will need to leave so be prepared on the gate, understood?"

Jazz nodded stupidly. He couldn't be seen by MI6 Dave, then on reflection he asked,

"I thought no one was going to come in or out tonight. Why a catering van?"

David was by now even more exasperated and, getting angry, shouted, "Mind your own fucking business, Singh! When I tell you to do something, do it!!"

Calming down a bit he added, "I know this is new to you but things happen. Someone here wants a particular meal and we don't have it so it's a delivery for the morning. We are catering for all nationalities and tastes. So, is that now clear?"

Jazz nodded again but added, "Yes, sir."

The van arrived exactly five minutes later and Jazz let them in. The van sped towards the house at what seemed sixty miles per hour or so; it wasn't hanging about. Jazz got back into the service box and found the walkie-talkie and called up Boomer.

"Hey, Boomer," he whispered. "Has the catering van arrived yet? It was speeding towards you and should have taken no more than a minute or so."

"Nope, nothing here."

"It's a catering van bringing something exotic or such to the kitchen. Would they go in through the back door where you are?"

"I can see the rear car park from here and nothing has arrived. You sure it's coming here?"

"Yup, MI6 Dave said so."

They waited a few minutes and still nothing arrived. Jazz was pacing and Boomer was unsettled. This wasn't right. In the silence, both were thinking what to do and who to contact. A decision had to be made.

"Fuck it! I am coming to you with the golf cart and we can decide what to do when I arrive. In the meantime, take a look around the other wing of the house, you know where Devious Derek was, and I will meet you there."

Boomer agreed and Jazz took off in the golf buggy extremely frustrated that the bloody thing didn't go more than fifteen miles an hour with his foot to the floor. He toyed with the idea that he could run faster but he knew that wasn't true. It didn't take long to reach the kitchen and he sailed past the parking area there going towards the wing where Devious Derek was. He could see the white catering van was there and stopped the golf buggy a distance away until he found out what was happening.

Boomer was by a tree to the left watching the van and Jazz quietly ran over to him.

"Are they caterers and we will look like useless idiots when they can't open the gates to leave when finished because I am here, or are we the dog's bollocks?"

Boomer, not taking his eyes of the van, said, "It has a man nervously sitting in the driver's seat at the moment but I think others may have left the van because he keeps fidgeting and looking up to the first-floor windows and that's the floor Devious Derek is on."

"We need to get in and see what's happening, don't we?" asked Jazz.

"Well," said Boomer who was watching intently the shifty driver of the van who kept looking up at the windows then looking around as if he shouldn't be there. "I don't think we can go in that door because that driver will clock us and we don't want that."

Jazz, anxious to get in to see what was happening (he had that bubbly feeling in his stomach that told him there was an adventure to be had, but if they weren't quick enough it would be over, and they would have missed it) had an idea.

"Get into the buggy and pretend to be drunk."

Boomer looked at him and was about to say something but Jazz slapped him on the back and whispered, "We have no time to waste, just come on!"

Jazz drove the buggy up to the van slowly and got out. He saw the driver looking startled and anxious. He had to act quickly, not sure what this man would do. So with a resigned look on his face, he went up to the van and through the open window grimaced, and whispered conspiratorially, "Fucking toffee-nosed people just don't know how to take their drink. Got to put this one to bed. Wouldn't mind but I am a waiter not a fucking nursemaid."

The driver, still suspicious but more at ease, just nodded in agreement and watched closely as Jazz grabbed Boomer none to carefully and dragged him into the building. Once inside and out of view, they both ran towards the stairs to see what was happening on the first floor.

They had no sooner got to the door which opened onto the first floor when it was flung open and a melee of men piled out. Standing on the landing with nowhere to go Jazz and Boomer tried to make sense of who was who in front of them. What they did see straight away were the three guns pointed at them.

Before either Jazz or Boomer could draw breath, Derek stepped forward and just shot Boomer in the chest. Boomer was flung against the railings of the stairwell by the force of the bullet and lay sprawled on the floor. Jazz, unable in that brief second to comprehend, to understand or to believe what had happened, just stood still, mouth open, and in total shock hearing nothing and only seeing Boomer lying still on the floor.

Derek had got hold of him and shook him.

"You stupid fucker, what are you doing here?"

All Jazz could say was, "Why?"

Derek, busy holding up McHenry just said, "He wasn't needed. He was in the way. Now do as you are fucking told."

Before Jazz could even think to answer, one of the three men grabbed Jazz and told him to move himself. He was expected to be on the security gate and they needed to be let out. The routine checks on him were due in ten minutes. House security did a routine call to ensure all was well in the security box and Jazz had now developed a jokey repartee with the caller. The last call had him saying he had let in twenty beauties who were on their way to pleasure the security men on duty. His caller requested the blonde one with big knockers.

Jazz was manhandled into the van with the comatosed McHenry guy. They had put a sack over his head, and he couldn't tell if the man was okay or not but his legs seemed to move so he was alive, he reckoned. Jazz, shocked and stunned, just couldn't think straight; everything was moving so fast.

"Before you try doing something you shouldn't, I have a call for you," whispered one of the men as he thrust a mobile phone into Jazz's face. Jazz hated Derek with a passion. He couldn't believe that Boomer went down. No, it couldn't be true, he told himself. He wanted to go back and get him, to call an ambulance, to fucking murder the man in front of him. His head was full of Boomer lying there slumped on the floor against the railings. *Where the fuck was MI6 Dave who was supposed to be watching this,* he asked himself? The sultry voice brought him back to reality. It was Scarlett, the S&M mistress.

"Listen carefully. You will go to the security box and let the van out. You will answer your security call checking up on you and you will stay there. If not, I have two very enthusiastic men sitting patiently in Mrs Chodda's kitchen with the boy and that woman Amrit. If I tell them so, they will happily shoot them all, then leave and have time to be on a flight to somewhere untraceable. You will never find them. Do I make myself clear? Three lives are in your hands."

Jazz, the colour drained, the hopelessness set in, agreed.

He opened the gates for the van to leave and sat and answered the security call. The security man on the other end thought he was a temperamental bastard. Earlier he was laughing and joking and now he was miserable and bad-tempered. The security call lasted only a minute and this now gave Jazz time to think. He was worried sick about Boomer; how was he? He couldn't possibly be dead, could he? The thought brought a tear to his eye which he angrily brushed away. Now he had his family to think about. How the fuck was he going to help them? Sitting like a chunk of misery in total silence he jumped out of his skin when someone tapped on the window of the security box. It was fucking Boomer. Jazz, in a state of shock, distress and joy jumped out of the security box and grabbed Boomer for a man hug.

"Oh my god, get off, my chest hurts, you big Jessie, and help me in," was a groaning Boomer's response.

"This Kevlar is brilliant but my god, that fucking bullet has bruised me through to my back and I dare not cough, it will kill me. Give me a swig of your vodka, I know you've got it in your pocket."

Jazz, beyond relieved, asked, "How did you get here so fast? You look like shit."

"That bloody golf buggy was outside and I used it."

Both took a swig and Jazz, relieved he had Boomer there to help, quickly told him what had happened and the phone call from Scarlett.

"They have my family hostage. What can I do?" said Jazz. That he called them 'his family' was not lost on either of them.

"And where the fuck is MI6 Dave? This has been the biggest cock-up ever and I don't know where they have taken that McHenry fella and what they are doing with him. Derek was with them too."

Boomer listening said, "First things first: Contact MI6 Dave and get him doing his job, for fuck's sake. He will have a plan to rescue your family, he owes you that. By the way, don't tell him I am here. I am dead, remember? And I think I should stay dead for the moment."

Jazz thought on that and agreed. He phoned through to the security desk and asked for David who seemed to be in the vicinity because he came on the phone very quickly.

Jazz told him what had happened and that Boomer was shot by Derek and McHenry had been taken and where the fuck was he when this was happening? "My family are under siege and what are you doing to protect them?" Jazz sounded a bit hysterical and MI6 Dave stopped him in full flow.

"Calm down, Singh. It's all in hand. We have tabs on everything. Stay where you are and I am coming to you in fifteen minutes. Talk to no one and act normally. DI Black (Boomer) is not where he should be so I don't think he is dead. Have you seen him?" asked MI6 Dave.

"Thank God!" said Jazz. "No, I haven't seen him, I just hope he is okay."

When he put the phone down Jazz looked at Boomer quizzically and calmly stated, "Something isn't right here. MI6 Dave seemed to know what had happened yet he's done nothing to stop it. I don't feel comfortable about him. He is going to be here in fifteen minutes so you had better hide out there in the bushes and move the golf buggy too."

A grumpy Boomer said, "Cheers for that!! So, give me your flask of vodka then. I need something to keep me warm and out of pain."

Having been in a situation that moved faster than the speed of light, Jazz suddenly felt slumped in a vacuum of nothing. His family were in trouble and he couldn't help them. McHenry was gone and Devious Derek was a fucking murderer and traitor and he could do nothing. MI6 Dave seemed at odds with everything and he could do nothing. He grabbed the flask from Boomer and took a big swig of vodka, hoping it would make him feel better and give him some ideas on how to get out of this and help his family.

He picked up his phone and phoned Wills on the mobile he had given him. Wills should have been in bed by now so hopefully no one would know he had a call. It was ten o'clock so his bed time. Wills picked up the call quickly.

"Hi Wills, just checking you are okay," Jazz said brightly.

Wills had a lot of street savvy and replied in a whisper.

"There are two men here with Auntie in the kitchen. I was told to go to my room. Don't think Amrit likes them. They are all smiley but when you catch them off guard, they look mean. They say they are security guarding us while you are away. They said you were a 007 and that's really exciting. I want to be a secret agent when I grow up."

Wills was prattling on, very excited at the thought.

Jazz, quiet now, realised it was confirmed that Scarlett had sent men to watch them as a threat. He knew he had to do something, frustrated for the moment and anxious that Wills didn't get on their nerves with his jumping up and down and excitement that might goad them into doing something he didn't want to think about. He urgently told Wills, "Stay in your room if you can, Wills. Feign stomach ache or headache. You stay safe and all will be okay, I promise."

Wills, confused but trusting Jazz, agreed and hesitantly asked if Auntie and Amrit would be okay and Jazz, full of bluster, said oh yes, he was sure of that and just to go to sleep. He would be back Monday and all would be good. Jazz put the phone down determined to get out of this place and back home as soon as he had seen MI6 Dave.

CHAPTER TWENTY-SEVEN

RETRIBUTION

Boomer and Jazz, for a few moments, were both nonplussed as to what they should do. Jazz, who was desperate to go home and Boomer, in pain from the bullet impact, who was wanting to do something useful like shoot Devious Derek, had left them both swigging a further drink from the second flask Jazz had in his other jacket pocket.

"Have you got your gun?" whispered Boomer.

"Yes, and I have loaded it. Why? Do you think we are going to need it?" asked Jazz in a whisper.

Neither knew why they were whispering; there was no one near them but it felt the right thing to do. As they waited for MI6 Dave who was going to be another ten minutes, Boomer made it clear he was going nowhere yet and said that there was no way was he sitting in the bushes until he had to. They would see MI6 Dave coming from the house by the lights on his golf buggy which appeared to be the only form of transport used by security in this place.

"You never know if you will need your gun," was the ominous reply from Boomer who was not making light of any of this so far. The usual banter had left and was replaced by a feeling of forlornness and doom as they waited for something to happen.

Just as Jazz put the cap back on the flask, he jumped as the door to the security box opened suddenly and in jumped Devious Derek. Instinctively, both Jazz and Boomer grabbed their guns but Derek was quicker. With a sneer Derek looked the pair of them up and down and snarled.

"You are a pair of fuck-ups and you are messing up this operation."

Boomer, glad to hear they had done something good and badly wanting to put a bullet in Derek's sneering, smarmy face bided his time and asked the fucking traitor, "Why are you here and why aren't you off with those other bastards?"

Derek looked at him and almost smiled.

"I'm here to shoot Singh. You are both expendable and you are supposed to be dead, Black, so I'm finishing the job with Singh. I shall be the hero who shot the traitors who helped kidnap McHenry. You are both a pair of patsies and will be seen as the traitors. My job is secure."

While Derek was looking at Boomer, who was doing a good impression of fidgeting and looking lost, Jazz had moved a little closer to Derek and in a movement he didn't think he could achieve, he lunged forward knocking the firearm out of Derek's hand. In another swift movement Boomer picked up the gun and pointed it at Derek. Boomer, not taking his eyes off Derek, said, "Singh, grab a pair of handcuffs out of the back of my trousers."

He saw the look on Jazz's face of *what the fuck – handcuffs?*

"Well," shrugged Boomer, embarrassed for the moment, "I thought they might come in handy."

Looking up he saw in the distance MI6 Dave's buggy coming their way. Boomer, in a hurry now, said he was going to hide outside.

"I'm supposed to be dead so I reckon I'll stay dead for the time being until we know what's going on."

Jazz nodded, and pushed Derek onto one of the chairs used by security guards. Derek looked for the first time scared and hurriedly wanted to talk before MI6 Dave arrived.

"Look, Singh, you've got this all wrong. I am on your side."

"You fucking bastard. You killed or rather you thought you had killed Boomer. You are not on my side and I'm looking forward to you getting your comeuppance. If left to me or Boomer, we would save them the job and just put a bullet in you – Bastard!"

Desperate now, Derek said, "I knew he had a Kevlar jacket on."

"How the fuck would you know that, you bastard? David will sort you out."

Derek, more anxious, blurted quickly before MI6 Dave came in. His buggy was nearly here.

"I knew because the idiot forgot to tie one of the tapes and the tape could be seen below his jacket. I wear them all the time so I know. I shot him because one of the others would have shot him in the head and he would have been dead for sure."

Jazz, not convinced said, "David will sort this out, not me. To me you are a lying traitor, a murderer and a bastard. I'm looking for an excuse to kill you myself so shut the fuck up."

Just as he said that MI6 Dave pulled up outside the security cabin. He was alone which surprised Jazz. With all that was going on he assumed he would have backup with him. Mind you, he presumed everyone would be going ape shit with McHenry being kidnapped. He wondered actually why there weren't more security men leaving and going off to find McHenry. It all seemed quiet and that wasn't right, was it? Before he could think further Derek got his attention. In a rush of what sounded like panic, Derek whispered, "Don't trust David. I'm telling you the truth."

Jazz looked at him and just whispered back, "Shut the fuck up, you traitor."

Jazz, relieved MI6 Dave was here to take over, for the first time for quite a while joked, "Fuck off, Derek, this isn't a whodunnit crime novel. David will sort this out."

MI6 Dave came into the cabin and there was a look of faint surprise to see Devious Derek in handcuffs. It was hot and cramped in the security box. It could hold comfortably two security men and there was a small area for making hot drinks but with the three of them standing there, it felt crowded.

"It's a little stuffy in here, don't you think? I would prefer we went outside," said David in his posh, calm and dulcet tones.

Jazz wondered if he ever got fazed or lost his temper and ranted and raved like normal people. Jazz kicked Derek in the shins and told him to get up and move.

There was a bit of a scramble to get out and Derek stumbled as Jazz kicked him again to get him to move quicker. Once outside, they stood for a few moments, not quite knowing what to do or what was going to happen. The air was cool and Jazz realised how hot it had been in the security box. He wiped his brow as sweat drops slid into his eyes and made them sting. Squinting now, he looked to MI6 Dave for a word or a signal to see what was going to happen next.

MI6 Dave looked Derek and Jazz up and down and with a sigh, he talked directly to Jazz.

"Is DI Black still missing? Have you seen him yet?"

Jazz shook his head and just murmured, "May the great Guru in the sky protect him and give him shelter in his loving arms." He hoped that sounded religious enough. MI6 Dave just stood nonplussed and looked at Jazz and after a minute nodded knowingly in agreement. Convinced for the moment, MI6 Dave believed that Jazz had not seen him and it was time to move on.

"Right!" MI6 Dave sighed again and added, "What do we do with a traitor, Singh?"

Without hesitation Jazz said, "Shoot the bastard."

"Indeed, a good idea," confirmed MI6 Dave.

Now Jazz, although wanting the bastard dead, didn't comprehend how an MI6 boss would want someone dead before they had talked. As MI6 Dave cocked his gun and aimed it at Derek, Jazz jumped in, confused and scared and in a panic said, "No, no, surely not, sir. He has information to give you. He knows where McHenry is and his life is in danger. We need to rescue him and move quickly; we must get that information from him. I'll kick the bastard until he tells us."

Seeing that this didn't seem to budge MI6 Dave who hadn't taken his eyes off Derek, Jazz added quickly, "He has to go to court to be judged. You can't kill him in cold blood. We are British, we don't do that."

Boomer listening to this wondered what to do. If it hadn't been so serious, he would have wondered where the British spirit had come from. Jazz was giving it his all.

Derek, looking between both of them, added urgently, "So, sir, when did you become a double agent? You caused all of this today. I have been watching you carefully and have suspected you were the high-level mole in MI6 for some time. My boss set this up to smoke you out." With quiet sarcasm, Derek added, "You are done for, sir."

MI6 Dave laughed. "How absurd of you. I am the hero here. You are the traitor and Singh helped you. In killing you both I have done a great service to the country. I am assured of a knighthood."

Jazz, listening to this conversation between Derek and MI6 Dave, cottoned on to what was said. In a flash he knew MI6 Dave was the traitor and he was going to kill them both. That's why he wanted them standing near the bushes outside the security cabin.

With no time to think logically, Jazz grabbed for his gun and shouted to MI6 Dave, "Put your fucking gun down now!"

David, startled for a second, looked at him, then at the gun and after a slight hesitation laughed and shook his head.

"An empty chamber, remember? You are not to be trusted with bullets."

He nodded in the direction of an arrangement of large and well-established rhododendron bushes in a corner and pushed them both towards the bushes. Why Jazz didn't just shoot him he would never know. He had actually never shot anyone and it's not like on films where if you have a gun in your hand, you automatically fire it. So, hesitating, Jazz stumbled forward and did what he was told. MI6 Dave, anxious now and not liking the pair of them moving slowly barked, "Keep moving towards those bushes. You are both a bloody nuisance."

He was going to shoot them and wanted their bodies hidden from sight for a while. His role was to get Derek back here and he would kill him and Jazz together. They would be blamed for the abduction and killed. Their work was done now so time to dispose of them (no honour amongst thieves, that was for sure). Everything was going according to plan except for DI Black; he was the fly in the ointment so the sooner he was found and disposed of the better. DI Black was never part of the plot and this was causing MI6 Dave to feel somewhat shaken. He was not used to things going against the plan. He was ready now to dispose of these two and move on.

Derek was blackmailed into helping with the kidnapping of someone who must never be compromised. McHenry was guarded 24/7 by the best and elite security. His coming to England was only allowed because MI6, which have a worldwide reputation for excellence, promised their best agents would protect him. This conference was going to change the world and help all countries work together to eradicate the evils of germ warfare. It had never been leaked through news items or the internet that the world had been facing a severe crisis from undisclosed terrorist organisations (and there were far too many to name in the world at this moment) but one of them had been tireless in finding and tracking the virus that would stop countries working efficiently and would eradicate all non-essential humans through the disease and McHenry was the key to this secret.

A vaccine would be needed to counteract the virus and this conference, led by McHenry, who had vital information at his fingertips to help this work, made him the most important man to kidnap. There were many laboratories working hard for the US on biological warfare antidotes. None of them knew the full picture but McHenry did which was why he was so valuable. His information could make a terrorist organisation invincible with the antidotes he had access to of known killer viruses and what labs created them. There had never been biological warfare used on western countries but with McHenry's information, they could arm themselves with an antidote and command governments to do what they wanted. McHenry was going to share information on antidotes and how, with other countries, they would be able to protect themselves. Plans were already in place by this terrorist organisation and they couldn't allow the conference to happen. They wanted all the information for their own use.

At the moment, only Derek and MI6 Dave knew who *they* were. *They* were a far-right neo-Nazi German terrorist group called Hedda Deutschland. They were not well known yet. Various government agencies were aware of them but they thought they were not a problem at the moment. With so much money and contacts in the right places, Hedda Deutschland were able to work tirelessly below the radar. Their aim was quite extraordinary; they wanted to dominate Germany and return the fatherland to its previous glory. They had many high-ranking people from various areas of the government, the army and big business supporting them and many English people of substance who wished for the same in their country.

England, once a proud nation, was now considered by many as a weak, woke, waste of humanity. England needed firm, strong leadership and many high-powered men had secretly joined Hedda Deutschland with the promise that they would return England to its full glory. Money was no object, they had millions of pounds, euros, and gold donated to their cause. They were ready to launch but they needed McHenry to provide them with access to the laboratories making the virus and the antidote. Until this conference no other person or country were aware of where these laboratories were. It was considered paramount to allow only one person to have access to details and knowledge of these laboratories. The USA knew if the information was leaked to any organisation life as they knew it would stop. There would be millions of deaths. There was a good stockpile of antidotes and they were about to be distributed in secret around Europe and the USA in readiness for any eventuality. So now McHenry was ready to share this information with the selected governments around the world and Hedda couldn't let that happen. Total control of the virus and antidote was required to effect the changes Hedda were about to embark on.

Derek, after his week's visit to Germany with Scarlett, was indoctrinated and to a certain extent brainwashed into believing what Hedda was doing was right and proper and the world would thank them. Derek was vital to the kidnapping. Blackmail was not enough. They had to be sure he would do exactly what they told him to without any worry that he would falter or confess to his bosses. They had worked on him through chemical force, injecting him daily and through mentally working on him. After a week of prolonged, some would say torture, Derek was their man and would do whatever was asked of him.

Was he brainwashed? To be fair he was. A part of him knew this but the larger part of him would always support Hedda as instructed. He had been tested over the weeks since returning. They needed to know he was their man and he didn't disappoint. He told them all the information they needed to know about the conference; what was happening at what time, the best time to take McHenry and how he could lure him to his room. He couldn't be more helpful. The plan was set and those involved trusted Derek was their man.

MI6 is a dark organisation and most things are not what they seem. When Derek returned from his week off, he was instructed immediately to report to a substation where he was expected to practise his skills on a firing range and in hand-to-hand combat. MI6 Dave had been told, as his superior, that this was to ensure he was fully trained and competent to guard McHenry. All the other security staff had attended this training on the week of Derek's *holiday* as it was called.

Actually, secretly, Derek, instead of attending a training course, was spirited off to a substation in a bleak outer perimeter of a Scottish island whose name was never mentioned and did not exist on most maps, to undergo de-programming. For three days Derek underwent an intense course which some might say was torture to de-programme him and ensure he was still their man. He was instructed to tell them everything they wanted to know about the conference and he was to wear a mic so the director of MI6 and his team would know exactly what was going on. This was going to be a double bluff to smoke out the top mole in MI6, take down Hedda Deutschland and save the world. These were the words said to Derek when his intense course finished. He thought he sounded a bit like Flash Gordon and would have laughed if the job wasn't so serious.

No one knew who the top mole was in MI6; the identity was never disclosed to Derek or anyone else. He was Hedda's star and he provided them with all the information they needed. MI6 Dave knew when any government agencies looking for terrorist organisations sniffed anywhere near Hedda, MI6 Dave alerted them and they hunkered down until the threat passed. No one knew how powerful Hedda was becoming but they would know soon enough.

David had caused the deaths of many agents abroad and noises about how safe MI6 was were being made by America, Israel and Germany. How MI6 persuaded America to trust them to protect McHenry at this conference, even David didn't know. Jazz moved slowly towards the bushes and turned around looking at MI6 Dave with contempt, and gaining his full attention he asked, "Why now? You could have kept Derek as your agent and he would continue to feed you information."

Jazz could see that David was getting fed up with all this talking and he knew they were not going to last much longer. The gun in his hand was itching to pull the trigger, so Jazz was surprised that David answered, "Someone has to take the wrap for this kidnapping and Derek is perfect and expendable. I am not expendable. I will have access to so much information as my role in MI6 grows."

Fed up now with all this talking, MI6 Dave pushed Derek into the bushes and aimed his gun at his head. There was a loud exclamation from a gun. David stood still, looked at Jazz in surprise and said, "But, how? You shot me."

With that David keeled over. Jazz stood and looked in stunned silence. He had never shot anyone before. Derek let out a sigh of relief, and shouted, "Take these fucking handcuffs off me. We need to get moving quickly. Move yourself, Singh."

He took a breath, and asked, "Why didn't you shoot him before? Why wait? We could have been killed."

Jazz, in shock still, raised his eyebrows and just shook his head and said forlornly, "I dunno."

With that there was a rustling and trampling of bushes as Boomer appeared red-faced and fuming. He headed straight for Derek.

"He should have shot you, you fucking murderer. You shot me."

Derek sighed; these two were getting on his nerves.

"I knew you had the new Kevlar jacket on, you let the slip show under your jacket, you cretin. I shot you because one of the others could have shot you in the head and your Kevlar wouldn't have been much good then, would it?"

Boomer looked across at Jazz who nodded in agreement. He immediately took off the handcuffs on Derek and clapped them on a wounded MI6 Dave. As he put them on, Boomer, stressed beyond belief and fuming, put his face up to MI6 Dave and spat the words, "You are a traitor, bastard, and I hope they hang you."

Jazz pulled himself together and asked, "What the fuck do we do now?"

CHAPTER TWENTY-EIGHT

CONCILIATION

Derek, now free and animated, pulled his phone from his pocket and called his boss. The words were urgent and staccato fashion lasting seconds. He turned to Jazz and Boomer.

"There is a window of opportunity that will last no longer than one hour. The plane to take McHenry leaves then and all traces of everyone involved will have left or been killed. I am supposed to be dead at the hands of David and he will have to confirm that is so, soon enough. DS Singh and DI Black would have been killed. Scarlett needs confirmation of these details – so you are dead and I am dead."

Jazz looked at him and said, "My family, I have got to save them, they will kill them if they find out I have helped you."

Derek, in control mode, said, "Right! For starters men are on their way to collect David now. A helicopter is going to be here in under a minute to take us to your home and arrest the men there. Your family will be safe. A group is undercover at the airport ready to take back McHenry and those holding him so everything has been organised now. This place is surrounded by our men. So, for God's sake, someone give me a cigarette, I need it after all this."

True to his word, they heard the helicopter arrive and it landed on the road leading up to the house. He managed three drags of the cigarette and threw it away as the three of them ran out and jumped in the helicopter. Three men had already jumped out of the helicopter and run into the security box to grab MI6 Dave. A car arrived at the same time and within two minutes the helicopter had taken off, MI6 Dave had been bundled into the car and spirited away. The area was now quiet and all that could be heard was the phone ringing in the security box as a guard was doing his check that Jazz was okay.

If he hadn't been fraught with worry and anxiety about his family, Jazz would have enjoyed the journey in a helicopter, something he had always wanted to do. The countryside at night was spellbinding but he was told in no uncertain terms by Derek 'to get your arse in gear and check your gun'. They spent the time looking at their guns and ensuring they were in order. Jazz still had a magazine of bullets; he had fired only once. Boomer had his trusty gun, a Browning Hi-Power 13+ round single-action semi-automatic handgun introduced in 1935. He had had it for years and it was from unknown parentage and its history was buried. No one asked and no one got told where he got it from. Derek had his Glock 17 and all three sat waiting for the helicopter to land. Jazz, with moments to spare, looked at Derek and asked, "What about Sarah, is she okay? Will they go after her?"

Derek told him not to worry. "They didn't need to hold her to ransom because they thought I was their man. Besides, Sarah has been intensely guarded since I started this. How do you think they found you? You were becoming a bloody nuisance so it was decided by those above that David should be told that you were poking around my home and room and that is why David incorporated you into this; mainly to keep an eye on you but also to use you and then dispose of you and put some of the blame for the kidnap on you. You were a gift and a great patsy for him."

Derek laughed at this.

"Well, this patsy saved your fucking life, arsehole," was Jazz's tart reply.

"Well, you were the one to handcuff me and caused me to nearly lose my life, arsehole," Derek retorted, then laughed and raised his hand and high-fived Jazz.

The journey took just ten minutes. Stansted to Ilford wasn't far as the crow flies. They landed in Valentines Park in the pitch-dark and scrambled to get out of the locked gate and run towards De Vere Gardens which was only five minutes away. They were doing well for time. When they got to the end of De Vere Gardens Derek stopped them. He said they had to orchestrate this with other units who were there to help. Jazz had the shakes; he was beside himself with worry and so much adrenalin he wanted to just go in and shoot the lot of them and save his family. Derek, obviously used to such things, calmed him down and told him to wait.

After a very long five minutes, Derek got the go sign and they moved stealthily towards Mrs Chodda's house. The streets were empty, a lone dog somewhere was barking. They heard the sound of a car coming towards them but it turned into another road before reaching them. They were all highly sensitive to every noise and even the night-time breeze startled them as it whipped up the leaves of a silver birch tree in someone's front garden. Skittish now and jumpy, Derek didn't want these two amateurs with guns and live bullets getting gun happy. He whispered that they must not use their guns unless they had no choice. There would be enough people to sort this out.

The idea was to call the men out of the house. Apparently, there were two of them so it shouldn't be difficult. That way Mrs Chodda, Amrit and Wills would not be involved in the capture. It made sense to Jazz and Boomer and they hoped it would go according to plan.

They were now within two houses of Mrs Chodda's and they stopped. They could see in front of them a group of men in total black. You just couldn't see them unless they moved as they blended into the deep shadows. The street lamp close by had been extinguished so the area was pitch-black; even the sky was full of cloud blocking the moon and stars. It was looking good.

The silence was deafening then the bloody dog started barking again. It had to be in the next road, not that close but still unnerving. The wind had whipped up a bit more and it blew through wires and whistled and moaned sounding to their over-sensitive ears like a tornado. He hoped the men inside the house weren't spooked by the noise. Jazz's shaking started again. He could hardly breathe with the thought of those men sitting inside with the power to kill them all.

Jazz, his eyes darting from the front door of Mrs

Chodda's home to the men silently surrounding the house, counted six of them, then he looked back to Derek who seemed to be orchestrating everything with hand signals. He turned to Jazz and Boomer and whispered urgently, "Don't fuck this up. Just do what I say and nothing else, do you hear?"

Derek, Jazz suddenly realised, seemed to be the leader of this and Jazz wondered if he had misread Derek all this time. Perhaps he was like a 007 secret agent. Jazz looked at Boomer who was also thinking something similar. They grimaced at each other and raised their eyebrows, they nodded to Derek, put their heads down, and did what they were told.

For a short while there was a brooding silence and no movement that Jazz could see through the darkness. Suddenly a woman appeared in the road. She was about forty years old and dowdily dressed with short curly hair, she had a dressing gown on and slippers. She athletically strode up to the door, but then stood still and appeared to shrink in height as she bent her shoulders and stooped forward. To Jazz, in those few moments, she seemed to have aged about twenty years. He looked enquiringly at Derek who just shrugged and then looked back to the door, mesmerised now by this woman. Who was she and what was going on?

The show was about to start and as she rang the doorbell Jazz and Boomer held their breath. It didn't last long. She rang the bell and they noted the door was opened by one of the men, and there appeared to be some sort of discussion and then the door was slammed shut. The woman turned and slowly walked towards Derek.

When she got up to them, Jazz saw her face which

read disappointment. In a whisper Derek asked what had happened.

"My job was to get him to leave the house and help me look for my cat outside but he looked at me like I was a piece of dirt and told me to fuck off and he shut the door. Sorry it didn't work."

She walked off and Derek looked in thought mode. Jazz, now agitated, realised the men would be a bit edgy now. She had created something out of the norm and if they were any good at what they did, they would be alert. Edgy men with guns was not something you wanted in a house full of his family.

"You can't storm the house; those men will kill my family without another thought." Jazz hesitated for a moment and added, "I have an idea."

CHAPTER TWENTY-NINE

RESCUE

Jazz and Derek huddled together in a tense discussion that seemed to escape into argument. Boomer listened as close as he could and liked the outcome.

Derek decided reluctantly for Jazz and Boomer to enter the house. Jazz assured Derek that he had to be the one to do it because he knew the layout of the house and Mrs Chodda, Wills and Amrit would not be scared if he appeared. If the men in black entered, they were likely to scream and alert the two men. Derek agreed with Jazz that the two men might be quite on edge with the aborted action of the woman. It had seemed a good try at the time but now realised it might have made the situation more fraught; two edgy killers with guns was not a good option. He was told in no uncertain terms he would wear a microphone and take instructions from Derek through a small listening device stuck in his ear.

Jazz had a plan and he explained that he needed Boomer's help too because they worked well together and understood each other's signals. Boomer thought that was a load of rubbish but nodded in agreement. He was up for an adventure and he wanted to get those two men. He was seething with a frustrated anger he hadn't felt before. He had been messed about, shot at and now his friend's family were in danger. He was het up and usually he shouted and stomped around and threw things to vent his anger, but now he had to be quiet and that was killing him, so the best he could do was spring into action and grab the two men and punch their lights out. He smiled at the thought.

The first part of Jazz's plan was to text Wills. He got a reply that Wills was in his bed pretending to be asleep. Jazz asked him to creep down the stairs and unbolt the cellar door. He told Wills to be careful and if seen by one of the men to pretend to feel sick and ask for Mrs Chodda or Amrit to help him, and Wills replied immediately *OK*.

The men in black had surrounded the house and couldn't be seen in the shadows as Jazz and Boomer crept around the front of the house and into the sideway. Jazz knew the men would be sitting in Mrs Chodda's kitchen because if she was up that was where she spent her time. In the sideway there was a hatch, like the ones you see outside pubs where the barrels of beer are pushed down into the cellars. Mrs Chodda had one installed years ago so she could put stores of oils and various things easily into her cellar. There was a ladder which helped although Boomer being a bit more on the large side, struggled to get in and down. Jazz would have laughed at the sight but being quiet was paramount. He whispered to Boomer to stop fannying around and get in as Boomer sat on the floor outside and tried to find where his feet could go to find the ladder. He whispered back something unprintable and finally found the step to stand on.

The cellar with a low ceiling and stark walls felt like a prison cell. It wasn't cold down there but they both shuddered. The small pencil light showed a full-up cellar with spare pots, gardening tools, memorabilia from India and broken chairs. They had to get past some big wooden, actually quite beautiful chests which Jazz recognised as the place you kept spare saris, materials and women's things like that. He preferred not to get involved in all that sort of stuff. His mother had a few of them in her spare room. The cellar, on inspection, looked like a dumping ground which surprised Jazz. Mrs Chodda kept a very tidy and clean, if a tad cluttered, house. He supposed that's why she had a cellar. Jazz and Boomer's problem was to find a route out of the cellar without knocking anything over and making a noise. Everything they were doing, they were doing in slow motion; watching where they stepped and what they might brush against.

They found the stairs up to the door which opened into the hall. Every step they took creaked and to them sounded like each step had a microphone and the cellar filled with the noise. Jazz was sure they could be heard in the kitchen and expected with every step to see the door flung open and for them to be standing with no defence and shot to death. There were thirteen steps and it seemed to take hours although realistically it took ten minutes to get to the top.

Jazz stood, hardly daring to breathe, listening for any noise in the hall. He tried the door and as quietly as he could opened the door a crack. He thought *well done, Wills;* he had got the door unlocked and Jazz hoped he was back in his bedroom. He could hear voices in the kitchen. Mrs Chodda was talking about Guru Granth Sahib who was the living Guru. Jazz could hear her quoting him again. '*He who has no faith in himself can never have faith in God.*' He heard two male voices, sounding a little bored but in agreement with Mrs Chodda. So now Jazz knew they were both in the kitchen and he could move as quietly and quickly as possible to open the cellar door, he pulled up Boomer who was struggling a little and then closed the door carefully and quietly.

They headed, tiptoeing lightly, up the stairs but as quickly as possible to get away from the hallway. Both were feeling very stressed. They got to Wills' bedroom, opened the door and this made Wills jump. Jazz quickly rushed to him and put his hand over his mouth as Wills was about to say something. He warned him to be very quiet. Wills pulled himself together and was now very excited at the thought that something covert was about to happen. He was a bit disappointed when immediately Jazz and Boomer sat down on his bed, sighed and sat for a few moments in silence while they gathered their breath and their nerves for the next stage. There was very little left in one of the flasks but Jazz and Boomer managed a sip each. They looked at Wills who was staring at them and Jazz whispered with a sigh, "We need this."

Phase two was going to be the difficult bit but Jazz was convinced Wills was the man for the job, or that was what Jazz said to Wills who, although a little scared, loved the thought. Jazz hoped he wasn't causing more trouble for the lad but he had to get the women away from the two men downstairs. He was surprised Mrs Chodda and Amrit weren't in bed already; it was late.

Jazz reckoned Mrs Chodda felt bad about leaving the two men on their own which he presumed was why she was talking about Guru Granth Sahib, a favourite subject of hers, to wile away the time. Mrs Chodda was a very considerate woman. He presumed Amrit was still up too, to keep Mrs Chodda company. He had to admit they were both wonderful women and for a moment his eyes pricked with the start of a tear at the thought. He reckoned he was maudlin and getting tired so better get on with what needed to happen.

Jazz, now in complete control and getting organised, said to Boomer, "If you go into the bedroom across the way, if one of the men comes up to see Wills or whatever or passes the door you can grab him and that's one out of the way. Have you still got your handcuffs?"

Boomer nodded that he had the handcuffs and said he very much wanted to grab one of the men if they passed by. The hour was nearly up and they both knew there could be something awful about to happen if the men got a phone call to say what had happened and that the plans had been ruined.

Jazz looked at Wills and asked again, "Are you sure, Wills, you can do this?"

Wills nodded and repeated what Jazz told him.

"Yes, easy. Don't worry, I will get Amrit up first as you said and from there Amrit will call for Aunty."

"You got this Wills. Well done and just get back here quickly".

Jazz looked at the little mite in his Superman pyjamas looking all skinny and defiant and the bloody pricking of the eyes started again. He needed to *man up* he told himself.

With a nod, Wills left the room and so did Boomer leaving Jazz alone and wondering if he was a fucking idiot or a bloody genius. Either way he worried for his family. Wills sat on the bottom step in the hall and called towards the kitchen door. In a childish sing-song voice he shouted, "Aaaaaamrit, I've been sick. Aaaaaamrit, I've been sick."

The kitchen door opened violently and one of the men stepped out. It was Graham. To be honest he was glad of the distraction. Listening to that Mrs Chodda going on about some fucking guru was driving him and his mate Manj mad.

"What's up with you?" Graham asked Wills aggressively.

At that, Amrit pushed past him, rushed over to Wills and felt his head. He felt fine but she said nothing. She asked Wills gently, "Where were you sick?"

"Over my bedclothes and the bed is yukky," sobbed Wills who was really getting into this.

Amrit thought this was not the usual Wills but, nonetheless, he needed her help. She turned to Graham and said, "The boy needs to go to bed with a drink of water and I need to change his bed."

Graham frowned and nodded in agreement.

"Go on then, I will follow you upstairs."

Amrit looked at him and said, "You don't need to come up too."

But Graham insisted and so they went upstairs. Amrit felt uneasy and she didn't know why. Considering he was feeling sick and unwell, Amrit thought Wills ran up the stairs a little eagerly and quickly. She tutted to herself and followed him with Graham just behind her. Wills had gone into the bedroom by the time she reached the top of the stairs and she turned to nod to Graham and suggested he waited outside. A sick bed was not something very pleasant to see or smell. Graham agreed.

As Amrit entered Wills' bedroom the door just closed behind her. Startled, she turned and saw Jazz. Before she could let out a yell, he put his hand over her mouth and made the sssh-ing sound. Wills was loving this and getting very excited, bouncing on his bed and starting to giggle so Jazz turned to him and mouthed 'be quiet you bugger'.

There was a mild scuffling noise the other side of the door in the corridor and both Amrit and Wills looked to the door in shock. They all froze in silence and held their breath for what seemed ages and only when the door opened quietly and Boomer came in did they all seem to breathe again. The relief was culpable.

Amrit was stressed, unable to understand anything or why she felt so stressed. These men were here at the behest of Jazz to look after them so why all this quiet and skulduggery? Wills' bed was perfect, no sick anywhere; there was nothing wrong with him, he was jumping about on his bed. Jazz was hiding behind the door and where the hell had that Boomer come from? She had so many questions and Jazz just told her to be quiet.

Boomer nodded to Amrit and whispered to Jazz that the guy was handcuffed to the bed and he had found a scarf which he had put across his mouth to keep him quiet. Jazz asked where he was and Boomer pointed in the direction of the room across the way. He was not going to be any trouble because Boomer had smacked him hard on the chin and the man was out for the count. Boomer was quite proud of this and ready for the next one.

Jazz looked at Amrit and said, "Now this is the dangerous bit. I need you to call down the stairs to Auntie and say you can't find any clean sheets; can she come and show you where they are?"

He looked at Amrit and asked, "Can you do this and sound authentic?"

Amrit nodded too much. She was about to ask a question when Jazz said, "We need to get Auntie away from the man still downstairs. Things could get difficult soon."

He didn't want to elaborate.

Derek was in his ear saying the time was up and he expected the men to receive a phone call very soon now to get rid of Mrs Chodda, Amrit and Wills. Scarlett, who was running the show tonight, would have discovered that Jazz had not done what she told him to and the body of David would have been found and she would be very unhappy indeed.

Tense but trying to look at ease (he didn't want to spook Amrit), he pushed her towards the door and whispered, "Just get Auntie up here quickly. No messing around or asking questions, it's urgent."

Amrit could feel the tension in the air and scared now nodded and left the room to call Auntie. Jazz told Wills to lay under his bed for safety. Wills thought this sounded fun and did as he was told. Boomer went back to the bedroom across the corridor and waited. He kicked Graham for good measure. The grunt from Graham was muffled behind the scarf tied across his mouth.

Amrit called from the top of the stairs.

"Auntie, Auntie, can you help me, please?"

Manj came to the door and asked what was up. Amrit, looking harassed, said plaintively, "The poor boy has been sick again in his bed and I have to change the bedding yet again but I have run out of bedding. I need Auntie to show me where it's kept. I don't know as they are Auntie's sheets."

Manj tutted and asked where Graham was. Amrit smiled and artfully answered, "Oh, he is so lovely, he is helping me look after Wills. I didn't want to leave him in case he is sick again so I asked Graham to just stay with him while I get more sheets and a bowl."

By now Auntie had come to the door on hearing what was being said. Worried and bustling at the door, she pushed Manj out of the way and in a busy, quiet voice uttered,

"Come on now, mind out of my way. I have work to do. The poor lad needs a clean bed and it's women's work. You can help if you want but I need to get this sorted and washing put on."

Amrit hoped the invitation to help wasn't taken up. She smiled at Manj and raised her eyes to the ceiling and sighed. "Goodness, it stinks up here of sick. I don't know what he ate to cause that."

Manj, on reflection, decided to stay downstairs and said his job was to look after them so he would give them a few minutes to clear up before he went upstairs. With a nod Amrit pulled Auntie's arm and pushed her up the stairs and into Wills' bedroom. Auntie was breathless and felt pulled about. She looked up at Amrit and was about to ask what was going on when she saw Jazz. Before she could say anything, Amrit put her hand over Auntie's mouth saying, "We have to be quiet for a moment, Auntie. Sorry, it's just a bit of a surprise." She saw Auntie's face and added quickly, "It's, a, erm, nice surprise. Jazz wanted to surprise you."

Auntie looked around, confused and unable to understand. Jazz turned his back to Auntie and whispered into the microphone on his jacket for the benefit of Derek who he hoped was listening to every word.

"Derek, come in: Manj is downstairs and DI Black has Graham tied up if you want to send your men in now."

Derek answered.

"On their way and will enter quietly so no one is aware."

It was over in under five minutes. A magnificent job. Four men entered Auntie's kitchen and silently grabbed Manj; he didn't know what was happening. Another four men quietly ran up the stairs and took Graham from Boomer who tried to kick the hitman again as the men in black strong-armed Graham down the stairs.

The house was silent again and Boomer entered Wills' bedroom to find total confusion. Auntie had no idea what was going on. She asked why was she up here. Wills' bed was clean. Why was Jazz hiding away? This was his home and he didn't need to hide, she kept saying, as she looked in puzzlement from Jazz to Amrit. A story needed to be concocted quickly and Jazz was working on it. For a moment the only thing that came to mind was Jazz saying far too brightly and raising jazz hands in front of him, "Surprise! I came home early and wanted to surprise you. Amrit was in on the surprise and so was Wills."

Auntie thought that rather silly but accepted what Jazz said. Amrit would have questions later and he knew she would not let him get away with such stupid answers.

He heard Derek in his earpiece say that just as the hitmen reached outside their phones both rang. Derek knew it was Scarlett with instructions to kill. They had been saved with only a few minutes to spare. Jazz, adrenalin on maximum and scared beyond scared and so relieved all at the same time, sat down on Wills' bed, unable for the moment to think clearly. Auntie, worried Jazz didn't look right (he was pale, and she felt his forehead), undid his tie and muttered he looked like he needed a good meal and a cup of tea. Back on form now, Auntie looked at Amrit and instructed her to heat up the curry and rice and pour a cup of tea and to get the pakoras out as they were Jazz's favourite. She was her old self and all this nonsense was forgotten for the moment. Food was needed. They were all going to have something to eat. Boomer looked on and thought that sounded a good idea and followed Amrit downstairs to the kitchen.

Auntie went quickly to the cupboard and got a flannel and wetted it under the cold tap in the bathroom and tended to Jazz. She scolded him and tutted for arguing with her because she said that he needed a cold flannel on his head to bring his colour back. Distracted for the moment, Auntie went to the bedroom door and shouted to Amrit to ask if Graham and Manj would like something to eat as well. Jazz called her back and said they had left. Auntie was very put out.

"What, no goodbye? How rude was that?" she stated and then added, "But they did a good job for you, Jazz. They certainly looked after us and protected us, from what, I just don't know, but they did."

Jazz laughed and as Auntie came to move the flannel on his forehead, he grabbed her arm and gave her a kiss on the cheek for which she blushed and told him he must be feeling better and to go downstairs for some food and drink. She told Wills that he should be in bed asleep but Wills was far too excited by everything that had happened and said he was hungry and followed them downstairs.

CHAPTER THIRTY

THEY SEEK HIM HERE, THEY SEEK HIM THERE!

It had been a late night and by the time everyone had eaten it was past 1 a.m.. Derek had knocked on the door and asked for his microphone and earpiece back which Jazz was glad to get rid of. Derek said that the next morning there would be a debrief and both Boomer and Jazz would be picked up at 8 a.m. and brought to the compound. Everyone was tired and glad to get to their beds for the night.

On the dot of 8 a.m. Pinky and Perky (Jazz's name for the driver and sidekick) picked up Jazz and Boomer. Boomer had fallen asleep on the settee and it was decided by Auntie that he best stay and sleep there. Auntie got him a spare duvet and covered him. Neither Jazz nor Boomer felt brilliant in the morning but relieved it was all over and still tired they dozed on the way to the compound in the back of the car.

There was coffee and a fried breakfast waiting for them. Jazz and Boomer looked like they had had a rough night of no sleep but Derek was pristine and alert and full of energy. He even had a clean, starched shirt on and trousers with a crease down the front, for fuck's sake! If Jazz had the energy he would have bitch-slapped the bloody darling Derek.

"Eat up, Jazz and Tom. By the looks of you, you could do with something inside of you," was the cheery comment from Derek. He ignored the glowering look both men gave him. Mind you, after a full English breakfast and several cups of coffee both of them felt much better and ready for whatever was going to happen now.

At 11 a.m. the big boss entered the room. He introduced himself as Richard (no surnames necessary, he had added). The debrief had taken an unusual turn, he told them. He explained that everyone they needed to keep hold of (Jazz thought that a strange turn of phrase) was in their custody apart from one person who seemed to have disappeared. Richard looked directly at Jazz and asked, "Any idea where Mrs Manson might disappear to?"

"Why the fuck, oh sorry, why would I know that?" asked Jazz watching his language.

"Because looking through paperwork in her office, most of which seemed to have been destroyed, we found paperwork with your name on it. It seemed to imply you had a few meetings with Mrs Manson and that the two of you seemed to hit it off."

Posh Richard was being very diplomatic but Jazz knew what he was inferring.

"I saw her a couple of times but only as a prelude to

my appointments with Scarlett. Why would she say that about me?"

Richard nodded and then asked, "Do you know someone called Pete?"

"Yeah, I know a Mad Pete, well, that's what I call him. He is my snout. Why?"

In a very refined, soft voice, Richard, who was now more interested in Jazz's answers leaned forward and said, "It would appear that Pete was working closely with Mrs Manson and we are trying to find her and him. Mad Pete, as you call him, is also missing. We have been to his flat on the Gascoigne Estate and he is nowhere to be found. Your name appears together with Mrs Manson and Pete on paperwork we found. Can you help us find him?"

Jazz sat and thought hard. Mad Pete was a rat and worked in some pretty awful places. He was the sort of villain who knew everything that was going on because no one saw him as a threat. He was a dirty, snivelling coward who could get you anything illegal that you asked for. But Jazz knew he was not into working with terrorists or those types of people. It just wasn't his style and they wouldn't touch him with a barge pole.

He explained this to Richard who listened attentively then dismissed every word and again asked, "Can you help us find him? It sounds like you have worked a lot with him and may know places he might hide that we don't."

Jazz did know Mad Pete had a history of providing Mrs Manson with any drugs she asked for. He wasn't her first go-to supplier but Jazz could see she seemed to have a soft spot for him when they all met. Jazz didn't understand that. Why would the lovely Mrs Manson ever sweet-talk

Mad Pete? He was a greasy-haired, stinking, long streak of piss and definitely not a Brad Pitt. Jazz wondered if perhaps there was more to their relationship than Mad Pete had owned up to. Was he her main supplier? Did he supply other stuff and more of it than he told Jazz? He was, after all, a consummate fucking liar and a devious bastard. Had he missed something, he wondered?

Jazz was aware that Richard and Derek were staring at him while he was thinking. He pulled himself together and gave his considered opinion.

"Mad Pete is a stinking rat who will go to ground at the first sight of trouble. He has a fucking huge streak of yellow. I don't believe he is with Mrs Manson. Why would that woman have him in tow? Having said that, he might have helped her find a place to hide away or got her some form of transport. I didn't think he would know of anywhere that was halfway decent but he is a fucking liar and might not have told me everything about what he does for Mrs Manson."

Jazz looked at Richard who nodded and said, "We have, shall I say, many avenues exploring where Mrs Manson might be but to date, there is no sign of her. We are rather hoping you can find Pete for us so we may question him. To date there is no sign of him in Barking or surrounding areas."

Jazz smirked and couldn't help himself.

"So, you are fucked then?"

Richard raised his eyebrows at this remark, ignored the inference, and again asked if he could help find Mad Pete. Jazz asked that he and Boomer should be left to go and find Mad Pete. He advised Richard that the areas Pete worked in would smell out his men before they turned the corner of any shithole in Barking. He reminded Richard that he was known as someone who was on good working terms with Mad Pete and tentatively accepted by the toerags on the Gascoigne Estate and surrounding area.

It was agreed, not very happily by Richard, that Jazz and Boomer would be given until eight o'clock that night to find Mad Pete and then there would be a rethink. Meanwhile his men were still hunting Mrs Manson.

Before he left, Jazz asked cheekily if they could borrow one of their nice BMWs. They didn't need a driver. They were going undercover. It was agreed and the car filled with petrol. The journey to Barking was great; they played with the radio and found a station that had songs they knew most of the words to. They sang their way to a greasy spoon on the A13 where they were going to have a bacon sarnie and a big mug of tea while they discussed what the hell they were going to do.

Jazz hadn't a clue where Mad Pete was. He knew the man and knew he would be hiding well away from everyone. If he was at all involved, even on the periphery, with any of what went down, he knew Mad Pete would be shit-scared, shaking in fear in some awful place, smoking spliffs and snorting coke to keep himself together.

The greasy spoon served fantastic food and they concentrated on eating the sandwich made of thick white bread with hot bacon dripping fat over their hands; it was culinary perfection. This place let them smoke at the table so when they had finished eating they ordered more tea, lit up and looked to see what to do next. The most sensible thing was to call Mad Pete on his mobile which Jazz did. It kept going to voicemail so Jazz left a voicemail message:

"For fuck's sake, you degenerate, diabolical wanker, answer your phone. It's me, for Christ's sake!"

Boomer suggested that Jazz's dulcet, friendly tone might not make Mad Pete feel good or a treasured friend and sadly he may well decide not to ring Jazz back. Jazz, after questioning Boomer's sarcasm, said he would send another message just in case it made a difference. He dialled again and it went to voicemail.

"Hi Pete, sorry about my last message. Just know I am worried about you. Look, you know me, we are partners and I am here to help you. Please just ring me back and let me help you get out of this mess. Please ring soon because I am worried about your safety."

Jazz looked at Boomer and said, "Well, how was that message?"

Boomer replied in two sarcastic words.

"You Jessie."

They both laughed, lit another cigarette and ordered another tea. To be honest, this was the first time in a few days they felt on form and more relaxed. The stress of the night before needed to be dumped and they sat enjoying the ambience of a safe place. It doesn't get better than a greasy spoon with a cheery lady ready to serve you anything you want in record time.

After twenty minutes, Jazz reckoned it was time for another message to be sent to bloody Mad Pete. There was no way he would lose his phone; it was his lifeline and contained all the information he needed for buying and selling. Then it occurred to Jazz that he would have to dump his main phone because MI6 could pinpoint where he was and they didn't know. Jazz looked through his phone to find out if Mad Pete had sent him any messages in the past on a burner phone, something not registered so couldn't be found. He reckoned he most probably left his main phone at his flat and that's why MI6 found where he lived.

After five minutes of looking, Jazz came across a message from another mobile number from Mad Pete. Don't know why he had used a different phone but to be honest, Jazz didn't care. He rang the number and to his surprise it was answered.

"Who is this and what do you want, you fucking parasite?"

Jazz recognised the voice and thought *fucking hell, it's his mother!* Mad Pete's mother was the scariest woman in the country. She hated everyone including her son, Mad Pete. If you looked her in the eye, she would nut you without blinking. She was the size of a sumo wrestler with a mouth that even bleach couldn't clean out. If she fell on you, you were dead and she would jump on you to make sure you were dead. This was one evil, nasty woman. There had been rumours that when she copulated with some unfortunate man to produce Mad Pete, she ate him afterwards.

In a little boy's voice Jazz said, "Hello, erm, is Pete there, please?"

"Mind your own fucking business. Come here and I'll cut your bollocks off and use them as earrings, you nosey arse wipe!"

Jazz, although feeling quite scared and apprehensive, thought quickly as to what she would be interested in and what would get him an answer. Of course, it was the universal door-opener – money!!

"Actually, I have a grand I owe Pete and I would like to give it back, with interest of course." He added, after

265

a deep breath, "Do you know where I can speak to him? This money is burning a hole in my pocket so I want to give it to him quickly before I spend it."

"Who are you?" she asked in a gruff voice, the nearest to normal she had ever sounded.

"Tell him it's Jazz and I am his friend."

She grunted at this and in a voice that was louder than anything that came through a speaker at a music festival she shouted, "Oy, Pete, get here, you bastard, and take this now! It's some cunt calling his self Jazz or summit like that!! He's got money for you and I want some of it, you useless fucker, you owe me."

With a heavily sarcastic sickly-sweet tone she added, "He is your friend."

Jazz looked at Boomer who was listening to the ranting. He mouthed '*he is with his mother in Beckton*'. Boomer had heard of Mrs Mad Pete and slumped in the chair. This was going to be a fucking awful job. There was a rustling on the phone and a dejected guarded voice said, "Yeah, what do you want, Mr Singh? I ain't doing nuffink."

"Pete, I am worried about you. There are some big men looking for you and I am here to help you."

At this, Mad Pete started to whimper.

"I ain't doing nuffink. I just want to stay away from everythink. Mr Singh, you gotta not tell anyone you found me."

"Look, Pete, let's meet. I will get this sorted for you."

With more bravado and less truth Jazz added, "Don't I always look out for you? If you are in trouble, don't I always get you out of it? We have been in some scrapes before but has anything ever happened to you? No, it hasn't, because I make sure you are okay. Is that true or not, Pete?"

Placated a little, Mad Pete had to agree.

"Yes, Mr Singh, you have always watched my back but this time is different. There are some awful fuckers out there and I am really scared."

Jazz could hear the panic in his voice and he needed calming down.

"We will sort this. I am on my way to Beckton and will be there in minutes. Meet me downstairs and Boomer and I will ensure you are safe and we will work out how to get you out of this fucking mess, okay?"

Mad Pete reluctantly agreed and said he would meet them downstairs. Jazz added, "And don't bring your mother with you. I can't handle her, for Christ's sake!"

Mad Pete grunted he would try and keep her in the flat.

Jazz looked at Boomer and told him to step on it and get them to Beckton housing estate quickly. There were blue lights on this car so Boomer switched them on and put his foot down. The siren could be heard for miles.

He knew Mad Pete was going to be on the verge of one of his druggy fits, he could hear it in his voice. Calmness was needed so Jazz told Boomer to act confident and friendly towards Mad Pete.

"He must be shit-scared to be staying at his mother's. That woman is the last person you would want to meet, let alone live with. Something has happened and we need to find out what."

CHAPTER THIRTY-ONE

NO HIDING PLACE

They arrived at the tower block and when they looked up to the fourth floor, they could see Mad Pete on the balcony waiting for them. They also saw his mother shouting something at him. In what seemed a blink of an eye, Mad Pete looked to have made a dash back into the flat. Jazz wondered what the fuck was going on. He took the precaution of opening the back door in case Mad Pete appeared. Within a few minutes Mad Pete, red-faced, sweating and looking like he was being chased by a man-eating lion, ran out of the tower block's communal door. He took one look behind him and then raced to the car and threw himself in. Panting and barely able to speak he shouted hysterically.

"Go, go quick, go. She is gonna come out that door any minute and we will all be dead. Just go."

As he said that, they saw the enormous frame of Mrs Mad Pete trying to open the communal door. In her temper she forgot she had to press the green button that opened the door. They watched, mesmerised, because she looked like she was about to rip the door off its hinges. She was beyond mad; she was mouthing words through the door that left no one in any doubt that she would and could rip them into pieces when she got hold of them. Jazz, without taking his eyes off Mrs Mad Pete, nudged Boomer and told him to 'go, go, go'. The car tyres screeched as Boomer, spooked at the sight of her, put his foot down and took off down the road. When they reached a safe distance of several miles, Boomer pulled over and they all exhaled. It had been a close thing but now they had Mad Pete, they needed to find out what was happening and if he knew where Mrs Manson was now. First of all, Jazz needed to ask, "What the fuck did you say to your mother to turn her into the Incredible Hulk?"

Mad Pete was snivelling now and wanting something to settle him which meant either some coke or a spliff. Jazz opened the window and told him he could smoke but to make sure it went out of the window. At the same time Jazz and Boomer lit up. It had been a stressful time. After a few minutes of puffing away and inhaling deeply, Mad Pete was ready to talk.

"Nah, Mr Singh, it wasn't me that upset her, it was you."

"What the fuck did I do? I was nice on the phone."

"You told her you had a grand to give me with interest. She wanted it all cos she said she gave birth to me and I owed her. Well, I knew you weren't gonna give me a grand so I scarpered quickly. If she had got to you she would have pulled your car to pieces until you gave her the money and then she would've started on you. I saved your life, Mr Singh," was the plaintiff response.

Actually, Jazz felt grateful. He knew what a mean, strong bitch she was and he didn't think even a gun would stop her. It was unanimously decided that they would go to the nearest McDonald's and have a burger and chips and coffee, and talk. Mad Pete wasn't so sure about the talking but Jazz again, in his unusual placating voice, reassured Mad Pete.

"It's gonna be fine, Pete. We are here to look after you and make sure you are okay. We are safer than your mother who looked like she was about to tear you limb from limb. We won't do that, will we, Boomer?"

Boomer shook his head and nearly smiled at Pete. He thought this was all getting stupid. Mad Pete just needed to tell them what they wanted to know but he conceded that Jazz could handle Pete and avert the druggy fit he was prone to if stressed so Boomer played along with the syrupy fucking sweet-talk.

They found a quiet corner in McDonald's and with food on the table and hot drinks they tucked in. After a five-minute munch it was time to talk. Mad Pete was settled and looked at ease; a McDonald's always calmed him down. Jazz had done the sweet-talk stuff and now he needed to get down to the nitty gritty.

"So, Pete, why are you hiding and why are you shit-scared? To stay at your mother's, for fuck's sake, it has to be something really bad!!"

Mad Pete squirmed a little in his chair.

"I can't tell you, Mr Singh. I want to tell you but I can't."

Jazz thought that was a good start and the way was opening up nicely. Gently but firmly and with encouragement he said, "I understand it's difficult. I think you could start at the beginning, then when I know what's happened, I can sort out something to make it go away for you so you can get back to your life."

He added for the final push, "You want to get back to your life, don't you, Pete?"

Pete nodded and looked about to cry.

"I got into a lot of trouble, Mr Singh. I ain't happy. I don't know who is after me but someone is. I left my phone in my flat cos I was getting strange calls and I wasn't sure who they were. What I say must go no further. I could get people into trouble and then they will kill me."

Mad Pete was tensing up and Jazz needed to keep him calm otherwise he would never get to hear the whole fucking story and it was beginning to piss him off. So again, he tried to calmly say, "Pete, it's okay. Just start at the beginning and we will work through it."

What was to unfold was devious, complicated and awesome.

"Well, although I only work occasionally for Mrs Manson, she knows whatever she wants I can get. Like, she needed a gun with no history and I managed to get it for her, no problem."

Gee thought Jazz, *what is this creature into?*

"So, she rang me last night and said she had a problem and needed my help. She pays very well and this was gonna be a big earner. She wanted me to get her out of the country undercover. Me? What does she think I am? The fucking Scarlett Pimpernel or summink? I told her no way. Not summink I do."

Mad Pete looked at Jazz and Boomer aghast.

"She then fucking threatened me."

Jazz and Boomer nodded, anxious to hear more.

"She told me to meet her in Barking. She drives a swanky big car and she reckoned it would be quicker for her to come to me to pick me up. She had never done that before and I was fucking bricking it. I knew there would be trouble but you don't mess with her, Mr Singh. I know she has done some bad things in the past. I knew she had used the gun I got her. So, I met her on the Gascoigne Estate just outside my place. It looked pretty good, people seeing me getting into a swanky car with a gorgeous woman. If it had been any other time, I would have showed off a bit but this was serious."

Mad Pete hunched forward and shakily rummaged for another spliff he had pre-assembled and put in his inside pocket. Jazz and Boomer sat and patiently waited for the first two deep drags of the spliff which seemed to settle him a bit and then told him to go on. Mad Pete, scared beyond sanity, was telling the whole truth because he needed help with this situation.

"Well, and it's all your fault, Mr Singh, she knew you were a wrong 'un. She knew I had taken you to her place. I was in deep shit and thought she was gonna kill me."

Jazz didn't think that was necessarily an exaggeration and tried to keep Mad Pete calm.

"I'm sorry, Pete, you got dragged into this but me and Boomer are here to help and save your scrawny arse." Again, with fingers crossed Jazz lied. "Haven't I always saved you from trouble?"

Mad Pete nodded and said, "Yes, Mr Singh."

After a few more deep drags of the spliff, Mad Pete, a bit calmer, continued.

"So, she says I have to find a way to get her out of the country. Apparently, all her routes were blocked at the moment and she knew I dealt with various people who she would pay handsomely but it had to be soon."

The story was getting interesting but Mad Pete stopped there and went off-piste which was infuriating for Jazz but he had to let him get it out of his system. Mad Pete's voice raised an octave and he whined.

"I didn't know you were fucking undercover when I introduced you to Mrs Manson. I ain't never grassed up a client. I don't do things like that. You messed up a good bit of business. Now she is leaving the country and that has cost me more money than I can say. I have lost a good earner and it's your fault. It's not fair!! I work hard for my money. Things don't come easy, you know. It takes years to build up my client base. Now everyone wants to kill me."

For fuck's sake, he sounds like an hysterical legit business manager thought Jazz. He needed to stop this whinging now.

"No one is going to kill you, Pete. If anyone is going to kill you it's gonna be me if you don't get on with what's happening."

Mad Pete shut up for a moment and rummaged in his pocket for a normal cigarette and lit it.

"She threatened me, Mr Singh. She said if I didn't help her immediately, she would see to it that I didn't see tomorrow and that the pain would be excruciating and I would want to be killed. I believed her, Mr Singh. She is a fucking evil woman if crossed, I know this. She wouldn't let me out of her car; she said I had to organise something now. I was beside myself, Mr Singh, but she had her hand on my cock and she started to squeeze and it hurt, Mr Singh."

He didn't know why but Jazz worked hard to not giggle. He could hear Boomer's breathing which told him he was trying hard not to giggle too. They looked at each other and just exploded into laughter. Mad Pete was certainly not impressed and mournfully said, "That's not nice, Mr Singh. It hurt."

It was so childish and Jazz and Boomer, ashamed, nodded in agreement. The tension was high and Jazz explained that laughter was just a way of releasing tension. Boomer thought that was a load of shit but Mad Pete seemed placated by it and with a deep drag of his cigarette continued.

"It turns out that all her avenues of travel, as she put it, were compromised. I gather summink dreadful had happened and she was wanted by police or villains, she wouldn't say. So, I had to do a quick think."

Mad Pete looked up at Jazz and said, "This ain't my area, Mr Singh. But she was gonna do summink awful to my balls if I didn't help her."

Again Jazz stifled a giggle and Boomer coughed away a giggle. Jazz was quite amazed this classy lady would even touch that area of Mad Pete. He was filthy at the best of times and fuck knew what diseases he was carrying. Jazz knew she must have been one desperate woman.

"Anyways, I came up with summink, Mr Singh, that was really good. I ain't no idiot and I had a massive brainwave."

Mad Pete paused for effect and Jazz, wanting to bitch-slap him into getting a move on, restrained himself and nodded interestedly.

"Look, Mr Singh. This is all confidential and if I tell you, you ain't gonna use it against me, are you?"

Jazz shook his head and said this would not get reported to the police. He didn't add that MI6 would have to be told but left that bit of information for later.

"Well, there's this small fishing boat that pulls in at Bradwell-on-Sea tonight and they bring goods from across the water for parts of London."

Jazz asked what goods and Mad Pete refused to say.

"They are going back to Holland straight away and I phoned a mate who arranged for Mrs Manson to be on board. She is staying at a small pub with rooms to let and is waiting for tonight. I am due back there to take her but I got one of the guys off the boat to go get her. I ain't going anywhere near her. She is gonna kill me," he whined.

"So, who has been ringing you, Pete?" asked Jazz. He needed to know what they were up against.

"I had loads of calls from some posh git who sounded all friendly but I know that tone. He was after me, I know it but I don't know who he is."

Jazz reckoned that was MI6. They were full of posh gits.

"Were there any other calls?" asked Jazz.

"Yeah, some foreign-sounding man who wants me to ring him immediately. I didn't like the sound of him. Sounded funny speaking and not like my usual foreigners who have a bit of a London twang. This one was just foreign and thick sounding. Not right, Mr Singh, just not right."

Jazz reckoned Mad Pete had a bit of a sixth sense. Most probably what had saved him on many occasions. He dealt with some pretty dire and scary villains.

"So, Mr Singh, I think there are lots of people after

me. What did I do? I ain't done nuffink except help you. It's not fair."

Jazz had to agree with Mad Pete, but he needed to think what to do now. Boomer suggested, "Fuck it! Let MI6 know and we can go home."

This spooked Mad Pete and Jazz spent the next five minutes placating him and giving Boomer dirty looks. This was madness. While all lit up and smoked and enjoyed a few moments of peace, Jazz made a decision.

"We are going to Bradwell to get Mrs Manson. She is a dangerous fucker and MI6 need her asap. Now we are going," and Jazz looked at a stressed Mad Pete.

"We are going," he repeated, "because we are looking after Mad Pete and keeping him out of trouble."

Boomer looked and screwed up his face and asked "How?"

"Well, the way I see it," said a now confident and very smooth-talking Jazz, "is we get underway and when we arrive, we nab Mrs Manson. When we are nearly at Bradwell we then contact 007 (Derek) at shitface MI6 and tell them where we are going so they arrive after us. They will see we have Mrs Manson and, hey presto! Pete is a hero because he took us there to find her. 'Nuff said!"

Mad Pete, scared but excited and scared again, sort of agreed. Boomer thought it sounded fantastic and said he still had his gun and cuffs in his pocket. So, the trio set off for Bradwell without a full plan in mind. When this was suggested, Jazz replied, "We don't need a plan. We can wing it."

THIRTY-TWO

BABY, IT'S COLD OUTSIDE

"I took her to the Green Man pub in Bradwell. Mrs Manson is a classy lady and she ain't gonna stay in no dive. She gave me money for a cab to take me home to get her some coke. She had a little bit but she said she needed more to help her tension." Mad Pete suddenly tensed up and started whining again.

"She was gonna be there all night and she said she left her home in a hurry. So I said yeah, I had stuff and would come back. Mr Singh, I didn't go back. She is gonna kill me. I don't wanna go with you. And Mrs Manson is the toughest woman I have ever met, and if she is scared then who the fuck is looking for her and then they will be after me for helping her. I am double fucked, Mr Singh."

Jazz was getting fed up with this whining and whingeing. He didn't know where the Green Man was and he needed Mad Pete to tell them and get them to

Mrs Manson's room unnoticed. Boomer was driving with the blue lights flashing and they were making good time and would be at this Green Man very soon so he needed Mad Pete calm.

"Look, Pete, we are with you. You are safe. Boomer has a gun so no messing around with us."

Mad Pete looked over at Boomer and for a moment was very impressed.

"But, Mr Singh," he started. Jazz told him to shut it and listen.

"You are our priority, Pete. We are guarding you like you are made of precious jewels." Boomer threw him a look of 'What the fuck are you talking about?'. Jazz ignored the look and continued, "We will be fronting this up. You just have to show us where to go and we will do the rest. Then shitface MI6 will turn up and take over and we will make sure they know you are the hero. See! This is going to be good for you."

Mad Pete, silent and thinking, nodded his head and mumbled "Thank you, Mr Singh." After a few seconds thought he added, "Will there be a reward for Mrs Manson, Mr Singh? Will I get any money for this?"

Lying through his teeth, Jazz confirmed there would be a huge reward for Mrs Manson and it was all for him. This did the trick and Mad Pete sat back satisfied and rummaged for another spliff.

The day was getting later, it was well after lunchtime when they arrived at the Green Man pub. It was a most imposing black and white pub that looked like you would have to wear a tie to go in there. It looked posh. Mad Pete was at pains to tell them that the landlord was really nice and helpful and not a posh git. Jazz thought if the landlord was pleasant to Mad Pete who always looked like a bag of shit, he must be very accommodating or blind.

They went to the bar and ordered a drink. Jazz had whispered he didn't want to walk in like it was a raid and put the landlord's back up. Jazz needed a drink. It had been a while and he needed to relax for a moment. Both Mad Pete and Boomer had a shandy. While they were supping at the bar, Jazz told the landlord that his pub had been recommended by their friend who was staying with him. They had come to visit her and wanted to sample the pub. After Jazz finished his drink, he said with sincerity

"This is a great pub. I'll have another vodka and tonic and perhaps we will go see the lady staying here. Is she in?" Jazz asked innocently. Of course, she would be in, she was in hiding. The landlord agreed she was in and said up the stairs, turn right and first room on the left. Jazz nodded with thanks. This was going well and he nearly smirked but that wouldn't have looked good.

Boomer and Mad Pete had sat down in a corner and were looking out the window. Jazz went to join them when he felt that prickling feeling that someone was staring at him. He turned to look through to the other end of the bar and sitting in a corner all relaxed and smirky was 007 Derek. Jazz walked over to him and sat down.

"What the fuck are you doing here?" whispered Jazz.

Boomer and Mad Pete watched as the pair got into a heated whispered discussion that seemed to go on for ages. Mad Pete got all fidgety and nervous and Boomer had to tell him quietly to 'stop fucking about and keep quiet and still, you stupid arse'. Boomer had an authoritative way about him and this instantly calmed Mad Pete. They sat and waited until Jazz came back. Boomer, anxious to know what the fuck was going on, let Jazz speak.

"They bugged the car, the fuckers," was the first thing Jazz said. Boomer groaned.

"They heard everything we said?"

"Yup."

"Fuck."

"Yup."

Mad Pete had that look in his eyes and Jazz knew he could go into one of his druggy fits which could alert the landlord and Mrs Manson upstairs as well as the whole of Bradwell. Jazz, quick to placate and keep Mad Pete calm, soothingly uttered, "It's all good, Pete, really it is. Derek has his men outside strategically placed in case she escapes, which is ridiculous. How would a woman in six-inch high heels and dressed to kill get away quickly?" They all smiled at that comment.

"Derek knows you are a hero, Pete, so no worries there. We have just one more thing to do and we are good and can go."

"What's that, Mr Singh?" asked Mad Pete, not sure what was coming.

Jazz, picking his words carefully, smoothly said, "Well, Derek has a great plan to get Mrs Manson because he doesn't want to cause any fuss here. You can see it's a lovely pub and a quiet area so Derek doesn't want anyone to know this is a raid: It might get reported to the papers and that would not be good. As you know, MI6 are undercover and never want the papers to know anything."

Mad Pete was getting suspicious now.

"So, what are you saying, Mr Singh? I ain't going near that woman if that's what you think. She could kill me with one hand or punch an eye out with her stiletto. You don't want me to do anything, do you, Mr Singh?" he pleaded.

"Well," and Jazz smacked his lips trying to think how to phrase the next bit.

"Derek thinks you have done good to bring us here. She would never have been found without your help."

He didn't mention that she was here because Mad Pete was a fucking toerag and brought her here and then tried to disappear, but that wasn't helpful now.

Boomer was struggling to stop himself getting exasperated with this fucking wimp, and trying to be diplomatic, definitely not his usual style. He wanted to help this situation and push it forward by agreeing with Jazz. He said, not sounding as convincing as he hoped, that Mad Pete was great, and how they would be lost without him. Jazz looked at Boomer and could see the man was fed up with Mad Pete's attitude and given half a chance would have gone up the stairs, grabbed Mrs Manson himself, cuffed her and brought her down. All this smooching and niceties were not his style but he was doing his best to help. Jazz nearly laughed but this was serious and Mad Pete was needed.

Jazz needed them to work with him. He told them both about his conversation with Derek who was sitting a distance away watching them.

"Look, here is the deal. Mrs Manson will get away tonight on a boat that is going to take her to Holland. Last night MI6 had a big round-up of all the people involved in this in the UK, except for Mrs Manson; she got away and they need her. Mrs Manson is meeting the big cheese in Holland that no one knows about, well, MI6 don't know who he is and they want him badly. They want to make sure that Mrs Manson isn't spooked and calls this man and alerts him. MI6 want to capture him. So, they bugged her phone and they know where the meeting will be in a fishing village on the Ijsselmeer (north Holland inland bay) called Volendam. MI6 and its counterpart in Holland are surrounding the area already. This is a very big deal and Mrs Manson making a call alerting this man would ruin everything."

Hoping he sounded patriotic and proud he added, "This is for our country and the world."

Mad Pete was impressed even if Boomer thought it sounded a bit over the top. Jazz continued.

"So, we need to get Mrs Manson before she can ring this man and warn him. She is definitely going to have him on speed dial so it's important to get her before she can touch her phone."

Looking admiringly at Mad Pete, Jazz added as convincingly as he could, "And Derek, our 007 man, reckons Pete here is our best option. She trusts you, Pete, well, she trusts you more than she would trust any of us. I have a plan which will work with your help."

Jazz stared at Mad Pete, giving him a nod and a smile. This totally unnerved Mad Pete but he carried on.

"No worries, Pete, you don't have to go and see her, honest."

This made Mad Pete feel a bit better, but not trusting Jazz asked hesitantly, "So what do you want me for?"

"Well, it's like this."

Jazz hesitated for a moment because he wanted to say it right and keep Mad Pete on board. Boomer leaned in further to listen to this.

"So, you will ring Mrs Manson and tell her you are outside and for her to come down and get the coke and hear the details for the boat tonight. You apologise for not coming back last night but a friend told you the police were looking for you and were watching your flat. Tell her it was to do with a cocaine bust and your name had been mentioned or something like that, and you had to hide out. Tell her you got a cab and made your way here today because you know she needed the stuff and needed to be taken to the boat. You look a state today because you haven't had time to clean up and didn't want to go in the pub as the landlord might throw you out because it was a posh pub with posh customers and you stink."

Mad Pete was about to say he was looking okay and didn't stink when Jazz added, off the cuff, "She will never know it's not true because you always look a bloody state."

Aggrieved, Mad Pete muttered, "That's not fair."

Jazz said he was joking but of course he wasn't. Mad Pete looked like he hadn't seen a bar of soap for years and his clothes were slept in. Jazz, after another smack of the lips in concentration, carried on.

"Tell her you got some good stuff for her. That the boat, as she already knows, is booked for her and she only has to wait a few more hours before it is dark and she can get away. So ring her on your mobile and go outside. She might look out of the window and see you so she won't be suspicious. You can do this, Pete."

Mad Pete, relieved he didn't have to face Mrs Manson, turned his mind to another question.

"What's in it for me?"

"Well, for a start MI6 won't fucking shoot you. That's one good reason," Jazz said.

"Another reason is Boomer won't shoot you either and trust me he has come close, I can tell you."

Boomer nodded at this and said, "Too bloody true."

"I could ask MI6 for you to see if there is a reward. If there is one, I reckon you would be entitled to it. Leave that one with me."

Mad Pete pulled a face, nodded his head and said, "Okay, Mr Singh, I'll do it. Just get her before she gets me."

"No problem, Pete, we have your back."

At that, Jazz went back to 007 Derek and told him the plan. Derek nodded and silently left. When Mad Pete and Boomer turned to look as Jazz came back, Derek had already left by the back door.

The conversation went well. Mad Pete was outside and Jazz and Boomer stayed in the doorway out of sight of the upstairs windows and listened to Mad Pete. They thought he was bloody good and very believable in his cowardly, whining voice that no one would think could ever be threatening. When the call finished, Mad Pete had been instructed to stay there.

Now Jazz and Boomer rushed to the gents' toilets just by the entrance door waiting for Mrs Manson to come down. They gathered from the conversation she had bought the story and was now on her way down to see Mad Pete. Derek and his MI6 mob would take over now. They just waited to watch and check that Mad Pete did what he was told to do and stay put.

Mad Pete was now over by the tables and chairs that were outside the pub for smokers and good-weather customers. The place was empty, it was too cold to be outside and perhaps too early for a lot of the locals who preferred to go to the pub after their evening meals and meet up with friends. He had sat down so Jazz was happy he wasn't going to do a runner. That would have spooked Mrs Manson and that must not happen. It was feeling very tense in the gents' toilets as they waited for Mrs Manson to make an appearance and go outside.

Mrs Manson was on a mission and breezed down the stairs and out of the pub as if she hadn't a care in the world; she was seeing Mad Pete after all. She had a lot on her mind and there were things that would need to be done to repair this disaster of what was supposed to be the kidnapping of the year. The power, prestige, notoriety and money this man would have brought to the group was meant to put them on the map. She had worked undercover for so long and now her rise to power with her man, the man of the century, the one who was going to change the world in one fell swoop and would do this without needing an insurrection, was bitter sweet. The power would be in his hands and every leader would fall at his feet.

She loved him and admired him and would do anything for him. She would meet him in Volendam, Holland, in the early hours of tomorrow. They had been lovers for many years and enjoyed clandestine meetings around Europe. He had said when the war was won, they would marry and he would introduce her to the world as his partner. She adored him and longed for that day. Very few knew who this mastermind was: but she alone had touched him, caressed him and listened to him and he loved her. This made her very powerful and she relished the knowledge she had.

Their meeting, for the first time in many months, was meant to be a celebration but now they needed to run.

They would find a safe place together and start again. Mrs Manson knew he would never give up his dreams and she loved him for his passion and commitment to the cause. She would do anything for him and the cause.

For now, she was experiencing more stress, worry and damn headaches and yes, she was scared of MI6 who were looking for her. She knew what MI6 were capable of and how tenacious and clever they were. She needed some peace of mind; her mind had been sprinting through all the past events and what that meant to the party. The headaches had been getting worse. All the work, planning, time, and watching her back and those of her team for fear of being discovered, were scuppered, ruined, buggered and destroyed. All her team had been taken, her cover blown and her ambitions thwarted. She really did need some coke to calm and pacify her and Pete was, in her opinion, the least of the problems she had to worry about.

All she wanted was just an hour or so of some peace to calm her thoughts. She hadn't got round to dealing with the disappointment and the intense feeling of losing yet. Mrs Manson had never lost: She had always thought she was a survivor and knew how to deal with men and any situation. Now she so needed the coke Mad Pete was bringing her and that was all she could think of in those five minutes of leaving her room to meet Mad Pete and he had the power to help her feel better and back in control.

The smile on her face faded quickly as she saw Mad Pete who by now was agitated and worried. Before she could think, make a decision, find her phone, Derek appeared from nowhere and grabbed her and grabbed her arms so she couldn't open her bag. She cursed and screamed and threatened Mad Pete with a damnation that scared the hell out of him. She tried to kick and bite Derek who spirited her away in moments before anyone could realise what had happened. The landlord heard the screams but by the time he had rushed to the door Jazz and Boomer were there looking around as if they wondered what the hell had happened too.

"Landlord, I think it was that mad woman. She looked weird to me. A car was here for her and she got in and was off."

Jazz thought that sounded plausible but the landlord who had seen much in his lifetime wasn't so sure.

"So who is paying her bill then?" he asked.

"She was someone I knew, so I will. I do have to tell you she has a mental issue. I reckon that was her brother who had come for her."

The landlord nodded half believing what he was being told but more interested in the bill being paid. Jazz made a mental note to get Derek to refund him when he saw him. Everything had gone quiet. Derek and his mob had left and Jazz and Boomer looked around wondering what the fuck they were to do now.

"Let's have another drink and then go home. Mad Pete could do with cheering up. She threatened to chop him up into little pieces so he's not very happy."

Jazz called Mad Pete over and said they would get something to eat in the pub and one drink for the road. He reassured Mad Pete with a confidence he had no right to.

"Mrs Manson will never again darken your door. MI6 will bang her up for ever. Trust me, I know these things."

Mad Pete nodded and followed Jazz and Boomer into the pub. After eating and a further drink, although

Boomer was drinking non-alcoholic beer to counteract Jazz's quadruple vodkas and tonic, the tension mellowed and all realised just how tense the past few days had been. All hoped life would return to normal. Boomer added, "There will be a debrief, I reckon. Perhaps we can get some questions answered. It's been really weird. By the way, the MI6 lads were good, I never saw anyone other than Derek, did you?"

Boomer and Mad Pete thought for a second and with a puzzled look shook their heads.

"Let's see what we can get from Derek when we see him."

It had been a long weekend and an even longer day today. Everyone was feeling overwhelmed by the ending. All the hype, the tension and now nothing. Derek had just buggered off and left them with no instructions on what to do next.

They got in the car Derek had left. He had taken theirs but that was alright. The bastard had bugged that car and they didn't want it anyway. This was a nice BMW and Boomer was happy driving it. Mad Pete fell asleep in the car on the way back which gave Jazz the chance to ask Boomer the burning question, "Who is this woman you are going out with and is she sane?"

Boomer laughed and called him a bastard.

"No truly, have you got a girlfriend, really?"

Boomer was embarrassed and for a moment concentrated on driving as if he hadn't heard the question. Then with a resigned sigh he told Jazz about her.

"Look, she is a really nice girl. I met her in my local pub and I accidently bumped into her and spilt my beer down her top and trousers. Not much, just a little, but oh boy did she go for me. She called me a fucking cunt with no manners. She's a tiny thing and to stand up to me at six-foot two I thought was champion. We started to talk. I offered to wipe the beer off her top but she declined." They both laughed at this.

"Well, she is a really champion girl. Got a good heart and likes me a lot. She is different from most girls I have dated, no hidden extras. What I see is what I get and I like that. I burp and fart, can't help it, and she doesn't mind. She can drink me under the table but only if pushed, lol. She is a lady when she needs to be and one of the lads at other times which suits me. Been seeing her for four months now and we sort of said we are dating now. Sounds bullshit, but sometimes you have to say these things."

Jazz nodded and thought Boomer had it just right.

"Am I going to meet her?"

"No way yet. She's still getting used to me, you might put her off me and that ain't gonna happen."

They both laughed at that. Jazz thought this sounded the most serious he had known Boomer to be about another woman. It made him think of Amrit. She was a good and feisty girl and it made him smile to think they were having Auntie on. He knew Auntie thought they were getting close but it was a joke both Amrit and him were playing on Auntie. He had to admit he was enjoying the joke, but for the moment, he hadn't got time to think about it.

He arrived home quite late after they dropped off Mad Pete and Boomer took Jazz home. Boomer was the driver so he kept the car overnight. Amrit and Auntie wanted to know what was happening, what had happened and

Wills was jumping around saying what fun it had been. Thankfully Auntie didn't realise the full extent of what had happened but she was beginning to wonder by Wills' antics. Jazz, tired, worn down and maybe a little drunk told them that tomorrow he would explain everything but now he needed his bed. He stood swaying just a little more from tiredness than drink and seeing how exhausted he was, Auntie, remorseful for haranguing him with questions, rushed to make him a milky drink and followed him up the stairs. He had started to make his way up the stairs but climbed slowly as he pulled his leaden-filled feet up each step to bed. Auntie put the drink on his bedside cabinet, checked if he needed anything to which he said with a watery smile, "No thank you", and left. The whole fiasco of the weekend and today was taking its toll. He sat for a few moments feeling neither awake nor asleep. He took his clothes off, took one sip of the drink and laid down. His bed felt like heaven. His head hit the pillow and he was asleep.

CHAPTER THIRTY-THREE

WHAT THE...

It was 3 a.m. when his phone woke him. The buzzing was driving him mad and, in his sleep, he thought he was in the middle of a bees nest. He awoke with a start, glad it was a dream. He had his phone on silent but the continual vibrating whining woke him. The voice on the phone was terse, to the point and loud.

"Get your fucking arse down here. The car's outside and the boss wants to see you now!"

Unable to challenge, confused for a second then, after a deep breath, immediately alert, Jazz grabbed his trousers and a jumper, picked up his shoes with his socks conveniently pushed inside and carried them down the stairs as quietly as he could. *What the fuck was this all about?* he asked himself but he knew at 3 a.m. it must be serious. He saw Boomer was in the back of the car. *So they have got him too* he thought. He had that feeling of foreboding; something was seriously wrong.

They were told all would be explained when they got

to Area 10 or Roswell as Jazz and Boomer irreverently called it. They looked at each other wondering what the hell this was all about. They expected a debrief but not at 3 a.m. When they arrived, they were shown into a different hut; one they hadn't seen before. Both recognised it was an interrogation room with a huge mirror at one end which they knew from experience would have someone on the other side watching them.

They were sat down together, they looked at each other and Boomer was thinking the same as Jazz. So, this was not going to be an interrogation where it would have been prudent to keep them both separated. They were given a mug of steaming hot tea and some biscuits by some non-speaking person who left the room immediately. They were being very nice to them and that seemed unusual too at three in the morning. It was getting interesting and they both relaxed and waited to see what was going to happen.

After what was a strange and silent time while they drank their tea and dunked and ate their biscuits, neither wanting to say anything and trying to look relaxed for anyone watching, the door was violently opened and they both looked around at someone they didn't know come in struggling with a box and seeming to juggle it to the table. Jazz wondered what that was all about. It turned out the box was some sort of recording equipment and the man proceeded to plug it into a socket by the table they were sat at. It looked pretty amateurish to Jazz and he wasn't impressed. His police station seemed to have more state of the art than this lot had.

After a few minutes of fluffing about, the man sat down, took a deep breath, smiled and introduced himself as Tony. Both Jazz and Boomer just gave a brief nod of acknowledgement and waited. Tony said he wanted to know exactly what had happened the day before in every detail. This was the debrief Jazz and Boomer expected but not at 3 a.m.

They told the story of finding Mad Pete at his incredible hulk of a mother's home and how they went to Bradwell-on-Sea to find Mrs Manson and how they had found Derek had bugged their car and was there before them. Jazz added as an aside that he must have broken every speed limit to get there before them. They told how Derek had his men hidden outside waiting for Mrs Manson who had to be duped by Mad Pete to come down from the room in the pub and that Derek and his men took Mrs Manson and headed off.

Tony asked the question, "Did you see any of Derek's men who he said were with him?"

Jazz answered that he hadn't seen any other men and thought they must be brilliant to be able to hide the way they did. Tony just gave a 'hmm' answer to that.

Another question from Tony was, "Why do you think he went through the charade of getting Mad Pete, as you call him, to call her down and he didn't just go up to her room and get her?"

It felt like twenty questions and Jazz knew the answer to this one and cockily said, "Because he said that Mrs Manson was on speed dial to the villain in Holland she was going to meet and if she knew there was a problem she would ring and alert him and he would disappear from Holland and your men who were waiting for him would have lost him."

Again, Tony just gave a 'hmm' as a response. He had one more question for them both.

"What did Derek say to you both when he left?"

Jazz looked at Boomer and they both shrugged. Boomer answered this time.

"He said fuck all, not even a thank you for your help, the ungrateful bastard. These questions are for Derek, not us. What has that fucker got to say for himself?"

Tony answered with another 'hmm' and got up and left the room.

Jazz and Boomer looked at each other and knew there was a problem. This just didn't sit right. They were left for what felt like an hour but was actually not quite half an hour. The door opened gently and in walked the boss. The boss man had some fancy parliamentary title that Jazz didn't need to ask about, and introduced himself again by saying, "Just call me Richard."

Jazz wondered where Derek was. They expected to have their own 007 Derek explain what the fuck this was all about. They reckoned as law officers they deserved to know. Richard said he would explain what he could and by the same token Boomer and Jazz were to answer their questions as veritably and succinctly as they could. Jazz thought he sounded like a toffee-nosed twerp; *who uses the words veritably and succinctly in this day and age* he asked himself?

The first question from Jazz was:

"Why on earth did you put McHenry, a very, very important person, someone who had been hidden from the masses and held life-threatening information that every fucking terrorist would want, into such an insecure position. Is McHenry alive and is he back with his Americans?" As an aside Jazz added, "I bet the fucking Americans are pleased with you and I bet they won't trust you again." He would have laughed if it wasn't so serious.

Richard was not used to such disrespect from a subordinate. Jazz was not one of his men but he expected respect for his position. Jazz saw the back stiffen and the chin tighten and noted the affront and added hastily, "I apologise. My manners are quite bad from working with the low-lifes in the East End of London. DI Black and I are not used to working with such high-standing officers."

He hoped that sounded polite and Boomer thought he sounded like a dickhead but nodded, smiling at Richard just to keep him humoured.

Richard nodded and said, "We are not that stupid, Singh. The Americans would never have let McHenry come to such a meeting when we knew there was going to be a kidnapping."

"You knew?"

"Of course, Singh. We are MI6 and we know most things." Richard added a little more quietly and with a sigh, "Sadly, we don't always know everything".

"The McHenry that was kidnapped was one of our men. The real McHenry came the following day to talk with those at the conference. We had by then arrested everyone involved in the kidnapping except for Mrs Manson, who you and your companions helped us find the following day."

"So, where is Derek? We thought he would be here. We did lots for him and aided his arrest of Mrs Manson."

Richard now looked uncomfortable and with a deep breath decided to stride to the window and after a brief survey of the tree outside turned and faced Jazz and Boomer.

"Derek has gone. He has taken Mrs Manson, we believe, to the man we had hoped to capture in Volendam in Holland last night. Obviously, the three of them were not in Volendam. We are unsure where they are at this precise moment."

Those words had been hard to say and Richard walked to a table with a carafe of water and glasses and poured a glass of water and drank it in the shocked silence of the room. Jazz was the first to speak.

"No, that can't be right. He has been a good sort and he was on our side. He helped save my family. Why would MI6 Dave want to kill Derek if he was a true terrorist and part of their party?"

"It's called a power struggle, I think." Richard, not liking this conversation but knew it had to be said, carried on.

"We have since found out, much too damn late, that our de-programming programme doesn't work. We knew Derek was being programmed in Germany when he was away for a week and when he came back, we put him on a de-programming course of sessions. We thought they had worked. But they hadn't."

Richard stopped for another glass of water and nodded to Jazz and Boomer wanting to know if they wanted some. Both nodded. Their mouths were dry and they needed a few moments' distraction. They all had a few moments to digest this information before Richard continued.

"What we do know is that Derek took Mrs Manson from Bradwell-on-Sea by himself. He did not have any men with him. He had thrown his mobile phone away so we couldn't track him and didn't know where he was that day. We still don't fully understand why Mad Pete and that particular charade happened and why he didn't just go up to Mrs Manson's room and get her without you there."

Richard walked up and down for a minute while he thought and Jazz and Boomer, mesmerised by this, just watched open-mouthed. Richard continued, almost talking to himself.

"Mrs Manson is a very canny woman. She, we think, is the true leader in this country. She was not going to trust anyone after the debacle of the kidnapping. She has cleverly stayed under the radar for quite some time and it is only now we have uncovered how this spider's web of intrigue and terrorist machinations has worked."

Jazz thought *those fucking words again, machinations?* Richard, seeing how perplexed both Jazz and Boomer were, added an explanation for uneducated idiots with a sigh of resignation.

"There were many people involved in this organisation and 'machinations' means a scheming or crafty action or artful design intended to accomplish some usually evil end."

Jazz and Boomer nodded still wondering why he used such candy-assed words and didn't just say 'they wanted to rule the fucking world!'.

"Her cautiousness has kept her safe. It would be true to say that Mrs Manson did not call any one of her network in case calls were being monitored so she wouldn't know who was arrested, killed, or who got away. I don't think Mrs Manson would have trusted Derek immediately because he had not been killed or arrested. He was supposed to have been killed by David and used as a scapegoat. So, Derek was never going to be a long-term fighter for their cause. They used him so why would Mrs

Manson trust him if he knocked on her door? We had arrested everyone involved but not Derek so she would have been even more cautious. There is one thing to know about Mrs Manson, she is a very clever woman and would not have trusted him. She would have rung Volendam immediately on seeing him. We are not even sure if she was armed. We suspect she carried a small firearm in her bag but that is not a certain fact. She would protect her leader and herself at all costs. We need to find them."

Boomer, now shocked, had to say, "But Derek saved us. Derek saved Jazz's family. Why would he do that if he was a traitor?"

"Questions we can't answer. There is no rhyme or reason for his actions. It would seem he was playing on both sides. Very clever of him. The kidnapping, according to Derek, was supposed to be Sunday morning but it happened Saturday evening. We always have undercover backup, something Derek didn't need to know about; we were watching the events as they happened so we were prepared. This put Derek under suspicion but there could have been a reason he wasn't aware of, so we continued seeing how events unravelled. He acted like our man until he disposed of his phone, enlisted you both to help and then with your information took off to Bradwell. We don't know where he is now."

Boomer, who had listened carefully to everything that was said and realised they had been given more information than was normal to anyone outside of MI6, wondered why. He wanted to frame his question carefully. He didn't want to upset MI6; they were not people to mess with so he asked gently, "Thank you for sharing all this with us. How can we help you?"

It was obviously the right thing to say because Richard became more animated and very pleased.

"We want to find Mad Pete who has also disappeared. We raided his home and he wasn't there and he appeared to have cleared out his essentials there. We found residue of drugs and drug paraphernalia but no actual drugs which is his area, we believe. We think and hope you will have an idea of where he is hiding."

Jazz asked why Mad Pete was of interest. He was a low-life scumbag and certainly not a terrorist. Richard, looking embarrassed at such failure, said, "We think that Mrs Manson would have told Derek that Mad Pete had ways of getting them out of the country. We had every port and airport and private airfield covered and they have not left the country legitimately. We have assumed Derek was not prepared for this eventuality and Mrs Manson has lost her contacts in this country because we have them all."

With a deep breath and a short walk around the room to think of his next answer, Richard added with great reluctance having dredged up as much goodwill in his tone of voice that he could, "We think Mrs Manson would have directed Derek to Mad Pete's flat to find a way out of the country. From what you told us he had already been able to arrange this for Mrs Manson so we have presumed he could arrange another covert boat to take them both to some part of Europe. We know that Volendam was not going to be the meeting place anymore because our men found no one there that fitted the profile of the leader we were looking for. He must have been tipped off in some way and not through Mrs Manson because we have her phone tapped and she had left it somewhere in Bradwell. We think she threw it out of the car as she and Derek took off."

Richard looked like he had a nasty taste in his mouth and proceeded to drink some water.

"This is most unfortunate for us and we need to get this back on track. We have noted through CCTV that Derek drove to the Gascoigne Estate so we presumed to see Mad Pete when he arrived back."

With a slight sense of humour Richard added, "I am sure other residents would not be blessed with their company."

At this point Richard stopped moving around and grabbed a chair nearest to Jazz and Boomer and sat down and looked at them earnestly.

"We need you to find this Mad Pete as you call him. We need to know what he has done. We have looked everywhere and cannot find him and you, Jazz, know him better than anyone. The car Derek drove was dumped in Barking so we lost him and Mad Pete. We have no idea where they went. We need your help."

Jazz looked at Boomer and saw a very slight nod. Of course they were going to help. They all realised there was a timescale on this. Derek and Mrs Manson would want to be out of the country as quickly as possible. Derek had burned all his bridges and was wanted, so how was he to get out of the country? Mrs Manson would have told him about Mad Pete and his nefarious dealings with smugglers. Jazz reckoned they must have been desperate to even think of using Mad Pete. Derek must be spitting nails to have to rely on someone like Mad Pete; he couldn't have had any other options. Jazz thought this made Derek more dangerous. Like a trapped animal he would go for the throat if cornered. Jazz knew that most of Mad Pete's deliveries were at night for obvious reasons so the hope was they had until the evening to get this sorted and find him.

Boomer, always using situations to his advantage, asked nicely if he could have one of the souped-up BMWs he knew MI6 had for their use, and he said he only wanted it for today, of course. This was agreed and Boomer was very happy. It was now 7 a.m. and they had been up since 3 a.m. and they needed some food to keep them going. A fry-up was organised and more hot, sweet tea brought to them.

Jazz said that they needed to work alone. Places Mad Pete may be found would not take kindly to the brute force of MI6 men. Their car was bugged, of course, they knew that, and they were given burner phones to use for this operation where MI6 could be fully informed of what was happening. There was no point in secrecy, the MI6 could hear every fucking thing they said, but Richard promised not to interfere in what they were doing. Jazz didn't believe that but this was serious stuff; MI6 were not the enemy, Mrs Manson and Devious Derek were. Jazz had dropped the 007 accolade for Derek, the bastard.

As they drank fresh, sweet tea which tasted so good, they started to relax. Both hadn't realised how tense they were on hearing what was going on. So, with a sigh, Jazz started first.

"Look, Boomer, I don't think he would go back to his mother's flat. She would still be pissed with him from when we took him away. He is scared, quite rightly, of her. She is a fucking animal. So, his first go-to place of safety is out."

Boomer nodded and said, "Copy that."

"He hangs around the community halls in Barking as well. It's his work area but also, the scrotes who frequent it for drugs and drink and just hanging around, would protect him."

Jazz saw Boomer nod at this and after a few seconds he had another thought.

"But he ain't gonna go there because MI6 have guns and would hurt him. Mad Pete would not feel safe in such a well-known haunt of his and he wouldn't feel protected by out-of-their-heads druggies. No, he would go somewhere else."

Boomer added, "He might be with Derek and Mrs Manson. They might hang on to him in case he did a runner on them. They sound desperate to get out of the country and Mad Pete is a fucking slippery scrote."

This made Jazz think for a moment. Would Derek and Mrs Manson keep Mad Pete with them? Not unless they had to. He was a scruffy bit of filth who you would not have in the car for too long as he stank and he would certainly draw attention to anywhere they were holding up.

"My immediate thoughts are that Derek would have got Mad Pete to give him details of a suitable drug runner. He would get Mad Pete to do the introductions and then organise himself where the meet would be. He would be able to chuck tons of money at them so no problem. Mrs Manson must have lots of money at her disposal, I would think. If she had got ready to leave as arranged when the kidnapping was successfully completed, she would have a stash on her. So, thinking of it, I reckon they told Mad Pete to fuck off, gave him some money to keep quiet and he scuttled off to the sewers somewhere."

Boomer nodded. "That makes sense. Derek seemed very organised and he obviously is an ace at ducking and diving. If he wasn't such a bastard, I would admire his techniques. I think finding him and Mrs Manson is quite impossible. I can see how this is for MI6. They trained him to be a master of manipulation and now he is manipulating them."

Boomer would have laughed but it was quite worrying. Derek was clever enough to outwit everyone and their only hope seemed to be on a low-life rat with no moral, honourable or patriotic sensibility and he was a total snivelling coward, too, who would sell his granny to any buyer if it saved him. He suddenly felt very depressed.

The breakfast came and it was humongous. The chef had fried everything he could lay his hands on and they tucked in with relish. When finished both felt so much better, relaxed and even more optimistic. Boomer burped and rubbed his stomach.

"That was an ace breakfast. I reckon we will find Master Mad Pete. Another cup of tea, a piss and a cigarette and I'm ready to go."

Jazz laughed.

"In that order?"

"Yup."

The tea arrived within a minute. They looked at each other and it confirmed that every word was being listened to. That was alright, they knew the score. Boomer burped long and hard and just for their listening pleasure adding a loud fart to the cacophony. Jazz looked disdainfully on the spectacle in front of him. All Boomer said in response to raised eyebrows from Jazz was, "I blame the black pudding."

After a few minutes of sipping hot tea Jazz, deep in thought said, "If Mad Pete is not with Derek and Mrs Manson, then the only place I can think he would hide apart from with his mother is the crack house in Newham. It's the shittiest, filthiest place you can imagine and it stinks to high heaven; it's the best place to hide if you don't want to be found. It's not even on the police radar. I found it by accident when I followed Mad Pete one day; he delivers crack to the crackheads. Just to make it clear how awful it is", Jazz added, "a sewer in London is a cleaner place to hide."

Boomer pleaded. "Please don't tell me we've got to go there."

"Yup! It's the safest place for him to be. No one would look there or get in there easily. Those crackheads can be vicious when not high."

"Fuck!"

"Yup."

"Even Mad Pete wouldn't stoop this low unless he was very frightened indeed. He has MI6 after him and me and you don't know what threats Derek has made to him. There is no way Derek would let him go without ensuring Mad Pete told no one where they were. He is gonna be very scared and he will not think anyone would find him in that cesspit."

Boomer wondered if that was their only option, this crack house. Jazz thought for a moment and added, "If he is not in the crack house then Derek has him close to him or he is somewhere else I haven't thought of at the moment. We will have to cross that bridge when we get to it but the crack house sounds the best option to start with and it's fairly local for him. His safe places are going to be known to him and local."

At that point Richard came back into the room and asked if they were ready to depart. Both Jazz and Boomer promised to keep in touch but they all knew that Richard would have tabs on them and there was no way they wouldn't be followed and tracked. Jazz said as they left that it was essential those following kept a good distance. He added,

"Crackheads can smell filth a mile off. I know I am one but Boomer and I are used to the scumbags in our area so can handle them."

With a cocky swagger, he walked off with Boomer to the car. Their exit looked good but when they got to the car both realised they had drunk far too much tea and needed a piss before they left. Somewhat humbly they went back and were silently observed by Richard and his cohorts as they searched for the toilets. They made their exit again, this time looking a little more sheepish. They lit up once in the car and took a few drags before Boomer asked where the fuck they were going.

"We are going to Newham, my man," was the grandiose answer from Jazz.

"There is a disused industrial estate off the A13 and one of the buildings is being used as a crack house. It's off the beaten track so anyone can come and go without being seen. There are quite a few who doss there. It's a shithole so put a scarf or handkerchief over your nose and mouth. The smell is the worst you will have experienced and that says a lot, cos we have experienced the worst. How many homes have we left wiping our feet as we go out cos of the filth?"

With a grunt of dismay at the thought, Boomer fired up the car and set off causing a wheelspin for those watching. Boomer was happy now in this poky, awesome car. It was a brand-new state-of-the-art BMW with a great satnav and heated seats as well, for fuck's sake, he thought. He was a happy bunny and the journey didn't hold them up too much. They blue-lighted through the rush hour traffic; something that always gave Boomer a thrill.

CHAPTER THIRTY-FOUR

GOTTCHA

They reached the industrial area in record time. Boomer wasn't messing around and cars got out of their way as they sped through Stratford and made their way towards the A13. It was now 9 a.m. so Jazz was pretty sure everyone would still be asleep in the building. They parked the car at the back of another old building that was far enough away just in case one of the thieving toerags was awake and out looking to steal something for drugs. Never trust a druggy.

The piece of loose corrugated iron standing against an opening which Jazz presumed was once a door waved a bit in the wind and made a tinny popping sound. They eased their way around it into the black abyss. The smell hit them immediately and Boomer gagged.

"Put something over your mouth and nose, it helps a little and watch where you walk. They don't care where they shit," was the only advice Jazz could offer.

Boomer growled a long, deep and distressed answer that got lost in the muffling of his mouth and nose. There were bodies lying against walls, some had bits of blankets and others had bits of cardboard to keep them warm. It was a pathetic sight of human beings who had degraded themselves to such an extent that the RSPCA would have put down dogs in that state.

One or two roused a little but after looking up, moaned and went back to sleep.

"It must have been a heavy night last night," said Jazz.

Boomer wondered if Mad Pete had helped the party and given these miscreants some crack to keep quiet. That made Jazz even more hopeful they would find Mad Pete here.

They picked their way through nearly a dozen men and two women. That was the most upsetting, to see women reduced to this level. In the darkness, Jazz spotted a black leather coat across someone. That looked like Mad Pete's coat and he went over and grabbed the man under it.

"You slime ball, I have been looking for you," was Jazz's greeting as he grabbed Mad Pete.

But when he looked down at the man's face, it wasn't Mad Pete.

"Where is the man whose coat you pinched?" asked Jazz, now losing his temper and wanting to punch this low-life. The man, scared and not fully focussing pointed to a corner and Jazz looked over at a pathetic ball of humanity curled up and lying on some cardboard. He started whining as he saw Jazz coming over.

"They took my coat and all my stash, Mr Singh."

Jazz looked at him. They had beaten him up and his face, all cut, bruised and dirty was a pathetic sight. Jazz was relieved to have found him but he was in a state, and he felt almost sorry for him. Shocked to see him like this, Jazz gently said, "Put your coat on, Pete, and let's get out of here."

He helped Pete get to his feet. He swayed a little and was unsteady standing. He looked like he had had a kicking too. Jazz put the black leather full-length Nemo coat around Pete's shoulders and helped him out. This coat was Mad Pete's trademark and everyone knew it was him by his coat. He was proud of it and saw himself at times like Nemo from *The Matrix*. He tried to walk with a swagger but the pain was too much.

"I think they broke my legs, Mr Singh, they don't arf hurt."

Trying not to smile Jazz reminded him that if they were broken, he wouldn't be standing and walking. He told him they were most probably very bruised.

They gathered up the few remaining bits he had around him. It looked like everyone had taken something of his including his phone. There remained an empty plastic bag and his diary; they couldn't sell that. They helped him out to the car where Jazz took a look at the poor bastard. Mad Pete was crying silently. He was grateful to have been saved and utterly petrified to have been found. He was gonna die and one of them would kill him.

Jazz rummaged in his pockets to find one of his flasks with vodka in it and offered Mad Pete a drink, hoping it might put some life back into him. He promised him a McDonald's breakfast from the drive-by on the A13. He quietly told him that they were here to save him because Jazz and Boomer were the only friends he had and the only ones he could trust. These soothing words worked and Mad Pete stopped shaking.

"Yes, Mr Singh. I just want to be left alone. They came for me. I didn't go to them, honest. They made me help them, honest. I got beat up last night and the bastards took everything I had. Obviously, I carry my stash with me. Can't trust no one to leave it anywhere and they took it all and they got my phone too. I am lost without my phone."

"Who took your phone?"

"The bastard who took my coat too."

With that, Jazz tapped Mad Pete on the arm and said to stay there. He looked at Boomer who knew what he was going to do and got out of the car with him. They found the bastard who had the coat and manhandled him which was easy. He had obviously dosed himself up and was quite incapable of defending himself. They searched him and found the phone down his pants which nearly made Jazz gag. They grabbed the phone and left with each wanting a handwipe to clean themselves.

Back at the car Jazz gave Mad Pete his phone.

"It needs a bit of a clean but looks alright," said Jazz.

Mad Pete took it and the relief could be seen.

"This has my life on it, Mr Singh."

Jazz nodded, glad to have put Mad Pete back together. Realising everything could be heard and he was worried that MI6 would suddenly appear, he said out loud, knowing the car was bugged, "Give us time to find out what is happening. If Mad Pete has a druggy fit, he is no use to anyone. I know this from experience."

Mad Pete looked up and asked, "Who are you talking to, Mr Singh?"

"No problem, Pete. I need to get you a hot drink and a McDonald's breakfast. How does that sound?"

It sounded good to Mad Pete, he was starving, he hadn't eaten anything since yesterday evening and with all the adrenalin he had used up he was shaking with fear and hunger. Boomer drove them swiftly out of the industrial disaster of a place, before anyone in the building got curious. They had made a lot of noise and didn't want to have to deal with anyone from that place.

Mad Pete sat in the car with his McDonald's breakfast and a steaming hot cup of coffee. Boomer decided to join him and ordered one for himself. Jazz had no idea where Boomer found the room for a McDonald's after such a big breakfast; he could only manage a coffee.

They sat for ten minutes enjoying the silence as Mad Pete and Boomer chomped their way through their breakfast and Jazz sipped his coffee while he thought how to do this. Nice or nasty, what was going to work on Mad Pete at the moment? He needed to be diplomatic and use the right tone to get the information he needed from this very scared low-life rat. Boomer finished the dining experience with an appreciative loud and long burp. Jazz used this as a signal to begin.

"So Pete, tell us from the beginning what happened last night. Remember we are here to be your protectors and to see that the right thing happens."

"He will kill me, Mr Singh. I can't tell you nuffink. He is very clever, more clever than you and he promised not to kill me if I keep stum."

"Are we talking about Derek?" asked Jazz.

"Yes, of course, Mr Singh. Who the fuck do you think I am talking about? The honey monster?"

He deserved a slap for being so disrespectful but Jazz had to keep him happy.

"Just checking, Pete, just checking. So, what happened last night? That's all I want to know. Not asking you about anything else. Did they kidnap you?"

Mad Pete liked that idea.

"Yes, they did, yes."

"So, what happened?"

"Well, Mr Singh, Mr Black had dropped me home and as I was getting my keys out to get in, there was Mrs Manson and that Derek standing there. I was very shocked. They made me go with them, Mr Singh. I didn't want to. They kidnapped me."

Jazz stopped himself smirking at the thought that Mad Pete was kidnapped but it was working well so far.

"They broke into a car and that Derek knows how to start engines without a key. He could've made a fortune down my way with that skill."

Mad Pete laughed at his joke and Jazz smiled. He was feeling more relaxed so hopefully they would get somewhere with all of this.

"So where did you drive to?" asked an interested Jazz.

"Not far, Mr Singh, he stopped the car and wanted my help but I can't say any more, Mr Singh. He said he would know if I ratted on him and he would come back and waterboard me. Oh my god, Mr Singh. He will do that. He said he was an expert in drowning me and bringing me back to life and doing it again. I couldn't stand that, I can't do that, never. No, I want to go home, Mr Singh."

Now Mad Pete was whining and getting into a state that Jazz knew could lead to a druggy fit that would cause foaming at the mouth, almost an epileptic fit that certainly would make him unable to talk for a long time.

Jazz, using his most soothing voice, something Boomer hadn't heard before and was interested to see how it worked, said, "Pete, my friend, you are safe with us. I would never, ever let anyone hurt you. I have saved your scrawny arse so many times. Remember, when was the last time you got arrested for dealing, fencing, and all the other stuff you do? – Right, never! Why? Because I protect you. Is that right?"

Mad Pete sat, looking down and thinking. It was a painful few minutes as Jazz waited for his reaction. From deep down came a sigh of resignation and Mad Pete reluctantly agreed.

"Yes, Mr Singh. You have saved my scrawny arse many times."

"So, Pete, now I am about to save your scrawny arse again because without the two of us someone will get you; if it's not Derek it will be the mighty force of the MI6 men."

"Oh gawd, Mr Singh. Why does this happen to me? I want none of this. I want my business back and just to get on with my life."

His business? This made Jazz bite his tongue. His business was illegal in every way but for now he commiserated with the unfortunate way Mad Pete had been used.

"I am here to help you get your life back. Know this, I have MI6 in the palm of my hand. They will do whatever I ask them to do and I am going to ask them to leave you alone to get back to your business and they will do that."

Boomer nodded earnestly in agreement. He wondered if Mad Pete was seriously buying this crap but so far, he had to admit, it seemed to be working. Carrying on in a soothing tone Jazz, with a deep breath and a sense of let's get this done said, "So, Pete, tell me what you have done for them. They wanted something from you. Remember you are safe with me, and Boomer has a gun if we need it."

Boomer nearly laughed at that extra bit of information. It sounded so cheesy but he did have his gun with him and handcuffs; *well, you just never know*, were his thoughts.

"Okay, Mr Singh, I will tell you. Can I have another cup of coffee?"

Boomer went and got it and they all had another cup. Jazz didn't want to get distracted from finding out what had happened so continued.

"While we wait, Pete, just tell me what they wanted."

"They wanted another boat to come for them and take them to Europe but I couldn't arrange that, it was too short notice."

Jazz's stomach fell to the floor, and he thought *fuck, what now?*

"But," continued Mad Pete, "I could get them to southern Ireland. I am a can-do person, Mr Singh." Now Mad Pete was looking very smug.

"Goodness, Pete, you are amazing. So, what could you organise?"

Mad Pete was now well into this and feeling in control and actually showing off to Jazz who sat with an awed look of appreciation on his face. He was playing the best game he had ever played and was himself feeling quite smug; this was going well and MI6 was listening to it all.

"I rang my friend Mick who does the odd job delivery to me from southern Ireland. He has a fishing boat and fishes off the Welsh coast and he was going to pick them up at Tenby. I didn't sort out the finer points as Derek took over. They drove through the night to get there and are waiting for the fishing boat to come into the harbour. I have nothing to do with it now, Derek and Mrs Manson are talking to Mick."

"Any idea what time of day that might happen?" asked Jazz, a little concerned now as this was a pucker fishing vessel so not needed under cover of dark.

"Nah, don't know nuffink. Derek gave me some money and threatened me. Said best I know nuffink more which I don't."

"Does Mick have a surname, or the name of his boat? Do you know anything?"

"Yeah, the boat's called, and it's really funny, it's called *Craic of Dawn*. Get it, Mr Singh? *Craic* is a joke in Irish."

Yes, Jazz got it and hoped MI6 did too. They could be halfway across the water now, depending on when they were being picked up. MI6 could monitor that. For now, Mad Pete, Boomer and Jazz needed to head for Roswell (Area 10) and see Richard, but just in case, he used his burner phone to check in and check they heard everything. It was confirmed they did and were working on it now.

With relief, Boomer was back with the coffees and the story was told to Boomer. It was decided that they would head off as soon as the coffees were finished. Mad Pete got a bit panicky at the thought but Jazz, again in dulcet tones, told him he was the hero of this adventure and should be proud. Mad Pete, not sure whether to believe such a thing but trusting Jazz, agreed he would go with them, but first, he needed to go home.

Mad Pete, scared, twitchy and babbling insisted he needed to go home. He needed a spliff and the crack fuckers had stolen everything he had on him. He whispered he had a small emergency stash in his flat for times like this. Jazz was going to say no, they needed to get to Area 10 to see what was going on, but Mad Pete was shaking so much now he didn't have the heart. So, first stop was the Gascoigne Estate and Mad Pete's flat. It only took them twenty minutes to get there and Mad Pete jumped out of the car and made his way to his flat. Jazz followed him to make sure he didn't do a runner. Jazz had to wait outside the flat door because his emergency stash was in a secret place. Jazz nodded and let him have his moment of privacy, so when he came back puffing away with a spliff in his mouth and he had cleaned his phone, Jazz could see he was more himself.

"Finish that before we get to MI6 otherwise they will take the stuff off you," warned Jazz.

"No, Mr Singh, no way. I got my phone and ordered some replacement stuff so by tonight I should be okay for everything. Thanks for the heads-up though."

This was a bit more information than Jazz actually needed to know. If DCI Radley knew he was condoning drugs and knew of a dealer ordering more, he would be frogmarched out of the police and into a prison cell. Never mind that Mad Pete was worth it. He coughed up so much information over the years and many cases were solved because of his help. Well, the word 'help' was an exaggeration, he had to be encouraged every time to help with information but Jazz always got there in the end. He patted Mad Pete on the back and said, "Let's get back to the car and no mention of dealing in drugs. You will get away with personal use but that's all as far as MI6 is concerned."

CHAPTER THIRTY-FIVE

THE END GAME

The journey back to Area 10 was filled with relief. They smoked their cigarettes, played loud music and felt good. They had saved the MI6 mob. They hoped for praise for their work and a good recommendation to their boss in the Metropolitan Police. Boomer hoped they would supply a good lunch too.

"You hungry already," asked an incredulous Jazz.

"Always hungry. This brain of mine needs feeding regularly, it's a powerful tool."

Jazz grinned.

"Yeah, right."

They parked at Area 10 and their welcome was very slick; as they got out of the car, they were immediately taken to one of the buildings. One man politely showed Boomer and Jazz to a building and Mad Pete was whisked off to a separate building by Ash.

Mad Pete knew Ash and went fairly comfortably with him although he looked over at Jazz for confirmation that

317

all was well. Jazz nodded to him and waved him on with a reassuring smile. Mad Pete was on a promise that there was a lunch for him and a drink and a first-aider would sort out the cuts and bruises for him. Jazz and Boomer were taken to a hut they hadn't been in before. They saw the top boss, Richard, and a couple of other men sitting in a huddle around a small table. They looked up as Jazz and Boomer entered and smiled.

"Well done, both of you. We have found the boat and we know that Derek and Mrs Manson are aboard. We are monitoring it as we speak."

"Aren't you arresting them before they get across the water?" asked an incredulous Jazz. "They will be under European law and they would have escaped, wouldn't they?"

"Nope, we are working with Interpol and other organisations who also want them and the leader captured so we are monitoring them. We will see where they go from Ireland."

"So, are we done now?" asked Jazz.

"Yes, and thank you."

But Richard felt the need to add more information. Jazz called it showing off. He suspected because MI6 had ballsed-up this kidnapping and resorted, in Richard's mind, to using rank amateurs, he was just trying to save face. He proceeded to inform Jazz as follows:

"We would have had difficulty finding Mad Pete as you call him, although his name is Peter Holmes for your information and he is the illegitimate son of Irene Lacey and a miscreant called Thomas Holmes who lives in Bermondsey on and off with a woman called Patsy. So, you can see we do know who he is."

With a smirk of embarrassment, he added, "We just didn't know where he was hiding."

At that moment, someone whispered to Boomer, who then left the room with Boomer following him out. There was a cosy three of them in the room and Jazz wondered what was going to happen now. Richard and another person pulled their chairs closer to the table and Richard beckoned Jazz to come forward.

"Sit down, DS Singh, we have an offer to make you."

Jazz wondered what the fuck was up now. He just wanted to go home. Richard's demeanour was relaxed but with a serious face, he leaned back in his chair and stared at Jazz. It felt quite chilling to Jazz.

"We are quite interested in you. I think you can work outside of the box so to speak, and we note you deal appropriately or inappropriately with every situation. With training and discipline, I think you would make a great MI6 operator. Would you be interested?"

Jazz wasn't expecting this, and sat digesting what he was being asked to consider. While Jazz thought about the offer, Richard added with raised eyebrows and a smirk, "After all, Jazz, you do have MI6 men in the palm of your hands."

Jazz laughed; they had heard the comment he had made to Mad Pete. This guy was a funny guy. Actually, Jazz was feeling very appreciated at that moment; he liked Richard and the way he talked and worked. This massive and prestigious organisation was offering him a job. It was a huge compliment to be considered and he basked in the glory of being headhunted, as he thought about the offer being made. After thinking further for a few moments, he asked, "Are you offering Boomer this as well?"

"No, I am afraid not. DI Black is an excellent DI in the Met but not MI6 material."

"Could I still use Mad Pete?"

Richard delicately answered, "No, I don't think that would be appropriate for the work we do, but," he added, "I think Ash, as we have come to know him, may be interested to stay as a technical officer, if that helps?"

Jazz actually didn't have to think for long.

"Nah, thanks anyway. I am very happy working with DI Black and Mad Pete. I don't think what you do is my bag. I am very flattered though and like the idea of being a 007 but it's not me. I know my area and I fit in."

Jazz stopped for a second and with a rueful smile added, "If you want to help me, I would appreciate it if you could sort out my fucking DCI Radley. He has it in for me and is a pain in the neck."

Richard smiled at that.

"You cost him his supposed promotion and DCI Radley is all about getting promotion. You are his fly in the ointment. Now, he would be very happy if you joined us."

They both smiled at that. Life was going to be what it was and to a certain extent Jazz could handle DCI Radley.

"Just don't let him put me on school-crossing duty again and that will do."

Richard winced at the thought. Such a waste of a resource. He might poke his nose into the Met and just tell them what an arse DCI Radley had been regarding DS Singh but he wouldn't mention this to Jazz. *No need to stir the bubbling pot of resentment,* he thought.

Both Mad Pete and Boomer had been taken off separately and debriefed again. Mad Pete's version was a bit garbled but by the end of the sessions all information had been gleaned and lunch was served to them all. They were told they would be released to go back to their duties at Ilford and Barking Police Station and their superiors had been notified that they would, after a recovery break of four days, report for duty.

Jazz asked, "What are you going to tell Sarah, Derek's wife? She needs to know what is happening. At the moment she only thinks Derek is a pervert who indulges in strange things with what she considers prostitutes. She is in for one hell of a shock when the truth comes out."

Richard raised his eyebrows and thought about that.

"I forgot to mention, all of this is highly confidential. You both have signed the official secrets act so you will never say a word to anyone about this. We will have a cover story for Sarah that she can cope with. You say nothing and tell her you found out nothing."

He added firmly, "It's a prisonable offence."

Boomer frowned at this.

"So we can't even brag about it? That's fucking unfair. Where the hell have we been for all this time then?"

Richard smoothly stated, "You have been exactly where you should have been, at the conference helping out. Your expertise was required. Just don't mention the incident that happened."

Both Jazz and Boomer agreed that would work, but Boomer muttered it would have bought him quite a few drinks if he could have told the lads the true story.

It was time to leave. Mad Pete had been cleaned up and his long, greasy hair looked almost clean and it had been brushed and given some sort of shape. Jazz stared at him and thought he looked nearly human. With an embarrassed look Mad Pete said, "I've been done over, Mr Singh. I think I look quite good."

"I think you mean you've had a makeover, Pete. Your face looks skinnier now the muck and dirt has been scraped off."

Resentfully, Mad Pete said, "That's not nice, Mr Singh."

"Just joking, Pete, just joking. You look good."

"Aww, thank you, Mr Singh. They have been very nice to me. You were right, they treated me good. I even get to keep this clean T-shirt they gave me. I told 'em my T-shirt was okay but they said it had bloodstains where I got beaten up."

Jazz thought that his T-shirt had much more on it than blood. It had months of filth, snot, slops of dinners and drink down it too. It was stiff with stains. Mad Pete was a happy bunny, holding his plastic bag.

"They put my bloodstained T-shirt in a bag for me to take home. That was nice of them, Mr Singh. They treated me good. I'll give it a wash and it'll be right as rain to use again."

Everyone was more relaxed; even Mad Pete was relaxed and usually in the company of anyone in authority he got very jumpy but even he was happy. They could go home and have a normal life again. They were thanked for their help and hands were shaken. This was the most recognition Jazz had ever had and it felt good. Yes, they had done a good job and they were needed and did a fantastic job for one of the biggest organisations in the country. Boomer pulled him towards the car. He could see Jazz was overwhelmed and getting far too big-headed.

"We worked well together, Singh, now is the time to go home and rest up."

The BMW was taken back and Boomer reluctantly gave up the keys. They were back to Pinky and Perky, the two MI6 men who chauffeured them, to take them home. Jazz had one request. He wanted them to stop in Ilford so he could do some shopping. He said he needed to buy stuff for the people back home who had put up with such a lot with those two men living in the house ready to kill them if Jazz put a foot wrong. In some ways it all seemed unreal.

They dropped off Mad Pete first and they watched as he scuttled into his block of flats. Now they wanted to get to Ilford and then home. Pinky and Perky waited in the car park while Jazz and Boomer went off to shop. Jazz bought a state-of-the-art Xbox with a few games that usually involved killing everyone on screen. He knew Wills would love it and they could play together. The kid had done good and he deserved a present. He couldn't wait to see his face. He bought Auntie and Amrit a huge bouquet of flowers and chocolates. From his limited experience of women, he reckoned they would love this.

With difficulty, Boomer and Jazz carried the stuff which was big and awkward back to the car. Jazz smiled all the way home. Wills was going to love his gift and so would the women. It had been a very long time since he had bought presents like this. Boomer thought he had gone overboard but as he said "It's your money but spoiling women and children is not a good idea."

Jazz replied, "I feel sorry for your new girlfriend. She doesn't have much to look forward to."

Boomer, affronted, came back with, "She has the best present any girl could have – me!"

They looked at each other in a moment of silence and then both laughed at that. Life felt good at that moment and they both sat back and relaxed as they were driven home. Jazz was dropped off with his presents and Boomer shouted goodbye and with reference to the Xbox games shouted, "Kill the bastards" as Pinky and Perky turned the car around and sped Boomer home.

CHAPTER THIRTY-SIX

CHECKMATE

Jazz watched as the car turned around and gave a curt wave as Pinky and Perky passed by with Boomer in the back. He just wanted to catch his breath before going in. He wanted to enjoy the pleasure of seeing their faces when he presented them with their gifts. He reckoned he should have bought some plugs for all the Xbox stuff which he reckoned would sit nicely in Wills' room. He thought he might buy them some proper chairs to game in. He was more excited than even Wills would be to play on the Xbox.

Auntie, who never seemed to get presents, would love the flowers and chocolates and he reckoned she would cook him her pakoras to spoil him. As for Amrit, well, he hoped she liked the flowers. She would want questions answered. He thought he might take her out for a meal to chat and just have some time away from the distractions in Auntie's kitchen. He would make sure she didn't think it was a date; more, a sensible place to talk. He nearly believed the last comment.

Standing on the doorstep, having a cigarette just thinking, was a happy moment for Jazz. He finished the cigarette, got his keys out and got ready to go inside to be greeted, he hoped, by squeals of pleasure as he gave out his presents. He felt good.

He just got into the hall and put the Xbox and stuff on the floor with the flowers on top of the box with the chocolates. He was going to knock on Auntie's kitchen door but it urgently opened before he could knock. Amrit and Auntie stood there with a look of anguish and despair on their faces.

Just as he screwed his face and shaped his mouth into a silent 'What?', Amrit started, just like someone had wound her up and now she was a mad woman as the words spilled out.

"They are taking Wills away, Jazz. The woman is here to take our Wills away."

Auntie, near to tears added, "He is so upset. I said no, they can't, and the woman said yes, they can. I don't know what to do. You speak to her; you tell her no."

Amrit continued, the words coming thick and fast.

"She has been coming round to check up on Wills and you were at work. She said she was happy with how he was being looked after. She just turned up, just like that and said he has to leave us. He loves it here, Jazz, she can't just take him away. You go talk to her and stop her."

Breathing fast, his eyes darted from side to side as he digested all the information and now he was mad, very mad.

"Where is she?" he asked with venom.

In unison they pointed and said, "In there, in the kitchen."

He brushed past them patting each on the arm reassuringly saying, "I'll sort this," as he went into the kitchen with all guns blazing. She saw him come in and knew there was going to be further trouble and that just wasn't going to happen.

"Before you start, Mr Singh, you have to listen to me. I have the responsibility of looking out for the welfare of William."

She raised her hand to stop him answering and carried on.

"He was only meant to be here as an emergency temporary home until I found the right foster parents for him."

Before he could answer again, she stopped him.

"Please listen before you answer. To be a registered foster parent you have to pass various tests. When designated a foster parent you are considered the right person to look after children. The foster parents I am sending William to are very experienced and have fostered for many years for us. They are kind and caring and have two other boys and a girl in their home so William will have companions his own age."

"But we love him and we have had him for ages so we thought we were doing such a good job you were going to leave him with us. We love him and he loves us," implored Jazz.

"You are not registered as foster parents and lawfully, something you should understand, DS Singh," she added pointedly, "my code of work is something you know I have to abide by."

"Can I register as a foster parent now?" asked Jazz.

"Yes, you can, it will take about six months to complete everything but I can put your name down."

"Can we keep him for now until then?"

"No, you can't. This is upsetting for the boy, and not fair. We have to go and I want to get him settled in his new home. I am doing this lawfully and don't want to have to call the police for their assistance."

That was harsh and Jazz realised he had no way of keeping Wills. One last try, and he asked.

"Can I have him after six months if registered?"

"Maybe, no promises."

That was going to have to do. Devastated but worried about Wills and how he was coping, he asked where Wills was. She told him he had gone to his room to pack and Amrit and Auntie had gone up to help him. Jazz waited in the kitchen for Wills to come down with his small suitcase. Jazz asked for a few moments to just talk to him, to say goodbye. The woman went into the hall to wait and Auntie and Amrit sat in the corner watching Jazz and Wills.

Jazz sat Wills in front of him and looked him straight in the eye. Wills looked everywhere but at Jazz. His mouth was clamped shut, his jaw was tight and his eyes darted to the ceiling. Jazz held his arms and tried to get him to look at him.

"Wills, we are so very sad to see you go. We have loved you but you are going to an excellent family specially chosen for you."

Wills didn't flinch or utter a word.

"I am going to do what I can to get you back. I am going to register as a foster parent to get you back. Auntie and Amrit and me, well, we love you and just want you to be happy."

Wills still wouldn't look at him and wouldn't utter a word. There was no expression of anything in his face and

Jazz didn't know what else to say. The woman, anxious to get going, came into the room and called Wills. Auntie and Amrit rushed past Jazz to get one last kiss and cuddle and Wills responded to them. Jazz watched as Wills left the kitchen with the woman not looking back at Jazz, just ignoring him as if he was nothing. The tears were close with Jazz who wondered what he had done for this reaction. Auntie and Amrit were crying and cuddling each other as they waited for the front door to open and for Wills to be gone.

Suddenly there was a flurry of activity in the hall and the kitchen door burst open and Wills came running in and rushed up to Jazz, nearly pushing the chair he was sitting on over as he threw himself onto Jazz and hugged him.

"I love you too, please don't forget me."

"Never!" was the only word Jazz could say as his voice was giving out on him.

Wills hugged him tight and cried a little into Jazz's coat. Jazz stroked his head and with a crackle of emotion in his voice said, "I love you little fella."

Wills looked at him and with nearly the start of a smile said, "Fuck off."

They both smiled at that. Wills disengaged himself and then turned towards the door, and now compliant, he left with the woman. They heard the front door open and close with that final click. They all sat in that silence of misery; the women quietly sobbing and Jazz, worn out and emotionally spent, got up and went to his room. He needed some peace and quiet and a drink. *What a fucking few days this has been* he thought.

After an hour of drinking and laying on his bed thinking about nothing and everything, the knock on his door was a disturbance he didn't want. He heard Amrit's voice, and against his better judgement he got up and unlocked his door and let her in. He wasn't in the mood for good, optimistic words. He wanted negative, 'I will fucking kill you' words although he didn't know quite who he wanted to kill at the moment but was working on it.

Amrit, not actually knowing why she had come to his room stood thinking what to say. She wrestled with thoughts for a few moments and Jazz watched bemused at her trying to find the right words.

"I have lost my son, too."

Jazz sat up. He remembered she had a son when he first moved in. He hadn't seen him for a long time. He thought she meant he had died and felt in those seconds dreadful for not asking about him. She saw his face and added, "No, no, he is not dead. What happened is my ex-husband who is my son's father took him on holiday to Bangladesh to meet relatives. I didn't want him to go but legally my husband had the right to have him for a holiday. That was nearly a year ago. I have been fighting through a solicitor to get him back. My husband came back to England to get on with his work but left my son with his relatives. He did it to spite me. I did a terrible thing in our family to divorce my husband and this is my punishment."

There was a silence. Jazz, not knowing what to do or say, just shook his head. She continued.

"When you came back a few weeks ago and I was a bit snappy, remember?"

Jazz nodded. He remembered, so unlike her.

"Well, I had been at my solicitors and they told me there wasn't much they could do and it would cost a lot more money to further this. I would need more expert help. The family refuse to let my son come back to England so I was very upset."

Jazz nodded again and murmured, "I bet."

She continued after a gulp. She needed to say this and with a determination she hadn't felt for a while said, "So, I have a son to bring back and so have you. We will get them both back. Fuck the lot of them. Let's join forces and do this."

What a woman! Jazz thought. Without thinking he got up and held her as she cried. He looked down at her and tenderly kissed her; it was long and sweet and something they both wanted and needed.

EPILOGUE

The first day back at Ilford Police Station was weird. Boomer had got in first and although he hadn't said what had happened, he had hinted more than he should have. The whole station was abuzz with misinformation and exaggerated stories. Jazz was classed as a hero and Boomer was obviously the bigger hero according to his version of events. It felt good to be back.

Jazz got called into DCI fucking Radley's office which took the smile and cheeky banter off the table. Boomer wished him luck and some bright spark said they had a spare lollipop man outfit ready for him. Jazz said he would rather join the French Foreign Legion than be a lollipop man again. In unison, Boomer's team all shouted "*Au revoir*" as he left the room. This made him laugh.

Sitting upright at his desk, DCI Radley motioned Jazz to sit down in the chair positioned opposite his desk. The meeting was painfully formal but the gist of it was a begrudging well done for the work he had achieved with MI6. He would now resume his duties as a DS and he would be assigned to the Murder Squad and work with DI Black. Ashiv Kumar would also be assigned to the Murder Squad. It had been noted that they had, in the past, worked well together and it was his decision this would continue. Jazz was told to move his stuff into the incident room occupied by DI Black's officers. Jazz thanked DCI Radley and left quickly in case he changed his mind.

Once outside the room he walked very quickly to where Boomer was and shouted, "Fucking hell, I am working with you, Boomer. This is going to be good."

The response wasn't what he expected.

"Geez, what the fuck did I do to deserve this? It's gonna be a bumpy ride."

"But an interesting one," was Jazz's retort.

"I've got Ash as well in my squad, now that is a bonus."

Jazz laughed and play-punched Boomer saying, "You bastard."

"Oy. I'm your boss now so a little respect if you don't mind."

With that Jazz gave him a sloppy salute and walked off to get his stuff. He felt happier than he had for a long time. His job was coming along nicely. He reckoned MI6 Richard had something to do with this; Radley would never have been so gracious. He wasn't quite ready to admit that the spring in his step might also have to do with Amrit and their liaison in working together. He wanted to replicate that kiss between him and Amrit. Neither had mentioned it again but he was working on that one. Could life get any better? He loved his family. Yes, he would get Wills back and Amrit's son too then life would be near perfect.

Ash had rejected the offer of working with MI6. He told Jazz that it wasn't really for him; far too dangerous. This made Jazz laugh because he remembered the dangerous situations Ash had been in with him. He reckoned Ash just couldn't work away from him and he would miss the banter they had. Jazz didn't need to know that the real reason was Ash wanted to go home each night to his wife and children and not work for an organisation that was dangerous and had bad hours. Also, perhaps, he had got used to working haphazardly with Jazz and Boomer and he supposed he would miss them. He didn't think the money was any better either.

It was about a month later that Jazz's phone bleeped a message. It was in the evening and he was just relaxing having a drink and a take-away McDonald's in his room. The message on his phone was unnecessary and threatening. There was no name on it and no particular reference to anything but Jazz knew it was from Mrs Manson. It said:

You cunt. I will be back. They will never catch me. I am more powerful by the day. Just watch your back, Singh. I will pay you and your cronies back for the trouble you have caused me. You are dead meat.